CURSED

LEGACY OF MAGIC
BOOK 8

LINDSAY BUROKER

1

_____

"THERE'S A NIGHTCLUB DOWNTOWN THAT WOULD BE A KILLER PLACE for a wedding," Dimitri said.

"A nightclub?" I eyed him as we navigated around pedestrians on busy Ballard Avenue. One sunny day in November, and people flocked to the outdoors. Even though I glowered often and carried my big magical war hammer slung over my shoulder, people bumped shoulders with me frequently, usually in a hurry to veer around the towering Dimitri with his black death-metal T-shirt. As if _he_ were the dangerous one. "Are you and Zoltan getting hitched?"

"No. Zoltan isn't even talking to me, on account of me sawing and banging during his sleep hours."

"Having a vampire for a roommate must be challenging."

"At least he doesn't threaten to incinerate me if I make too much noise."

"Having a _dragon_ for a roommate must also be challenging."

"It is. What I meant is that you and _Sarrlevi_ could have your wedding at the nightclub. Val said you two are planning one." Dimitri raised his eyebrows—asking if it was true?

I hesitated, now wishing I hadn't said anything to Val, but she was my across-the-street neighbor and friend. Who else was a girl supposed to confide in when her significant other said he would be willing to be married in the *Earth* way if it would make her happy? And her *family* happy.

They—especially my sister—cared more about the formality than I did. Sure, it might be nice to have an excuse to wear my sparkly peacock dress, but Sarrlevi and I already considered ourselves fused, as he called it. Like two trees that had grown together in the woods.

"We're just talking about getting married," I said. "Nothing is planned yet. But I don't think a nightclub is the venue we'd have in mind." Mom and Dad wouldn't bat an eye, but I couldn't imagine bringing my grandparents and my prim and proper sister and her kids to a glorified bar for my wedding. "My priority is getting the twenty tiny homes built for Mikki the Wrench so he doesn't undo the favors he did for me."

Thanks to the goblin crime lord, there were no longer assassins after me, and my father was no longer wanted by the authorities. It was glorious, but I had no doubt The Wrench could snap his fingers and undo everything if I didn't fulfill my part of the bargain. He hadn't threatened to do so, but I worried that I wouldn't be able to enchant the homes to his satisfaction. After all, I was only a half-dwarf. I would never have the power or expertise of my full-blooded dwarven mother.

"I'm excited to see how you enchant them," Dimitri said, "and I'm even more excited that you're going to let me use a corner of the building you're buying so I don't have to do my noisy crafting projects at home. Then Zoltan and Zavryd won't have any reasons to complain about me."

"No? They approve of the Costco-sized boxes of Pop-Tarts that you fill the pantry with?"

"They're indifferent to my Pop-Tarts." Dimitri pointed toward a corner. "The address is that way."

Relieved to veer off the busy street toward Shilshole Avenue, I jogged around the corner, almost clubbing a hanging basket of flowers with my hammer. Who put out flowers in November?

"I'm looking to lease a warehouse for a few months," I said, "not *buy* it. And didn't you say you would chip in?"

"Sure, Matti. But how much do I have to chip in for a corner? I'm only making yard art and door knockers, not twenty tiny homes."

"You're awfully cheap for a guy with three roommates and a thriving coffee shop in Fremont."

"I'm saving up to buy a house. I have to economize."

"Are you going to move in on the same street as Val and me?" I checked the GPS on my phone as we turned to follow Shilshole and passed a hulking sand-and-gravel building. Though Ballard had long ago turned more commercial and residential, the area along Salmon Bay had the remnants of an industrial vibe, and I started looking for the address.

"I'm not sure about that. I've had materials go missing since all those goblins moved in down the street."

"I thought Zavryd's wards kept intruders out."

"They were in my van out front. Zavryd doesn't care about warding that."

"Maybe he would if you kept some racks of ribs in there. That's the address." I pointed to a graffitied warehouse.

The brick building had a loading dock with a handful of parking spots against the wall, all oddly empty, considering the busy restaurants and shopping area a block away. Signs all over the building read, *No Trespassing*, and one on the door read, *No Ghost Hunters*. What might have been bullet holes riddled the door and the signs. Wrought-iron bars covered the sole visible window high on the wall, one of the glass panes shattered.

"Ghost hunters?" Dimitri asked.

"I'm beginning to see why it's listed with a below-market rent and the landlord is willing to do a short-term lease."

"If this is like Val's house, there might be a vampire living in the basement."

"Let's hope not, or you'll have the same problem here as at home." As I approached the metal door, seagulls squawked over the nearby bay, and an answering caw came from a power line. A crow with beady black eyes watched us.

It was not, I told myself, an omen. There were crows all over the Seattle area.

There wasn't a lockbox, but the landlord had said he would leave the door open. When I gripped the knob, however, it didn't budge.

"You said you have an appointment, right?" Dimitri asked.

"Yeah."

The crow cawed again.

"Maybe the roll-up door?" Dimitri suggested.

I hopped onto the cement dock and tried it. It also didn't budge. I checked the time, making sure we hadn't shown up early. Nope. We were two minutes late.

I debated on calling the landlord, but... "I can unlock doors with my enchanting magic."

"Or your huge badass hammer." Dimitri nodded to it.

I do not have an ass, Sorka said, presumably only to me.

As far as I knew, my hammer didn't communicate with anyone else on Earth. She hadn't even spoken to *me* for the first thirty years I'd known her.

It's a compliment, I told her telepathically. *He means you're amazing.*

Her *Hm* sounded skeptical.

Out loud, I said, "I would prefer not to damage the building I might lease."

Returning to the front door, I rested my hand on the metal

near the knob and examined the lock with my senses. As I did so, I detected magic inside the building. Not a lot, and it seemed to be underground. Strange. The listing hadn't mentioned a basement. Maybe the previous renter had left a magical artifact behind.

It was *not*, I told myself firmly, a ghost. Though if there was magic present, that could explain why mundane humans had believed the place haunted.

My magic thwarted the lock, and it *thunked* open. The door creaked as I pushed on it, and the crow cawed three times in protest, then flew off in a huff.

"*Not* an omen," I muttered.

"Oh, good. Because I was thinking it seemed a little ominous." Dimitri waved for me to go first.

The scents of dust, mildew, and spilled oil met my nose when I stepped inside the cavernous, empty space. A couple more barred windows existed high on the far wall, but little illumination made it through the grime coating them. I fumbled for a light switch. When I flipped it, nothing happened.

"Guess electricity isn't included in the rent." Nose wrinkling, Dimitri peered inside without committing himself to stepping across the threshold.

"As long as it's available. I'm not building tiny homes without power tools."

I eyed the roll-up door, debating if it would be tall enough to move the homes-on-wheels out once they were complete. It looked like it, but I reminded myself to take measurements before committing. Now that my business partner, Abbas, and I had sold the homes on the subdivided five-acre property in Maltby, I didn't have space for building large projects. Since the rainy season had also set in, it made sense to find something indoors. This place wasn't that far from my home in Green Lake, so it would be perfect. Assuming it wasn't haunted. "I'm going to find that artifact that I sense."

Dimitri nodded. "I thought I felt something too. But..." He leaned farther in, looking left and right. "I don't see it or even know where it would be, unless back there." He waved toward an office built into the far corner of the warehouse.

A whisper of cold air wafted through the building as I headed toward the back. Something unearthly about it made the hair on the back of my neck rise, and I paused to look around. I wasn't the superstitious type, but I'd seen a lot of magic these past months and knew better than to dismiss my instincts. Something about this place was off.

Halfway across the cracked cement floor, I looked back at Dimitri. He lingered in the doorway. Maybe I should have waited until Sarrlevi was back on Earth to check this place out. But it hadn't occurred to me that the warehouse I wanted to lease might be *haunted*.

"Everything okay?" Dimitri asked.

"Just wishing Sarrlevi was here."

He squinted at me. "Because you don't think I'm tough and would have your back in a fight?"

That was exactly what I thought, but I said, "Because he brings me cheese, rubs my head, and knows a lot about all things magical."

"Oh. That makes sense. Where is he?"

"On Veleshna Var learning how to be a noble."

"Isn't it all about being haughty and pompous? What's he got to learn?"

I thought about defending Sarrlevi, the elf I loved and hoped to have kids with, but he *was* haughty and pompous. It had taken me a while to see past that. "Something about managing his family's lands too," I said.

"Haughtily and pompously?"

"It's the only way elves do things." Another cold draft whispered past, and I continued toward the office.

We had better figure out what was up with this place—and whether we could put up with it while we worked. Otherwise, I would have to lease something farther away. Since I hadn't yet purchased a new truck and only had my Harley for getting around, closer would be better.

Shutters instead of glass covered the large office window, so I couldn't see inside until I pushed open the metal door, another door riddled with bullet holes. They also perforated the wall next to it and had knocked slats off the quirky faux-wood shutters. I envisioned a ghost making a last stand behind a desk in the office.

But the small room was empty, save for a lone dusty toilet squatting in the back corner and a dome-shaped light fixture that had fallen from the low ceiling, bulb shattered on the white-painted cement floor amid desiccated rat droppings. The magic I'd sensed outside was stronger in the little room but definitely belowground.

There weren't any exterior windows, so I muttered, "*Eravekt*," and Sorka flared silver-blue to illuminate the space.

A scuttling sound came from the toilet, and I hefted the hammer in case an animal ran out from behind it. The rat came not from *behind* the toilet but out of the drain in the empty bowl. Claws scratching, it pulled itself out, then saw me and ran around the office two times before darting between my legs to escape.

I lowered my hammer. "Better than a ghost, but I doubt you're what people were shooting at."

Leaving the rat to race across the warehouse, I stepped into the office, looking for a trapdoor in the floor.

A scream came from the front, and I leaped out in time to see Dimitri dart outside as the rat scurried past him.

"*Definitely* should have waited for Sarrlevi," I murmured, then searched the rest of the office for a trapdoor.

I didn't see one, but it *had* to be there. Unless the artifact I sensed was in the plumbing leading up to the toilet? I imagined the previous owners, besieged by gunmen, flushing their valuable whats-it before they were overwhelmed.

"Sorry." Dimitri stepped back into the warehouse doorway. "That startled me. Uhm, I'm not sure about this place, Matti. It's close to a lot of good restaurants, but is that reason enough to lease it?"

"The fact that the rent is affordable is a good reason. If I can find whatever artifact is here and get rid of it, the weirdness may stop. Then it'll be fine, and we'll be getting a good deal."

Again, I walked around the office, peering at the floor. My instincts told me that what I wanted was underneath it. I was on the verge of dismantling the toilet when I remembered the spy kit my mother had given me for my last mission. Some of the items I didn't carry with me, but a couple of the trinkets had been small enough to go on my keychain. Including one that could highlight hidden nooks and doorways.

After I rubbed the trinket, the narrow blue outline of a square appeared in the corner opposite the toilet. Not so much a door but an access panel that must have been sealed and painted over at some point.

"Hah." I called to Dimitri, "I'm checking the basement."

"Okay. Be careful."

I knelt and ran my hands along the glowing blue lines but didn't feel any creases. I didn't even sense any magic beyond that coming from the artifact below. Not deterred, I rested my hand on the panel and willed my own magic into it, envisioning the sealed edges as similar to pipes that needed to be unblocked. Imagining my power working like a toilet auger, I thrust it into the floor all along the outline.

"This is why Sarrlevi teases me about being a plumber," I murmured, but my imagery worked.

Mortar crumbled. Using more magic and raw strength, I levered up what turned out to be a heavy panel, then shifted it aside. Stale, musty air wafted up, and the mildew scent grew stronger.

A faint purple glow came from somewhere below, and an urge to check it out came over me. A *strong* urge. It almost made me jump down before investigating.

"Let's not be stupid, now." I lowered Sorka, her light revealing a dusty cobblestone floor that looked older than Seattle. The two closest walls of the warehouse were visible, forming the same corner below as above, but the rest of the basement stretched away, open space, save for brick support posts.

Be wary, Sorka said as I dropped my head and shoulders through the hole, trying to see the source of the purple light. *I believe that is dark-elven magic.*

Really? I thought of Val's stories of having tangled with their people in tunnels under Seattle. That had been south of Lake Union, hadn't it? I'd never heard of tunnels under Ballard.

The urge to get closer to the artifact swept over me again. Since it was behind one of the support posts, I couldn't see it.

Those posts appeared stable, so I lowered myself down, landing in a crouch on the cobblestones. Only when I looked up did I realize the drop had been seven or eight feet and that I might struggle to climb out. The hole wasn't that close to any of the walls, nor was there a handy rope or ladder.

Sorka sighed into my mind.

"Dimitri will help me out if I yell for him," I said.

Nothing good ever comes of dark-elven artifacts.

You've run into a lot of them?

No, but I know the reputation their species has.

Well, if we get rid of this one, maybe the creepiness will go away, and we can use the warehouse. Nodding to myself, I strode toward the light. I caught myself almost *running* toward it.

Be wary, Sorka repeated.

But I barely heard her, other than to keep my hammer raised in case I encountered a threat.

The artifact that waited for me, resting on a marble pedestal behind a post, was *beautiful*, not threatening. Made from glass or maybe crystal strands that knotted together in a complex design, it made me gasp in admiration.

A voice in the back of my mind pointed out that I'd never gasped in admiration of *anything,* but this artifact was so amazing that I had to reach out and—

The shadows stirred beside me, and I jumped in surprise. But it was only Dimitri, also drawn down by the artifact. So much so that his eyes were glazed.

"It's beautiful," he whispered and reached out to touch it.

"We'd better not." I lifted my hand to block him, though I'd been thinking of doing the same thing.

His face twisted with surprising rage, and he knocked my hand away to grab the artifact.

"*Mine,*" he snarled, jerking it from the pedestal.

Afraid that something horrible would happen if we removed it before checking for traps, I swore, lunged, and grabbed it. He started to spin away, but the artifact flared with heat and light, startling us both. Something seared my hand, and I jerked back, letting go. Dimitri also let go, and the artifact clanked to the stones.

I winced, certain it would shatter and unleash devastating magic. But not so much as a chip flew off the crystal. It did, however, start throbbing ominously.

"Uh." Dimitri lifted his hands and looked at them. They glowed.

Miniature versions of the knot design marked each of his palms, and purple light emanated from them.

Certainty curdled in my gut as I turned my own palms over. I was also marked.

2

DIMITRI AND I SAT CROSS-LEGGED ON THE MAIN FLOOR OF THE warehouse, the artifact resting between us. It still glowed purple. So did our palms. After we'd touched it, the intense urge to do so had faded, as if it had accomplished what it desired. To mark us.

To what end?

"It just seems like a magical doodad to me now," Dimitri said. "I'm sorry I got all crazy over it."

"I know. It was affecting me too, some kind of powerful compulsion. Sarrlevi always tells me that my dwarven blood allows me to resist mental magic better than most, but I guess not this time."

Dimitri shook his head ruefully. "I have dwarven blood too, and all it did was let me know how gorgeous that was and that I had to have it."

The artifact *was* gorgeous. But my palm itched, unpleasant warmth under the mark it had left on my right hand. Poor Dimitri had a mark on each hand, but I'd only managed to grab it fully with one.

He glanced at my phone. "How long until Val gets here?"

"She said she was going to pick up Willard on the way since she's a repository of information."

"*She'll* probably lecture us."

"Probably." I was more worried that Val and Willard would also be drawn to touch the artifact, and that I would have to fight them to keep them away from it.

Dimitri rubbed his palms against his jeans. "My hands itch."

"Mine too. I hope it fades soon."

Sorka sighed into my mind. Because she believed that was a naive hope? Or because I'd failed to heed her warning? I hadn't *wanted* to ignore her. The artifact hadn't given me a choice.

"Maybe we should take our minds off it with some food," Dimitri said. "There's a good barbecue joint near here."

"I don't think I've ever seen you eat anything but pizza, Pop-Tarts, and barbecue."

He looked at me and started to nod, then paused. "Oh, that *was* your point."

"Yeah." I smiled faintly but couldn't judge him. It wasn't as if I enjoyed the most healthy dietary options.

"For your information, I also like gyros."

"I'm not shocked. Abbas's new favorite dish is gyro-meat pizza."

"Zavryd has recently discovered gyro meat too," Dimitri said. "I believe it's *his* new favorite food. Several mornings this week, I've woken to the smells of a haunch dripping juice in Val's rotisserie oven."

"Not quite the same as bacon and eggs, but I can see the appeal." Sensing Val's half-elven presence outside, I rose to my feet and stood between the artifact and the entrance so I could block her if necessary.

Val and Willard appeared in the doorway, outlined by the wan autumn sun. Much like Dimitri had, they paused on the threshold to peer inside before committing.

As usual, Val was armed with her sword in its back scabbard and her semiautomatic pistol in a thigh holster. Willard carried an iron box that I hadn't seen before.

A caw came from beyond them. The return of the crow? Maybe the artifact drew it too.

"No ghost hunting allowed?" Willard asked in her Southern drawl. "What kind of place are you trying to rent, Puletasi?"

"One plagued by dark-elven magic, apparently," I said.

Willard groaned.

Val walked toward us, her gaze locking on the artifact behind my legs, its purple glow making it hard to miss.

"Val?" I asked warily.

Her eyes were as glazed as Dimitri's had been, and she stretched a hand toward it as she approached.

"Val, don't touch it." I didn't want to threaten her with my hammer, but I shifted so I could block her. "Ma'am," I blurted to Willard, though I didn't know what *she* could do.

"Val, don't." Dimitri rose to stand beside me, adding his bulk to our defensive wall. Would we have to tackle her?

Val drew her sword.

Hell.

"*Hygorotho*," I blurted, willing Sorka to raise a barrier that would protect Dimitri and me.

"I'm on it." Willard surprised me by running past Val.

Was she affected by its magical pull as well? No, her eyes weren't glazed.

Having Willard sprint past didn't keep Val from striding toward Dimitri and me with her magical Dwarven blade poised to strike. Though she never took her eyes from the artifact, she swung swiftly and accurately toward my head.

Not certain Sorka's barrier would be strong enough to deflect another powerful dwarven weapon, I swung my hammer up to deflect the blow. Val's sword didn't get through, but the barrier *did* weaken under the strike. When Val snarled and drew her blade back for another attack, I willed some of my own power into it.

"Get out of the *way*," she snarled.

This time, Val feinted toward my hip first before whipping her sword toward my head. It was as if she didn't quite grasp that a barrier protected me.

"Val, stop." The last thing I wanted was to club her—or try. Her elven blood gave her lightning-fast reflexes, and I'd rarely bested her when we sparred. "You do *not* want that artifact. Trust me."

I took a hand off Sorka long enough to show her my palm. Though she couldn't have missed seeing the glowing mark, she didn't glance at it, instead swinging again as she focused on the artifact.

A clank sounded. Willard knelt behind me, and she'd opened that box.

"I have to have it." Val tried to step past me as she swung toward my head again.

Her sword is strong, Sorka said as I shifted to block Val again. *I won't be able to keep my barrier up indefinitely.*

I'm crossing my fingers you won't need to. I risked glancing back at Willard.

She wore heavy-duty rubber gloves, gripped tongs and a spatula, and reached for the artifact with the tools.

"Let me touch it," Val snarled. "I just want to— I need it."

Her next slash pierced Sorka's barrier. Luckily, I was ready. Metal clanged as I parried her blow.

With tongs and spatula, Willard picked up the artifact. It pulsed purple light, illuminating her dark skin and the concentration on her face. Once she had it, she tossed the artifact into the iron box with the hurried movement of someone flinging a snake out of the garden. That done, she slammed the lid shut and fastened the lock.

Afraid that wouldn't do anything to diminish the artifact's

power, I braced myself to parry another attack. But as soon as the lid shut and the purple glow disappeared, Val stopped swinging. The fury left her face, and confusion replaced it.

"Phew." Dimitri wiped sweat from his brow, though Val had never taken a swing at him. "I thought she was about to start calling it *my precious* and making plans for it in her will."

"What happened?" Val looked at her hand and seemed surprised to find her sword in her grip. She peered around the warehouse, as if searching for the enemies who must have attacked.

"Puletasi found a dark-elven artifact," Willard said, "and was thoughtful enough to invite us over to experience it with her."

"Just be glad you didn't touch it." I showed them my palm, then waved for Dimitri to do the same. "It didn't have a draw over you, ma'am?"

"Not that I noticed," Willard said.

"It must only affect people with magical blood." Val eyed our palms for the first time, then looked at her own, probably not remembering if she'd managed to reach it. "Thanks for keeping me from getting to it."

"No problem. I wish I'd been able to keep *myself* from getting to it." I grimaced.

"And me," Dimitri said glumly as he rubbed his palms against his jeans again.

My mark itched in commiseration.

"What prompted you to go hunting for evil magical artifacts on a Saturday morning, Puletasi?" Willard asked.

For the first time, I noticed she was in running clothes. Val wore her usual jeans, T-shirt, and leather duster, so she always seemed on-duty, but Willard must have been taking the day off— like a normal person.

"I came to check out a warehouse for lease," I said. "The artifact was a delightful bonus."

"You have a giant new house. What do you need a warehouse for?"

"She's gotta build Mikki the Wrench twenty tiny homes," Val said. "Apparently, there's not that much room in her backyard."

"Not if I want to build more than one at a time and be out of the rain," I said.

My goblin friend Tinja also hadn't yet moved *her* tiny home out of the backyard. Recently, she'd taken ownership of a house down the street, and it was overflowing with goblins eager to help her turn it into an urban sanctuary, but she was still living out back and visiting my kitchen to drink my coffee and eat my cheese.

"Well," Willard said, "if there are no objections, I'll take this back to the office and do some research. I'll have to be careful since we have other operatives with magical blood."

"Yeah," Val said, "I don't want Gondo going crazy and braining people with your stapler to get at it."

"I was thinking of Corporal Clarke and Captain Summers. They've got fae blood. And I don't know what waltzed through Biggs's bloodline, but he's a hairy tank."

"Orc," Val offered. "His wife is lucky he doesn't have tusks."

"Uhm." I raised a finger, not that concerned about the heritage of Willard's troops. "What are *we* going to do?" I lifted my palm again before pointing to myself and Dimitri, who nodded vigorously with concern in his eyes. "What if these marks don't fade?"

"You won't need to turn on a light when you have to pee in the middle of the night," Val said.

"Funny."

"I'll see what my research turns up," Willard said, "but you may want to consult Zoltan and your mates. I assume they know more about dark elves than you do."

"My mate?" I mouthed, though I knew she meant Sarrlevi. Even though we'd been discussing wedding ceremonies, it felt strange to have someone use that term for him. I'd been thinking of him as my boyfriend—my handsome, loyal, cheese-bringing, now-retired-from-being-an-assassin boyfriend.

"Even with her hand glowing like a bioluminescent mushroom, she gets lovestruck eyes when she thinks about him," Willard observed.

"I think bioluminescent mushrooms are green, not purple," Val said.

Willard waved in dismissal. "You'll have to ask around, Puletasi. In the meantime, are there any *more* artifacts in this place?" She looked around. "Why would a dark-elven artifact have been in an abandoned warehouse in Ballard? There isn't an entrance to a warren of secret tunnels in here, is there?"

"I hope not," Val said. "From what I've heard, they cleared out of the Seattle area after Zav and I dropped a car through the roof of their underground temple."

"There could be tunnels." I pointed toward the office. "There's access to a basement in there. It was hidden until I used magic to find it. Dimitri and I didn't go farther into the basement than the artifact."

"I didn't want to go *that* far." Dimitri eyed the iron box distastefully. "But its magic compelled me to visit it."

"Show me." Willard tucked the box under her arm, then pointed toward the office. "I better stick with you, since it's not compelling me to do anything."

"Good idea," Val said, "you can crack us on the head with those tongs if we get glazy-eyed again and wander off."

"Those aren't the sophisticated tools I'd expect an Army colonel to be issued to deal with magical artifacts." I headed for the access panel.

"It might surprise you to know," Willard said, "that tools aren't issued for such tasks."

"Even to your office that specializes in dealing with all things magical?" Val asked.

"I suspect it's because my higher-ups don't know *what* to issue. We're lucky we get guns and ammo and not EMF meters and ghostometers."

"Those might have been useful here." I paused inside the office, realizing I no longer felt the cold draft or creepy sensation. Maybe the artifact *had* been causing it. Too bad my palm still itched. Maybe I needed to start wandering around with tongs, spatulas, and iron boxes.

Without the purple illumination coming from below, the basement was pitch-dark.

Willard thumbed on her phone's flashlight app while Val and I ordered our weapons to glow. Dimitri didn't join us; he'd probably had enough of that basement.

For the second time that morning, I hopped down onto the dusty cobblestone floor. Val, Willard, and I split up to search along the walls for evidence of tunnels.

Here and there, rats scurried away from our approach, but we didn't see anything more disturbing until Val said, "Ugh."

Willard and I joined her to find a skeleton lying on the cobblestones near one of the brick walls. Its size made me believe it had been a man, but there wasn't much evidence to prove that. A few shreds of clothing and a camp lantern were all that remained beyond the bones. In the nearby wall, a doorway had been boarded over, the wood attached to the brick with crudely slathered cement.

"What prompted you to want to lease this particular place?" Val prodded the rib cage with the tip of her sword, tiny teeth marks visible from the rats and who knew what else had feasted on the guy.

"It's close to home, and the rent is cheap."

She snorted. "We really must stop being drawn to places because they happen to be inexpensive. There's always a reason."

"I know that, but I thought it might be like your house. Didn't you get it cheap because it came with a vampire and was haunted?"

"Yeah. Were you hoping for a vampire of your own?"

"Not exactly," I said, "but I was willing to deal with a few quirks to pay less in rent. Since The Wrench got the assassins off my back, I'm doing his work at cost, and it's going to take months."

"You should have haggled more. You need money. You've got a wedding to pay for." Val punched me in the shoulder.

"I'm sure Sarrlevi will chip in if we decide to do something expensive, but I'm not planning on that. I don't want a huge ceremony, just for my family to know I'm legitimately married. Mostly my sister. She would give me a hard time for having a kid and not being married."

"How prudish and 1800s."

"You've met her."

"Will she object if your hand glows like a lava lamp at your wedding?"

This time, I punched *her* in the shoulder. Hard enough to rock her off balance. She deserved it and must have agreed because she only grinned.

"If I were judging only by the bones, I would have guessed this person died a long time ago, but..." Willard picked up the collapsible black lantern the guy had presumably been carrying at the time of his death. She closed it and opened it. It was dusty, and the light didn't come on, but it looked like something that could be purchased today off the shelves at REI. "This isn't that old."

"His skull is cracked," Val said. "Someone might have bludgeoned him."

"As in with a dark-elven artifact?" I asked.

"Or a big hammer, maybe."

"You two figure out what's behind there." Willard pointed at the boards and brought up her contact list on her phone. "I'll call someone to collect the skeleton, and we'll see if we can figure out who this was."

I interpreted *figure out what's behind there* as knock down the boards with my hammer. Since the itching and warmth of my palm was making me cranky, I smashed Sorka into them with relish.

Once more, she sighed into my mind.

I thought you didn't object to being used to tear down doorways into enemy strongholds, I thought to her.

I sense no magic beyond the boards to suggest that enemies are near. This is reminiscent of when you used me to demolish walls and cabinets.

Sorry. That didn't keep me from gleefully destroying every last board covering what turned out to be a brick archway. *If it helps, I'm not planning to renovate this place after we demolish it.*

That does not help.

Val watched in bemusement as I obliterated the boards. Willard had moved away from the noise to make her call.

"You get almost as gleeful-looking when you destroy things as when you think about Sarrlevi," Val observed.

"Both activities fill me with joy."

Too bad there wasn't much to see. A dusty tunnel extended about ten feet before a dirt-and-rock cave-in completely blocked it.

"The bay and the street are in that direction," Val mused, pointing toward another wall, "so this tunnel is—or *was*—under the alley between this building and the next, right?"

"I think that's right," I said.

"I parked over there," Val said. "The alley was normal—no sinkholes or anything. I bet this cave-in happened a long time ago."

"Before this guy came looking for... whatever?" I waved at the skeleton.

"Maybe." Val looked toward Willard, who'd finished her call and was walking back over.

She stepped into the tunnel, eyed the caved-in rocks, and walked back out. "While I'm researching the artifact, I'll see what I can find out about tunnels and dark elves in Ballard. This might be collapsed now, but it must have led somewhere once."

"Zav is coming." Val pointed upward. "Maybe he'll know something about all this."

I reached out with my senses but couldn't detect the dragon's aura yet.

"Sarrlevi is with him," Val added.

I blinked. "Like flying on his back?"

"I believe so. Maybe Zav has forgiven Sarrlevi for the egregious crime of moving in across the street."

"That seems unlikely. Unless they've realized that they have a common enemy to worry about now and need to band together." I still didn't sense Zavryd or Sarrlevi. It was strange that Val had been able to so much sooner than I. We were both half-bloods and had seemed to have about the same range before.

"Are you talking about the goblins?" she asked.

"Yup. Didn't you say you caught one peeing on the rose bushes just outside your defenses the other day?"

"He was *squatting* suspiciously. I'm not sure urination happened."

"It must be a joy to live in your neighborhood," Willard murmured.

Finally, I sensed Zavryd flying in this direction. And, yes, Val was right. Sarrlevi was with him.

Are you all right? Sarrlevi asked into my mind.

That wasn't his usual greeting. And... did he sound worried?

Uh, I think so. A flutter of dread attacked my stomach, and I turned my palm up to look at the glowing knot pattern. *Why do you ask?*

He hesitated. *Your aura isn't as strong and bright to my senses as it normally is.*

The flutters turned into a boulder dropping. What had the artifact *done*? Could it have poisoned me as well as marked me?

Something did happen, I admitted, not able to take my gaze from my glowing palm. *To me and Dimitri. I hope you or Zavryd have some ideas about how to fix it. How much do you know about dark-elven artifacts?*

Only that they're as evil as those who create them and can be deadly.

I swallowed and eyed the skeleton. *Yeah.*

3

I WASN'T IN THE MOOD FOR BARBECUE OR ANYTHING ELSE, BUT WHEN Zavryd landed, he recognized the area as being close to a restaurant he liked and declared that he would study the marks Dimitri and I had received while suitable amounts of meat were delivered to him. Now, I sat inside at a table for four with an extra chair dragged up as Sarrlevi clasped my hand and Zavryd examined Dimitri's palms.

Val sipped her water, not giving any indication that she minded being left out of the hand clasping. Willard had gone to her office, and Val had her phone out, waiting for updates.

I was glad we'd kept her from being marked, but I wished Dimitri and I had also managed to avoid this fate. Even though the artifact had magically compelled us to touch it, I couldn't help but feel like an idiot for being lured in.

I am uncertain how to remove the mark, Sarrlevi spoke into my mind.

For the third time, his healing magic flowed into me, cooling my heated skin and soothing the itch, but it did nothing to diminish the glow. As soon as his magic faded, the itch returned.

But you are certain it's done something to me? To my aura?

Sarrlevi hesitated, his blue eyes concerned as he held my gaze. *I am not... certain it has done permanent harm, but I can feel that your aura is diminished, as if you are ill.*

Ill or poisoned? I grimaced.

Possibly. If the dragon can't heal this, we may need to consult the vampire alchemist. He can take a blood sample to examine.

Won't that be fun? I leaned my head against his shoulder.

"This mark was most certainly caused by dark-elven magic. I have tried but am unable to remove it." Zavryd squinted at Sarrlevi and then down to my hand. "You have also failed, assassin?"

"I lack the knowledge to remove a dark-elven mark," Sarrlevi said coolly. "That is not a *failing* on my part, nor am I, as I have reminded you several times, an assassin any longer."

A waiter came over to the table, noticed the lack of hand-holding between Val and anyone else, and smiled at her. "You without company, babe? I can bring you something from the special menu."

Zavryd's eyes flared with violet light, and he surged to his feet. "You dare suggest interest in *skylitha* with my mate?"

"What with your what?" The waiter looked blankly at him.

"He and I are married." Val showed off her ring finger and pointed to Zavryd.

"Oh, really?" The waiter looked at Dimitri's hand, though Zavryd had dropped it when he rose. "I thought those two were a couple."

Dimitri shook his head and scooted his chair farther from Zavryd.

"Sorry, bro," the waiter said, "but you were holding his hand, and that robe... Well, you can't blame me. Menus?"

Zavryd cast an exasperated look at Val. Some steam might have wafted from his ears.

"We're regulars," Val said. "We don't need a menu. Just bring—"

"Meat," Zavryd said. "Meat without breading or dipping sauces or inferior dish sides."

"Side dishes," Val corrected, "and I'll take his sides."

"I like sides too," Dimitri said. "And cornbread. Lots of cornbread."

"Bring us a variety," Val told the waiter.

"A variety of *meat*." Zavryd squinted around the table as if he would object more vociferously if too many nonprotein dishes ended up on his table.

"You're *sure* you're with him?" the waiter whispered to Val.

"Yup." She grinned and patted Zavryd's hand.

He settled back into his seat, disgruntlement twisting his lips, then snatched up Dimitri's palm to try something else.

I do not sense any foreign magical substances within your blood-stream, Sarrlevi told me telepathically.

His focus remained on my hand, and I wasn't sure he'd heard the food discussion.

I hope that's good, that this isn't anything serious. I threaded my fingers between his.

His eyebrows drew together, but he didn't refute the idea. Because he believed it or he didn't want to worry me?

"You don't think the marks could be transmissible, do you?" Val asked.

Zavryd dropped Dimitri's hand with a thunk. I wouldn't have expected a dragon to worry about dark-elven magic, but maybe the subterranean elves had power enough to threaten his kind.

Sarrlevi either wasn't worried about transmissibility, or he was willing to risk it, for he kept holding my hand.

"That is unknown," Zavryd said, "but I have heard of dark elves placing security artifacts around the perimeters of their lairs and sacred places, especially if they are not frequently used, to keep out trespassers."

"Keep out or *kill*?" Val checked her phone for messages from Willard.

When we'd left the warehouse, I had wanted to go straight to Val's house to roust Zoltan from his coffin, but she'd pointed out that he'd gone to bed recently and charged much more if he had to work outside of what he called sane hours for a vampire. She'd also reminded me that days were short this time of year, so I wouldn't have to wait long until dusk.

"They are indifferent to the deaths of people from other species," Zavryd said.

I shifted in my seat.

We will find a solution, Sarrlevi told me. *You will not die. I will not permit it.*

I didn't know you had the power to prevent death.

I am a noble now. I have many powers.

Oh? Like what?

Sarrlevi hesitated. *I can collect property taxes from those who live on my land.*

Is that a lot of people? Where is your land?

It is not greatly populated, no. Do you remember the boiling pools that you visited outside the capital?

I didn't visit them so much as I was fired at and knocked into one. Don't tell me you own those.

Yes. A great swath of land in that area. Due to the scalding, sulfuric water that seeps out of the ground there, it has little value to any but scientists and some species of animals that do not mind such an environment.

Did you grow up there?

No. We had a home in the capital. Though, due to my lack of popularity with my people, Mother suggested I might build a domicile out there now. She pointed out it would be easy for her to visit me there.

I wrinkled my nose at the idea of a treehouse built into branches extending over scalding water, with toxic fumes wafting into the bedroom. *Maybe you should keep your chalet and get your mom a portal generator for Christmas.*

Such items are rare.

My mom made one for a school project.

Your mother is an exceptional enchanter with rare power.

If you bring her some cheese, maybe she'll make a portal generator for your mom.

He raised his eyebrows. *Does she also have a soft spot for gifts of fine fromage?*

We actually haven't discussed her feelings on cheese. I guess I assumed food cravings are in the genes.

As the waiter and a waitress he'd wrangled into helping brought our trays of food, Val's phone rang. I glimpsed Willard's name on the screen before she answered it.

"Hey, Willard." Val gave me a thumbs-up and put the phone on speaker mode. There weren't any diners at the table next to ours, and once the food was delivered, the servers hurried away. "Any updates? I'm having barbecue with Matti, Sarrlevi, Dimitri, and Zav, and they're listening. Nobody's been able to magically remove the dark-elven marks."

"My people are working to identify the man who died," Willard said. "With Gondo's help and some digging, I've been able to determine that there was a period of a couple of years when young women disappeared in that part of Ballard. Their bodies would be found weeks or months later, mutilated and floating in Salmon Bay or Lake Union. The police believed a human sicko was responsible, but they never found the perpetrator. The magical community believes the deaths were a result of ceremonial sacrifices by dark elves in the area. There were nocturnal sightings from Ballard up to Carkeek Park."

"How many years ago was this?"

"Back in the seventies."

Val scratched her cheek. "So, were these dark elves tied in with the ones hanging out in the Seattle underground?"

"Nobody knows, but it's been a long time since there were sightings in Ballard. And nobody's seen the dark elves you tangled with since the Mt. Rainier incident last year."

"So, Matti and Dimitri may have stumbled into a booby trap they left behind? And it doesn't necessarily represent a current threat?"

"It represents a current threat to *me*," Dimitri grumbled.

I nodded.

"That's our hypothesis, but I've got agents asking around."

I leaned closer to the phone. "What about the artifact itself, ma'am? Dimitri and I are still glowing like we're radioactive, and it's possible we're suffering health effects. Our, uhm, auras are diminishing." Despite having been immersed in magic and magical people these past few months, I felt silly talking about such things to mundane humans. But if any pure-blooded human knew all about the magical world, it would be Willard.

"Meaning you're losing power?" she asked.

Zavryd and Dimitri dug into brisket, pulled pork, and ribs, ignoring the collard greens and coleslaw that had come with the meals. Dimitri did alternate his meat consumption with bites of cornbread.

"Well, probably, but also... vitality, I guess." I thought of how weak Sarrlevi's mother's aura had been when I'd first met her and shivered at the idea that mine might diminish until I also was lying on a sickbed, too weak to get up.

"I don't have a specialist in magical artifacts," Willard admitted. "Now that you're learning about enchanting, *you* might be the best I've got."

"That's depressing," I said.

"But since you, and it seems anyone with magical blood, are drawn to touch the artifact, I can't give it to you to study."

I didn't know anything about dark-elven devices anyway but said, "I was less mesmerized by it once it marked me. I might be able to investigate it without further repercussions."

"Where? In your house? You'd have legions of goblins knocking down your door, drawn by its power. Not to mention Sarrlevi and Zavryd."

Zavryd's head went up, barbecue sauce smeared on his chin. "*I* would not succumb to dark-elven mind-manipulation magic."

"A minute ago," Val told him, "you were worried handholding with Dimitri would result in the mark being transmitted to you."

"That is not the reason I released his hand." Zavryd eyed Dimitri as cornbread crumbs tumbled from his mouth to his T-shirt.

"What?" Dimitri asked.

Val waved in dismissal. "What about Zoltan, Willard? He's got defenses to keep intruders out of his basement, in addition to our wards around the property, and since he's undead, he might be immune to the artifact's effects. He can study it."

"I doubt an alchemist would be more capable of determining the use of an artifact than an enchanter."

"I don't know about that. He has enough books on magical stuff to fill a library, and he likes research."

"He likes to *charge* for his research too," Willard said.

"True, but Matti gets a discounted rate from him right now. She can say the work is for her."

I nodded, willing to pay *any* rate if it would result in the removal of the mark.

"How did she manage to get a discount?" Willard asked. "As frequently as you and I make use of Zoltan's services, he ought to offer *us* one. A punch card at least."

"Buy nine potions and the tenth is free?" Val asked.

"Something like that. I guess if you want to come collect the artifact, I won't stop you, but you'd better promise me you won't let anyone else touch it. I don't want zombie hordes with glowing hands roaming the streets of Seattle."

"I'm not going to turn into a *zombie*, ma'am." I looked at Sarrlevi and whispered, "I'm not, right?"

"I would not guess that would be the outcome, but the dark elves are so secretive that few know much about their magic. They were driven from the elven home world before I was born, so I've had few interactions with them."

"I'll take that responsibility, Willard," Val said. "I just got a decent neighbor across the street. I can't let her die."

"What about me?" Dimitri thumped his chest. "Wouldn't you be a little upset if your roommate bit it?"

"I suppose, though I wouldn't mind getting your pantry space."

"Funny, Val."

Sarrlevi, who hadn't touched any of his food, brushed my shoulder and nodded that he would like a word in private. I left Val hanging up and digging into her meal—the brisket had disappeared from her plate when she hadn't been looking, replaced by extra greens and cornbread—and followed him outside.

"While the alchemist contemplates your affliction and the artifact," Sarrlevi said, "I will attempt research of my own. As distant relatives of the dark elves, my people have more material and historical data on them than most. There also elves old enough to remember when they lived in tunnels under our world. I will consult them—those I can convince to speak with me. Despite the king removing my exile status and making me a citizen again, I am not beloved."

Even though his words made sense, and I wanted a solution to this problem as quickly as possible, I hated the thought of him leaving, of lying in bed alone at night, worrying about this strange illness that might be sapping my life as well as my power. I had to fight the urge to grab his hand and beg him to stay at my side, to help me keep my mind off my concerns.

Instead, I forced myself to smile and nod at his plan. "You'll have to make an effort to charm them the way you did me."

"By bringing them cheese and rubbing their heads?"

"Well, cheese at least. I might get jealous if you start rubbing heads other than mine. Especially if they belong to vivacious elves who are attracted by your great beauty."

"Most of my people old enough to remember the dark elves lack in vivaciousness."

"If we're talking grannies with walkers, I guess I could survive knowing you were giving them scalp massages."

"I'm hoping gold will suffice." Sarrlevi clasped my hand, then bent to kiss me. Telepathically, he added, *I won't be away for long.* A trickle of his power flowed into me, bringing thoughts of bedroom activities to mind. *I'll return soon to keep your mind distracted from your worries at night. To distract your whole body.*

I always appreciate that. I wanted to clasp more than his hand and make the kiss linger.

I know this.

Way more than the elf grannies will appreciate it. I rested a hand on his chest and willed a trickle of my power into him, wanting to make sure he had plenty of reasons to hurry back.

Though I was able to do so, it seemed harder than usual, as if I were trying to use a pen, but something was stopping up the ink flow. It took a moment before the trickle started, teasing his nerves and making him lean into me, basking in the pleasure I gave him.

A brush of fear swept through me as I realized I could lose the power to be able to tantalize him with my magic. Even though I knew he loved me, and I'd had sex my whole adult life without *magic* playing a role in it, an unreasonable worry ricocheted through me. What if he wouldn't be as drawn to me if I couldn't use my power to make his nerves sing with desire?

The dragon has finished consuming everyone's meat. Sarrlevi sighed and stepped back, breaking our kiss as he released me. *I will leave now so that I can return as soon as possible.* His eyelids drooped as he gazed at me. *Tonight, perhaps.*

I made myself smile, but what if by the time he returned, my power was gone? What if I was too weak for sex?

We will find an answer, he assured me, waving his hand to create a portal.

My palm itched. I tried not to find that ominous... but failed.

4

THE NEEDLE SLID INTO MY VEIN WITH A SLIGHT STAB OF PAIN. I didn't object. Dimitri had already endured his blood draw.

We were in Val's basement, the sun setting outside and Zoltan attending us. Usually, his black hair was swept tidily back from his widow's peak, but we'd been too impatient to wait for his ablutions, so he had a severe case of bed head. As he kept reminding us, he hadn't had breakfast yet, and that made a vampire hungry.

Surprisingly, he hadn't suggested that we could be polite and allow him a taste of fresh blood from our veins. Or maybe, given that our palms were still glowing, it wasn't that surprising. Who wanted to eat radioactive food? A few times, he *did* eye Val's wrists speculatively.

"I will examine the artifact after I look at your blood under my microscope and start some tests." As Zoltan took the samples to his equipment-filled counter, he nodded toward the iron box we'd retrieved from Willard.

Thus far, nobody had lifted the lid, so we hadn't had to deal with magical beings showing up, drawn by the artifact's power. Since my senses informed me that Tinja and numerous goblins were in my house, we might soon find out if Val's wards were suffi-cient to keep them all away. I worried that they might, drawn by the artifact, ignore the buzzes of warning that informed strangers of the threats and step in front of the topiaries or trigger other defenses.

"I am not an expert on such matters, you understand," Zoltan continued, "but I am adept at research."

"Yup," Val said, "that's what I told Willard."

"And she agreed with this assessment? She is always so vitri-olic when she must employ my services. I do not believe she truly appreciates my gifts."

"It's your rates that she doesn't appreciate. But you'll be charging *Matti's* rate, right? And you've agreed she gets a discount, right?"

"For bringing me the delightful formulas of the dwarven alchemist? Wondrously exotic and powerful formulas that I am still studying and learning about? Yes, she receives a discount. However, is this not as much a problem for your business partner and roommate, dear robber?" Zoltan gestured at Dimitri. "Not one but *two* of his hands are marked."

"Meaning he should pay twice what Matti pays?" Val asked.

"Twice what she would pay if she did not receive a discount."

"I'm not that rich," Dimitri protested.

"Did you not say that you almost have enough money saved for the down payment on a domicile that is not a van?" Zoltan asked.

"Yeah, but I need that money. You guys are great, but I don't want to live here forever. I want to be able to bring dates home."

"We've never said you can't do that." Val pointed at her chest, then waved toward her bedroom in the turret, though Zavryd had left to learn what he could about dark-elven defense artifacts from other dragons.

"Zoltan complains if I make noise," Dimitri said.

"My complaints revolve around you making the noise of beating metal and sawing wood during my sleep hours. I care not what you do with guests in your bedroom during the night. Am I not already forced to endure the overly exuberant cries that come from the turret?"

Val rubbed her face. "They're not *overly* exuberant. They're... appropriately exuberant."

"Maybe you should convince all of your roommates to move out," I murmured to her.

"I'm not sure how to do that."

"I can't give you lessons, since my roommate who now owns a house down the street is still hanging out in my kitchen." As if the words had summoned her, I sensed Tinja heading in this direction. I glanced at the box, making sure Zoltan hadn't lifted the lid when I hadn't been looking.

"It's hard to convince roommates to leave when their favorite foods are always stocked in your pantry," Val said.

"Your pantry lacks *my* favorite food, dear robber." Zoltan glanced at her neck.

She pointed at his microscope.

Matti, Tinja spoke into my mind from the front yard. *I have something to show you. Are you able to talk? I do not wish to risk my veins by intruding upon the vampire's domicile.*

Though I wasn't in the mood to ooh and ahh over upgrades to the goblinator, I couldn't do anything until the results of Zoltan's tests came back. *Sure. I'll meet you in the backyard.*

Are you ill? Your aura is not as robust as normal.

I grimaced. Hell. Even the goblins could tell.

It's a long story, one that involves me vowing not to consider leasing anything listed under market value. I should have known better.

Yes. There is a human saying: you get what you pay for.

Tell me about it.

I waved to Val to let her know where I was going and headed

up the stairs. She stayed back, taking her duty as guardian of the artifact seriously.

Tinja trotted into the backyard carrying a tablet and a rolled blueprint. "I have crafted plans for the urban-goblin sanctuary. There will be extensive remodeling required. Since I am now a monied goblin, I can pay you well if you will do the work."

"I'll help, but I have to finish The Wrench's order first." I had to *start* it, something that had seemed far less daunting before I'd been marked.

"Understandable. You do not want to cross him." Tinja shuddered.

That tendril of worry trickled down my spine again, the fear that he could undo the favors he'd done if I couldn't give him all that he wanted.

"That is why I have also prioritized my work for him." She held up her tablet. "I recently finished a class on computer drafting, so I was able to customize the tiny-home plans he ordered completely online. I will send you the files."

"Good. Thanks. I'll get started building them as soon as..." I looked at my glowing palm, then pushed my hands through my hair. "Soon."

Tinja saw the glow and gaped. "What happened?"

"I foolishly touched a dark-elven artifact."

"Matti, why would you do such a thing? Their people are evil, and nothing they make with their magic is wholesome."

"I know. There was magical compulsion involved."

"They are not targeting you for some reason, are they?"

"I hope not. I think this was an old booby trap that I stumbled across." I almost wished an enemy *were* targeting me. Then I would have someone to hunt down. I might have needed Sarrlevi's help to deal with dark elves, but he would have given it. We could have captured the guilty party and forced them to remove the mark. "Zoltan is researching the artifact and trying to figure out what this does." I waved my palm.

"Maybe the half-dark-elf tracker friend of Val's mother would know."

I started to shake my head, well aware of how little Val and I had known about our magical blood and the heritage of those who'd given it to us, but wasn't it possible that Arwen had grown up differently? Maybe she'd learned from her dark-elf mother or father. I knew so little about her that I didn't even know which of her parents wasn't human. And was the person dead or alive?

"I can check with her if Zoltan doesn't come up with anything," I said. "We haven't spoken much, but I sent her ribs and lemon bars after my barbecue."

"What if she did not like the food?" Tinja's eyes widened, and she gripped my arm. "What if *she* was responsible? What if she found your offerings so loathsome that she arranged for the artifact to be placed where you would chance across it and die horribly?"

"Come on, Tinja. Arwen is shy, introverted, and hangs out with Val's mom. She's not trying to murder me. Besides, nobody finds ribs and lemon bars loathsome."

Tinja touched her jaw. "That is true. Such foods are wondrous, even to goblins who have grown up eating other fare."

Other fare, such as roadkill. I shuddered at the memory of her fellow goblins trying to toss some onto the grill next to my burgers and hot dogs.

My phone rang, and I yanked it out, hoping Willard had learned more. But my sister's name popped up.

"What's up, Penina?"

"Josh asked me when you and *Uncle Sarrlevi* are going to visit."

"Uhm, probably not this week."

"I called to ask you why my son knows you're making wedding plans with your quirky boyfriend, and you haven't told me."

"Haven't I?" I hadn't told my nephew either, but Sarrlevi and I had been talking about human *mating ceremonies* at the barbecue when the kids had been playing nearby. Josh must have gotten the gist.

"No, you have not," Penina said tartly.

"Well, we haven't set a date or anything, but we're thinking about making things official."

"Official. Matti, that doesn't sound romantic at all. Has he proposed?"

"No, he doesn't know about proposing. He's not from Earth, you know."

"Don't remind me. How will a wedding with him in it even be legal?"

"We haven't gotten that far in the planning yet."

"Do you want *help* with that? You do want to make sure it's a grand and proper wedding, right? Please say, yes, Matti. This is important. Grandma and Grandpa *adored* my wedding."

"Your wedding at that hoity-toity country club with the waiters in white suits who sneered at me for having a grass stain on my shoe?"

"*Yes*. It was magnificent, wasn't it? Remember the cake? It was epic. And the gifts we shared? Everyone loved them. And the bridesmaid dresses. Do you remember them?"

"How could I forget?"

There had been *eight* bridesmaids at my sister's wedding. A ridiculous number, I'd thought, but Penina had been worried, lamenting that it was too few. Our grandparents' traditional Samoan wedding, back before they'd immigrated to the US, had apparently involved a more respectable twenty bridesmaids.

"Oh, and my friends still talk about the talented musicians and the tasteful selection of music, not to mention how beautiful the flower arrangements were. I had to give out the cards of my florist to more people than I can count. I'll make sure to hook you up."

"That's very generous," I murmured, turning toward the door to the basement as it opened.

Val stuck her head out and waved for me to return.

"Are you going to marry in the spring? A spring wedding would be *perfect*. Though there's not much time. I can call the club and see if they have any openings. Our father and, uhm, your mother will come, won't they? Don't let her wear anything... odd. And maybe you and she can go to the hairdresser together and get her frizz tamed. Oh, and why don't you start growing your hair out? It's so tomboyish right now."

"I have to keep it short so it doesn't get in my eyes when I fight." I trotted down the stairs, telling myself not to expect that Zoltan already had an answer but hoping he did.

"I trust you won't be doing as much of *that* once you're married. And you're going to have children, right? You shouldn't wait too long. You're not getting any younger, you know. Right now, Josh and Jessie are still little enough that they could play with your children. Jessie, anyway. Oh, I've always wished we would both have kids and that they could play together. And that you would settle down and stop working so hard. You will, right? You'll *have* to. You can't be pregnant and slinging that hammer around."

I scowled at the phone as I navigated through the double doors of Zoltan's light-lock and groped for a way to end the conversation.

"I need to go, Penina, but I'll let you know when we have a date."

"If you have some flexibility, it will be easier to get a slot at the club."

"I'll let you know about that too." Since I could *hear* Penina scowling at my vagueness, I hurried to say goodbye and hang up before she could launch into the virtues of her chosen venue.

"Like a country club?" Val asked, having caught the end of the call.

"Some kind of golf and social club that they belong to. It's where Josh takes tennis lessons."

"Is it snooty?"

"Yeah."

"Sarrlevi might fit in." Val looked at my jeans and Henley but did not comment on my look or attire. Her daughter would have called it *Grapes of Wrath*. The staff at Penina's club would have even more acerbic comments about it. "You might do better with an outdoor wedding. Mine was in the woods near the goblin sanctuary on the way to Granite Falls. It was great. We got attacked by trolls."

"Romantic."

"Yup." She winked.

Zoltan cleared his throat. "When this female jibber-jabber has concluded, I can share my findings."

"It's called girl chat," Val said, "and it's important, but go ahead."

"Thank you vastly for granting your permission." Zoltan faced me.

I tried to plaster a hopeful expression on my face, but Dimitri, who'd never left the basement, slumped in one of the wingback chairs with his face in his hand. That didn't portend good news.

"I have examined your blood and found no evidence that there is a poison or anything foreign coursing through your veins. I believe that your affliction is wholly magical." Zoltan patted a book written in a language I didn't recognize, but a page held a large drawing of what might have been a similar artifact. "Unless I am mistaken, you have been cursed."

"No kidding," I said.

"I refer to a *literal* curse, not some spitting of oaths at an enemy. This will, over time, affect your health."

"How *much* time?"

"The literature that I have painstakingly translated does not say."

"How badly will it affect my health?"

"That is also not stated explicitly, but dark elves are known to wish ill on those who presume to trespass on territory they have claimed, especially religiously significant territory."

"So it might kill me." I looked at Dimitri, but he didn't lift his head.

"It may, yes."

"Is there an antidote? A cure? If there's a list of ingredients, I'm sure I can find them. Sarrlevi can help me. He's great at finding things."

"Yes, your new beau has the nose of a truffle hog, a desirable trait in a mate, I am certain. But, no, my pugilistic half-dwarf, there is not a *list* or an antidote at all. The curse must be removed by the person who placed it upon you."

"Uh." I glanced at the iron box. "It wasn't a person."

"In this case, I would assume the maker of the artifact could remove the curse."

"Zoltan," Val said, "this artifact might have been in that warehouse for decades. The maker probably isn't alive."

"Dark elves are as long-lived as surface elves," he said.

"Yeah, but these dark elves had a car-filled street fall through their base after a dragon and I tore into them. I'll admit we didn't wipe them *all* out, since they put together a sizable infiltration of Mt. Rainer, but... there hasn't been any sign of them around lately."

"It is possible that you need not find the maker of that particular artifact but only a powerful dark elf with the general knowledge of how to make such devices."

"Did you hear the part about how there hasn't been any sign of dark elves?" Val asked. "At *all*?"

"Is your mother not a tracker?" Zoltan asked. "Perhaps she can locate their current warren."

"Couldn't a magically gifted person from another species learn about the artifact and how to cure Matti and Dimitri?"

"I suppose anything is possible, but dark-elven curses are quite powerful, and one of the tomes I researched said that *only* a dark elf would be able to remove one."

"Ugh." Val slumped.

So did I. If Zoltan was right, neither Sarrlevi nor Zavryd would find an elf or dragon who could help. Not unless they knew where in the Cosmic Realms a sect of artifact-making dark elves was hunkered down.

"I will investigate the device further," Zoltan said, "and let you know if I learn anything helpful, but I deem it unlikely that it can reverse the effects it imposed. It likely only has one enchantment, to apply the curse to enemies."

I eyed the artifact box. "So, if I used my hammer to smash it into a thousand pieces, it wouldn't do anything?"

"To help you? No."

"What about to make me feel better and be an outlet for my frustrations?" I rubbed my hammer's haft, tempted.

Val lifted a hand to stop me. "It's rarely a good idea to break artifacts. Trust me. I know."

"I suppose you're right." I looked around the basement, longing for *something* I could pummel to pieces.

"Ah, dear robber." Zoltan must have recognized my expression of frustration—he'd seen it before, after all—for he lifted a hand and pointed to the doorway. "Please take your belligerent friend out of my laboratory before she menaces the many valuable and *breakable* items present."

"Come on, Matti." Val rested a hand on my shoulder. "You look like you need a beer."

I needed a solution.

"Dimitri," Val added, "are you interested?"

He wasn't menacing anything, but Zoltan also shooed him out.

"I can't sit around and do nothing, Val," I said.

"I'll call my mother, and we can go look at the remains of the dark-elf lair Zav and I trashed. Maybe by now, a few of their people have moved back in. After all, Seattle is a happening place. Where else are you going to find quality people to sacrifice?"

"Your humor can be dark at times," I pointed out.

"What did you expect from someone called the Ruin Bringer?"

5

When Val's mom said she refused to track dark elves in underground lairs in the middle of the night, I took the opportunity to use the portal generator in my office to visit Dun Kroth. Though uncharacteristic fatigue made me want to head to bed early instead, I worried that I didn't have a lot of time and had better not waste it.

Zoltan's implication that only a dark elf could lift the curse didn't lead me to believe my mother, powerful enchanter though she was, would be able to heal me. Still, she had a lot of knowledge and resources, so maybe she would be able to do something. Besides, even if she couldn't help, I felt compelled to let her know about my problem. In case...

Just in case.

It turned out to be night on Dun Kroth, as well, or at least the period in which the lights in the dwarven capital and surrounding tunnels dimmed for sleep. The escort that always accompanied me after I arrived took me not to the smithy, my mother's usual spot, but to the royal quarters. She led me through the hallways carved from salt to Mom's quarters.

When we reached a stout wooden door, the escort didn't knock or pull the chain, instead frowning at a series of thumps that came from within.

"Oh, good. She's up." Never certain how the days lined up between Dun Kroth and Earth, I didn't know how late in the night I'd arrived. Switching to telepathy since the dwarf didn't understand English, I pointed to the chain and said, *Sounds like she's crafting something. Do I pull that instead of knocking?*

The dwarf opened her mouth, as if she might correct my assumption, but merely shook her head and waved to it.

As soon as I tugged it, she took off at a jog. Worried that Mom would be angry because of an interruption? That didn't seem like her.

The thumps stopped after I pulled on the chain, but long seconds passed without an answer. My senses still worked well enough to let me know that Mom was in there, and I didn't detect anyone with her. Unless...

A premonition crept over me as I remembered *who* might be with her and wouldn't have a detectable aura.

The door opened, my mother in a sleeveless lacy nightie, sweat gleaming on her bare skin and her frizzy hair wilder than usual. Penina's suggestion that I take Mom to a salon before my wedding came to mind.

"Hello, *Nika*." She frowned as she looked me up and down.

"Hi, Mom. Are you, uh, crafting?" I looked at her bare feet.

Her eyes twinkled. "No." She glanced back, and my father stepped out of a side room wearing a pair of jeans and nothing else.

I blushed, having a feeling he hadn't even been wearing *those* a minute ago.

"Sorry," I blurted. "I didn't mean to interrupt. I didn't think you would be here, Dad. Weren't you just visiting Grandma and Grandpa? I know Grandma mentioned that to me earlier." I looked at the doorframe instead of at him—at *them*. Even though they were both somewhat dressed, I was flustered.

"Yes, but they fall asleep after *Jeopardy*," he said. "Your grandma *did* mention that you might be marrying Sarrlevi though. I wanted to see if your mother knew any details yet."

Word of the wedding I hadn't told anyone about was spreading faster than a goblin foraging team in a junkyard. This was what I got for discussing such things in front of grade-schoolers.

"Which clearly led to the two of you..." I waved toward the doorway to the bedroom, the rumpled covers visible, some of them on the floor.

"Talk of love puts everyone in the mood. But *Nika*." Mom's gaze caught on my hand, the glowing mark. "What's happened? Is that *dark-elven* magic?"

"A curse, yes."

She took my hand and examined the mark while I summarized what had happened. While listening, Dad fetched his shirt and socks.

"I remember being given samples of the dark-elven language when I was studying the linguistics of the magical communities while in the Army," he said, "but my superiors told me that it was unlikely I would ever run into one. There aren't many left in the Cosmic Realms, much less on Earth."

"It doesn't take many to cause trouble." Mom's magic trickled into my hand, much as Sarrlevi's had earlier. It soothed the itch but did not remove the mark. "How long has it been since you received this, *Nika*? You realize... or do you?" Her frown lifted to my face.

"That it's diminishing my aura, and I could die if I can't find someone to remove the curse? Yeah. It's putting a real damper on the wedding plans."

She blinked at my sarcasm.

Maybe it wasn't appropriate, but I would have cried if I let myself ponder how I really felt.

"You are truly planning a wedding already?" Mom asked as she returned to examining my hand, again probing it with magic, not healing magic this time but something that made the itch intensify.

I resisted the desire to yank my hand away. If there was any chance she could help, I would let her. "No, only fielding unsolicited suggestions."

"You could have it here. Your grandfather—your *dwarven* grandfather—would enjoy being a part of it."

"Would he enjoy *Sarrlevi* being a part of it?"

"Well, perhaps not as much, but he wouldn't try to break you up, and the drink would flow copiously." Mom retracted her magic.

If anything, the glow flared and intensified. Was it my imagination that the knot-pattern had grown larger, filling more of my palm?

"I'm not sure my grandparents, the human ones, could handle Dwarven alcohol or the trip to Dun Kroth," I said, "but I'll keep your offer in mind. You don't know where any dark elves might be found, do you?"

"They never dared make a home on Dun Kroth."

"Because dwarves are so fearsome?"

"Fearsome, noisy, and they already occupied the tunnels here. We also have the magic to detect intruders like that and rush promptly to wherever they arrive and drive them out. Most of the magical races can do that. It's why dark elves often end up on the wild worlds, making a living where the populations are small or inept when it comes to sensing magical threats."

"Like humans," Dad said dryly.

"Yes. Are you offended?"

"That my species is inept or that you're pointing it out?"

"Either."

"Given how much, ah, *joy* being with you has given me, I shall not take offense, no."

"*Joy*," Mom said, winking at me, "is not what he was begging me for moments ago."

"*Mom.*" I blushed again. Dad ran a hand over his face and looked embarrassed too. Maybe it was a human thing to find such frank discussions of sexuality with one's children discomfiting. "The only information I came for is about dark elves."

"Well, I doubt much brings *them* joy. I will ask around and see if any of my father's staff or advisors have any idea about where to find dark elves. Someone was just mentioning—" Mom looked thoughtfully toward the wall behind my head as she tried to dredge up a memory.

I leaned forward, barely resisting the urge to grab her by the shoulders and try to shake loose whatever it was.

"Ah," Mom said. "I remember where I heard about dark elves recently. A *half*-dark elf. But that won't do you any good."

"What?" I didn't grab her shoulders but did clasp her hand.

At this point, I would welcome any lead. She couldn't be referring to the half-dark elf Arwen, could she? I couldn't imagine when they would have met. After helping find the organization's underground lair on the Olympic Peninsula, Arwen and Val's mom had left before the battle, so my parents hadn't ever encountered them.

"You'll recall that my people are upset because the half-elf–half-dragon criminal Starblade found and released a few other half-dragon soldiers that were also put in stasis chambers at the end of their war."

"Yes," I said, "and that King Ironhelm is grumpy with King Eireth over it, and you're building weapons and defenses for Dun Kroth in case Starblade starts something."

But what did that have to do with dark elves?

"We believe there are only four half-dragons left from that time, so four in total, including Starblade. Few of the half-orc-, half-troll-, and half-ogre-half-dragons that were made during the experiments reached adulthood. Those who did died during the fighting. But one of the remaining half-dragons is a female half-*dark* elf. Whether she has the knowledge of those people, I don't know—she might have been raised by the same elven commander and scientist who created and raised the others to be soldiers. But she would certainly have the *power* to remove such a curse."

"Oh." I didn't know whether to get my hopes up or not. "Power isn't enough though. Zavryd tried to heal us, and he couldn't. Zoltan, the vampire alchemist who lives across the street, said it would take the dark elf who created the artifact, or someone with the same knowledge, to remove it."

"That's possible. You should bring the artifact to me. Perhaps by studying its magic, I could learn how the curse works."

"I would, but it might compel you to touch it, and then you'd be cursed too."

"I believe I could resist such a compulsion."

I grimaced, still feeling like a fool, or at least a weakling, since *I* hadn't resisted anything. "It's at Val's house if you want to take a look. It might be better to check it out there than to bring it back here. In case not all the dwarves in the city have your ability to resist mental compulsions. Just guard your veins when you go."

Mom blinked before catching on. "Because the vampire alchemist would waylay them?"

"He might try."

"You have interesting neighbors."

"I know. I'd better get back. I'm expecting Sarrlevi."

"Good." Mom smiled at me. "It is good that you two have each other. He can comfort you during this ordeal." She rested a hand on my shoulder, her smile turning a touch mischievous. "Did you try the *zesh shaylesh* on him?"

Heat scorched my cheeks.

"The what?" Dad asked. "That's not an Elven term I'm familiar with."

"The Earth Army did not educate you as thoroughly as I expected." Eyes glinting, Mom smirked at him.

"Please don't tell him what it is," I whispered, mortified.

"No," Mom agreed. "I see that such talk with your parents distresses you."

Talk of magical cock rings might distress my *father* too.

"Yeah," I said.

"But you did use it, yes?"

I rubbed my cheeks. "Yes."

"Excellent. I trust he enjoyed the experience." Mom squeezed my shoulder and released me. "As I said, I will ask around. No matter what I find, I will come soon to check on you." Her gaze grew somber as she looked toward my hand.

I curled my fingers, feeling the need to hide the mark, to hide my shame at having let myself be afflicted with it.

"We will find a dark elf who can lift the curse." She nodded firmly toward me. "I have not been reunited with my daughter after three decades only to lose her."

"Thanks, Mom."

6

Rain fell outside, darkness shrouded my bedroom, and my palm glowed like a purple beacon.

Though Sarrlevi had returned for the night and helped distract me for a couple of hours—bless his elven stamina—now that we lay quietly, sleep eluding me, it was hard not to notice the mark. Even when I pressed my palm against the blanket, the glow seeped out around the edges.

Sarrlevi dozed at my side, an arm draped over my stomach, so I tried not to shift around much, and resisted the temptation to jam my hand deep under the blankets. I didn't want to wake him. *Someone* should have a peaceful night's sleep.

As fatigued as I was, with my eyes gritty and sore, I'd expected to doze off quickly after we made love. Instead, I lay staring at the ceiling and wondering what would happen if I couldn't find a solution to this.

Would I truly die? Or simply grow frail and lose all my power? Nobody had a concrete answer, at least that they'd shared with me, but I'd caught Val and Sarrlevi eyeing me with grim concern when they didn't think I was looking.

My power had already started to wane. Usually, Sarrlevi and I both used our magic on each other to tease and titillate during foreplay, but I'd struggled to be effective with mine tonight. He hadn't said anything, but he had to have noticed. And had he been disappointed?

Probably worried, I told myself, because he cared, and the decline in my ability was an indicator that I wasn't well. Still, how would he feel if I survived but I permanently lost my power? If I became, despite my dwarven blood, no different from a mundane human? Would he find sex with me boring? Would he be driven to seek another more stimulating lover?

No. I scowled at myself. He'd said he loved me numerous times and didn't want to hurt me. And he'd said he was fine with a monogamous relationship.

Of course, lots of people said that, and over time, things changed...

In my case, things had changed since breakfast.

You find sleep elusive, Sarrlevi spoke softly into my mind.

I turned my head to find his eyes open as he watched me. So much for not waking him. Had he been reading my thoughts? My doubts? I didn't want to offend him with them. He'd never given me *any* reason to doubt him, and I wouldn't have voiced my concerns. Sometimes, it was hard having a boyfriend who could read my mind.

Yeah. I lifted my palm to show him the mark. *I have a hard time sleeping with the lights on.*

Understandable. Sarrlevi brushed his fingers along my jaw. *My love for you and interest in being with you is not conditional on your performance in bed.*

I know. But I figure it's a perk that keeps things interesting.

You keep things interesting. He rested his hand on mine, covering the mark. *Even when you should not.*

I do have a knack for getting into trouble.

So I've observed.

But, hey, you've had more people—more extremely powerful people, including dragons—after you than I have.

More *people? Are you certain? A great many assassins were hunting you.*

Yeah, but one dragon has to count for ten or twenty assassins. They're all from lesser species, after all.

Lesser. Really.

I shifted onto my side to face him and slide my arm over his muscular chest. *I'm trying to be better about not letting my thoughts be full of insecurities, but today has given them a reason to rear up again. I'm not sure that, deep down, I really believe I'm enough for you.* Or enough in general? Sometimes, such as when the photographer and journalist came to do a magazine piece on me, I felt that I was, that I did good work and was succeeding in my business. Other times, I still felt like Penina's screw-up of a younger sister who'd barely graduated high school, had dated all the wrong guys, and who lost her temper on a dime. *Especially now that you're a noble.* I smiled to let him know I was joking. I shouldn't have brought this up at all.

Yes, my inheritance of the sulfuric pools that can slay any who fall into them has elevated me to a status that must make all around me feel inferior. Sarrlevi brushed his fingers along my jaw again. *You are enough for me. I hope that one day you will be enough for yourself.*

Me too. I smiled wryly. *Thanks for coming back tonight. I didn't want to say anything, but...* I rubbed my thumb over the itchy mark. *I didn't want to be alone.*

I did not wish you to be alone either.

Glad for his touch—for him—I turned my face into his hand. *I hope you aren't offended when my insecurities run amok in my mind. I do love you, and I trust that you won't leave me.*

Do you? He didn't sound irritated or confrontational, simply curious. *I think that if you trusted me fully, your insecurities would not voice themselves to you.*

I winced. Was that true? Was a lack of trust why I worried he would eventually be bored with me and seek stimulation elsewhere? Deep down, did I believe he couldn't want me forever?

I'm sorry. I'll keep working on that.

It will come with time, I suspect. That is how trust forms, not in a spurt of passionate lovemaking and a few evenings spent together but over months and years when people prove themselves to you again and again in small ways. Also, it is easier for me to trust you, because I can not only hear your words but see your thoughts.

Yeah. Have I mentioned how completely not fair that is?

Sarrlevi chuckled. *Perhaps if you read my mind and witness how I see you, you would feel more secure?*

I don't know how to read minds. That's not enchanting magic. The only time I saw your thoughts was when you took that truth drug and showed me how excited you got by me jiggling naked while swinging my hammer at your laundry device.

Yes, that was *an exciting time.*

I swatted him on the chest.

He captured my hand and held it against his heart. *Right now would not be the ideal time for you to attempt to learn new ways to use your power, but you are not limited by what is considered enchanting magic. You easily learned telepathy. I believe it would be a simple matter for you to read people's thoughts.*

Don't you and most powerful magical beings protect your thoughts behind mental barriers?

Yes. We learn to do so at a young age, as a protection from others who can read minds and might use our desires against us, and also so we do not inundate those around us by projecting our thoughts. Many elves are especially sensitive and would know, for example, when you're wandering around craving cheese.

I blinked. *I'm projecting my cheese cravings to people without knowing it?*

To those sensitive enough to pick up on such things. My mother isn't extremely powerful, but she does have a knack for capturing people's thoughts.

So I've smothered her with my cravings? Maybe *I* needed to learn how to protect my thoughts. If it was no more challenging than mastering telepathy, it might not be that difficult.

I don't think she minds. She likes knowing that you also crave her son.

Hell. I imagined thoughts of me lusting for Sarrlevi bombarding his mother. Hopefully, I hadn't been around her that often when I'd been thinking about such things.

I also like knowing that you crave me.

As if you weren't completely sure about that two seconds after we met. Even a rock could have read the attraction in my flustered burbling to him that first day.

Perhaps, but if you would like, when you are better, I can show you how to protect your mind. I can also lower my barriers to let you read mine. Sometimes, that happens regardless, when we're intimate and I'm relaxed.

Such as the times you've stuck images of us having sex against tree trunks in my head? Most of the glimpses I'd had of his thoughts had come when we'd been intimate. I'd thought he'd been intentionally sharing them, but maybe it had been more that he'd let his guard down, and I'd... read his mind? Accidentally?

Such as. Here. He threaded his fingers with mine and closed his eyes. *Try to see what I'm thinking.*

I couldn't sense that anything about him had changed—mental barriers had to be different from physical barriers—and I didn't know how to start. When I wanted to communicate telepathically with someone, I pictured their face in my mind. Maybe if I imagined Sarrlevi's face and then sliding my power past it to sift through his thoughts?

When the dragons mind-scoured me, it felt like talons raking through my brain matter. I didn't want to do anything like that to Sarrlevi—or anyone. But if my power could hover gently above his head, cupping it like a satellite dish, might I detect the thoughts floating out?

A satellite dish receives a signal? Sarrlevi asked.

Yeah.

That is likely an apt analogy, though you might have to burrow in, since I am not attempting to project my thoughts outward.

Hm. I tried the satellite first, mentally placing it on his head like a bowl. I didn't want to *burrow*. That sounded too much like mind-scouring.

Seconds passed, with nothing happening, and I was about to give up and try something else when I caught feelings of patience and support coming from him. It was like when Sorka emanated her moods at me. Except if he wasn't *projecting* that, I had to be picking it up?

Next, a feeling of approval came from him. I didn't catch words, not like when we used telepathy, but simply sensed his feelings. Some of his deeper-down concerns started to come to me.

He was worried about me and disgruntled because none of the people he'd reached out to on Veleshna Var had known where to find current dark-elf camps. He felt his time going back to his world had been wasted and that he should have stayed with me in case I'd needed him. He'd come to care deeply for me, and he would resent the universe if he lost me after we'd been together for such a short period of time.

I swallowed, touched that he cared, but also distressed that he was as concerned about the mark and what it meant as I was. I'd hoped he would be confident that we could find a way to fix it.

Reading thoughts, I realized, might be a two-edged sword. One edge might deliver useful information but the other could reveal things I would prefer not to know.

At least I sensed that everything he'd told me was the truth, that he loved me and would stick with me. That he wanted to be with me for all the years we could have together, and that he was even willing to endure what he feared would be an insipid Earth wedding ceremony if it would make me and my family happy.

I snorted softly, tempted to protest the word *insipid*, but hadn't I also sneered at the wedding suggestions people had made?

Eloping is also something people occasionally do on Earth, I told him.

I see you are effectively reading my thoughts.

Yeah, about the insipidness of weddings.

I do not mind elven *weddings. I find most of your human cultural practices either puzzling or...*

Insipid?

Yes. Dwarven weddings, where all the guests grow inebriated, don't appeal that much either. I admit even elven wedding ceremonies can be tedious, and since my mother is the only family I would wish to invite... Sarrlevi shrugged. *Perhaps you should tell me more about this* eloping.

Maybe so. I couldn't imagine flying down to Las Vegas to marry Sarrlevi over a weekend, but maybe, if we could magic some official-looking paperwork into existence for him, we could visit the local justice of the peace. *Would you want your mother to come to whatever ceremony we might have? Or anyone else?*

My mother might be pleased to witness our joining, even if it was not in the elven way. His telepathic voice grew amused when he added, *I would not be inclined to invite Assassins' Guild acquaintances.* He envisioned a surly collection of men and women, some tusked, some green-skinned, some with pointed ears, all with weapons and armor.

Such attendees might alarm the person marrying us.

Yes. Sarrlevi smiled at me. *I did not project that image toward you. I am pleased that your efforts to read my mind are working.*

With my imaginary satellite dish cupping his head, I sensed that he *was* pleased, the feeling coming through with the words. He was also... proud of me and the progress I'd made learning to use my magic.

It'll be easier when you get your power back. We'll try again then. A sense of sadness came with his words, a fear that we wouldn't find a solution in time and that I *wouldn't* get my power back.

Bleakness crept into me. Maybe this hadn't been a good time to practice mind reading.

But it allowed me to see that he was upset that he might lose me and also that I wouldn't be able to continue with the enchanting work that was bonding my mother and me together after so many years apart. As far as I could tell, there wasn't anything in his mind about sex or how it might be disappointing if I couldn't use my power on him during it.

"Thank you, Varlesh." I snuggled closer, wrapping both arms around him and kissing him.

You are welcome. He slid a hand under the covers to rest on my hip, fingers brushing my skin. *Perhaps, since you have not been able to find sleep, you wish a further distraction from your concerns.*

Though my fatigue hadn't gone away, my body still roused easily to his touch, and I smiled against his mouth. *Yes, perhaps I would.*

His kiss deepened as his fingers explored. *Excellent.*

7

Dawn found me on a dock on Lake Union near Gas Works Park, the sky clear but fog wreathing the nearby houseboats. We weren't looking at them but at a two-person submarine that could supposedly fit three if we squeezed. Well, make that *four* if the golden retriever was willing to hop in.

Val and her mother Sigrid were with me, as was Sigrid's dog Rocket. A few early risers who lived in the nearby houseboats looked curiously toward the submarine. We'd all been bemused when it had been delivered not by an Army vehicle but by a pair of goblins with a steam-powered jalopy and a trailer made out of rusted metal and recycled beer cans. Apparently, Gondo had arranged everything.

I'd invited Sarrlevi to come, but he and Zavryd had gone off together to search a few locations that Zavryd had learned of where dark-elven artifacts had been found in the past. It had amused me to watch them snipe at each other, proclaiming how vile and inferior the other was, and then fly off together with Sarrlevi riding on Zavryd's back.

"I don't think Rocket is willing to get inside that, dear." Sigrid gripped her chin as she studied the submarine, the canopy open and waiting for us.

"I didn't ask *Rocket* to come along, Mom," Val said. "What dog wants to track in half-collapsed tunnels? Also, I don't have the shirt off a dark elf's back to give him. He's not going to be able to follow any trails down there."

"Didn't you say you had an artifact?"

"Yeah, but it might be fifty years old. It's not like it would have a fresh scent. Besides, a team of dwarves showed up at the house this morning, asking to be allowed on the property so they could look at it." Val looked at me.

"My mom sent them. She's probably coming too, as soon as my father has satisfied all her needs in bed."

Sigrid stared at me, her mouth opening in an O.

"Matti and her mom openly share with each other about their sex lives," Val told her.

"My, isn't that... healthy," Sigrid murmured, horror lurking in her eyes.

"Mom does more sharing than I do," I admitted.

Sigrid turned back toward the submarine, which Rocket was sniffing, his tail out rigid. He'd wagged it delightedly at the pile of duck droppings we'd passed on the dock, but this machine was clearly more suspicious.

"Are you positive there aren't any other entrances to these tunnels?" Sigrid asked.

"No," Val said, "but this is the only one I'm certain still exists. The old buildings with access to the underground have long since been demolished or sealed off, and, after our battle, the Washington State Department of Transportation filled in all the holes and the ceremonial cavern the dark elves had carved out under the city."

Val climbed into the submarine and waved for us to follow. I settled gingerly in one of two seats, not much more excited about this mode of transportation than the dog. Rocket *did* get in, but only after Sigrid climbed in behind the two seats and waved a piece of salmon jerky under his nose.

The curved hatch that came down to seal us in was made from clear glass, or maybe something stronger, but that didn't keep the inside from feeling cramped. Especially when a dog tail whacked me in the side of the head. It whacked Val too.

She only sighed. "We'll be in deep shit if I have to summon Sindari too."

"I would hope you wouldn't do that *inside* the submarine," Sigrid said.

"If we're underwater, I'm not going to instruct him to pop up *outside*. Or even on the surface. He complains if he gets wet in the rain." Val familiarized herself with the controls, then steered us out toward the middle of the lake.

"I assume we won't run into trouble and need furry allies until we get into the tunnels," I murmured, leaning away from the tail again.

Rocket whined and was too nervous to wag it, but it was long, and there wasn't much room.

"Probably not," Val said. "I haven't heard any reports of krakens lately."

I looked at her face for signs of humor. "Was that a joke, or have you actually fought a kraken?"

"Right here in this lake the *last* time I went to see the dark elves. The krakens can get in through the Ballard Locks."

"Do they enjoy freshwater lakes full of house boats?"

"They enjoy when the dark elves feed them." Val grunted as Rocket turned around, his tail whapping her in the cheek. "Mom. Matti was hoping you'd bring *Arwen* along, not Rocket."

Sigrid gave me a betrayed look, as if there was no greater offense than not wanting Rocket.

I shook my head and patted him on the back. "I don't mind the dog. I didn't say anything about him. As to Arwen, well, I was cursed by a dark elf and thought she might know something about how to get rid of it." I showed her my hand.

Sigrid pursed her thin lips in disapproval. At my hand? Or at her daughter's lack of appreciation for her furry companion?

"Val, if you wanted me to bring Arwen, you should have said so."

"I said it would be great if you could bring your tracking friend."

Sigrid's gaze fell to Rocket, who was now sniffing my hand, either wondering why it was glowing or hoping to find treats in it.

Val rolled her eyes, much as her daughter often did to her. "Sorry, Mom. I should have been more specific about *which* tracking friend I wanted."

"Yes," Sigrid said.

"She sleeps with Rocket," Val told me. "They're besties."

Rocket woofed.

"In the bed?" I considered his furry head. "That's not problematic when it comes to..." I trailed off, remembering that Sigrid had never mentioned her werewolf lover to me. It was through Val's sparring-time gossip that I knew most of the goings-on in her family, and Val had been adamant that her mother and the werewolf across the street were most definitely *not* dating. "Relations," I finished lamely as Sigrid turned her pursed lips toward me.

"At my age, *relations* don't take long," Sigrid said.

"The relations you're *not* having with Liam?" Val smirked over her shoulder as she pushed a lever, prompting bubbles to rise to the surface as the submarine's tanks let out air and we descended.

"That's none of your business," Sigrid said.

"Are you going to get married? Matti is getting hitched to Sarrlevi soon. Maybe you could combine funds and go in together on a venue. Have back-to-back weddings."

"*Venue*," Sigrid mouthed, as if horrified.

Since I'd never seen her with shoes on, I guessed she might be the kind of person who would also detest the idea of a country-club wedding. Or going to a country club for *any* reason.

"I explained the concept of eloping to Sarrlevi last night," I told them.

Sigrid nodded, as if she believed it a perfectly reasonable thing to discuss, while Val gave us both an aggrieved look.

"Mom has never been married. She shacked up with Eireth for a summer, and that was it. I thought she might enjoy an actual wedding."

"I would not," Sigrid said tartly, "and I'll thank you to stop sharing my personal life with your colleague."

"Matti is my across-the-street neighbor now," Val said. "We're practically besties. Like you and Rocket."

"Uh, except for the sleeping together part," I murmured.

"Yeah, Sarrlevi might object to that."

"Not as much as *your* mate would object," I said, thinking of Zavryd's jealousy over the flirting waiter.

Val snorted. "That's the truth. All right. Let's see if I can find that tunnel entrance."

We'd descended a couple dozen feet below the surface. Wan morning sunlight trickled down from above, and we could make out the rusted hull of what looked like a World War II–era ship resting on the bottom.

"I didn't realize there were wrecks down here," I said.

"Oh, sure. There's a dive shop nearby and everything. People come to check them out all the time."

"Even with all that traffic, the dark elves had an entrance to their lair down here?"

"They only came and went at night." Val turned on a headlamp and sent the submarine to what I believed was the south, but I'd already lost my bearings.

When I reached out with my senses, I couldn't detect any

magic in the area. What my range was now, I didn't know, but Val hadn't mentioned sensing anything either.

What were the odds that we would get lucky and stumble across a dark elf living in the collapsed tunnels? A dark elf with the power to remove my curse?

My phone buzzed with an incoming text.

My cousin, Mikki the Wrench, wants to know if you've started work on the tiny homes. With winter coming, he wishes to ensure the rural goblins on his forest property are well-provided for. Also, more hunters have been reported stalking among the trees out there. The Wrench wants to make sure your enchantments will keep humans from finding the goblins.

My gut knotted at the reminder of all I'd promised. Before, it had been daunting but doable. Now...

I could still build, I told myself. It was only the enchanting that would be problematic. If I had to, I ought to be able to convince my mother to come to Earth when the tiny homes were done, and *she* could enchant them. Making self-cleaning countertops and shower stalls that don't leak ought to be easy for someone of her caliber. And she surely knew how to camouflage a dwelling.

But what if the war the dwarves were preparing for came to pass? What if the half-dragon Starblade was out there doing a lot more than setting other prisoners free? By now, he could have amassed armies to lead, to settle a grudge against the dwarves who'd locked him up for centuries.

"Who's texting you this early?" Val kept her focus on the route ahead. We were now meandering under houseboats, carefully avoiding the chains that anchored them to the bottom.

"Cousin Vinnie."

Eyebrows arching, Val glanced at me.

I sighed. "Vintok, The Wrench's cousin. They're checking on my house-construction progress."

"Have you started any of them?"

"I ordered lumber."

"That's a no, right?"

"Yeah."

Her second glance went toward my hand. "Are you going to let him know you've got a problem that's going to delay things?"

"Ideally not. Because we're going to solve it soon, right?"

"Right." Val pointed at a nearly vertical slope that was more rock than dirt.

Was there a slab there, or was that my imagination? The faintest trickle of magic plucked at my senses.

"That's the spot," she said.

"A door?"

"Leading into an airlock, yes." Val nudged the submarine forward and pressed a button, extending a tool. "Let's see if this works. Last time, I had to use Storm to pry the door open, but I don't think the dark elves have been here to keep the locking and illusion magic fully up. It's faded."

I grimaced at the reminder that we probably wouldn't find anyone here who could solve my problems. The best I could hope for was a lead about where the dark elves might be now. Did evil demon-worshippers leave forwarding addresses when they cleared out of their destroyed bases?

"Do you think Arwen would mind if you gave me her phone number?" I asked Sigrid.

That earned me a blank look.

"Doesn't she have a phone?" I asked.

"My *mom* doesn't even have a phone." Val stuck her tongue between her teeth as she maneuvered the tool—a cross between a wrench and a chisel—into a faint crack along the stone slab.

"I do so have a phone," Sigrid said. "I'm not a Luddite."

"Oh, please, Mom. You are the exact definition of a Luddite. Your *rotary* phone is glued to the wall and has a cord you could strangle intruders with. It's the most sophisticated piece of technology you have. And the most recently invented."

"Really, Val. I have a car."

"Cars were invented over a hundred years ago."

"I also have a clicker."

"A clicker?" I didn't think Val's tool would work and attempted to funnel some of my magic into the slab, examining it for a locking mechanism.

"For dog training," Sigrid said. "They were invented in the nineties."

"I'm sorry, Mom. I was wrong. You're a state-of-the-art woman."

"And *you're* a pain in the ass. To answer your question, Matti, Arwen doesn't have a phone, as far as I know. I don't think her father does either."

"Her father? Is he... human?"

"Yes. He has a farm near Carnation and keeps to himself. He's a former soldier with a lot of PTSD issues, though I think that's more from his time with the dark elves than any wars. Arwen grew up with him and still stays there when she's not in the wilds. You'd have to stop by the place to see if she's around. If she's not, her father might know where she is and when she's returning, but he's... twitchy. I wouldn't take your assassin friend with you when you go."

"He's retired from being an assassin," I said, more to let her know than because anything about Sarrlevi had changed. He still wore his two longswords everywhere he went and oozed deadly menace. "He's a noble now."

"He's ominous looking," Sigrid said.

"Good thing Matti's into that." Val cursed as her tool slid off the crease without doing anything.

My palm itched as I used my magic to trigger the locking mechanism inside the slab. At least I hadn't lost everything yet.

"Hah," Val said, as if her work with the tool had accomplished the task. But she gave me a thumbs-up, so I assumed she'd sensed my tinkering.

The submarine whirred into a water-filled chamber. Val rotated it, the light playing over slimy cement walls inside as well as an inner door. Using the submarine's tool, she pulled a lever. The door behind us closed, and a gurgling sounded as the water in the chamber drained.

"I'll give you directions to Arwen's father's farm when we're done," Sigrid told me.

"You said he doesn't have a phone either?" I asked.

"I think Arwen once said it's broken. I've had to go by their place when I've wanted to see her. Or she comes by mine now and then."

"Luddites," Val whispered to me.

"I find her quite restful," Sigrid said tartly.

"I'm sure you do, Mom."

"*She's* not a pain in the ass."

"Maybe you can adopt her."

When the water finished draining, Val hit the button to open the hatch above us. Its seal broke with a hiss, and it barely avoided hitting the low ceiling.

Some water remained in the chamber, and we climbed out into six inches. Rocket leaped out and ran around, his tail wagging. To me, the chamber was claustrophobic, but maybe all a golden retriever needed to be happy was water to splash around in.

"Good thing I haven't brought out Sindari yet." Val touched the cat-shaped charm on her leather thong as we plodded to the inner door.

It opened but only a few inches before sticking. It took all three of us pressing our shoulders against it to move it another few inches, revealing a gap barely wide enough for us to squeeze through.

Rocket lost his tail wag and growled into the darkness beyond. After drawing her sword and calling upon its light, Val led the way.

Rubble was the reason the door had been hard to open, and more of it filled the tunnel beyond. A *lot* more. If someone hadn't cleared a lot of it, we wouldn't have been able to continue.

"Did the dark elves do that?" I waved at rocks that had been melted to slag or shoved to the walls.

"Zav did," Val said. "This place looks about the same as the last time we were here."

Scents of must and mildew filled the passageway. I had a feeling nobody had been here since their battle.

When we came to an intersection, one way had been filled in by the rubble of a rockfall. Another had been bricked in. That appeared recent and the work of human construction workers, not dark elves.

With no other options, we continued forward, eventually reaching another intersection. In this one, the side tunnels remained open.

"If I remember right, that's the way to what was the ceremonial chamber and their laboratories and such." Val pointed down one passageway.

Rocket stepped into the other, his nose lifting and his nostrils sampling the dank air. He whined and looked back at Sigrid.

"What's *that* way?" she asked.

"I don't know," Val said. "I didn't take the time to map the place when we visited last time."

Rocket turned a circle, came to me, pressed his nose into my hand, and then pointed his snout down the tunnel again. I looked at my palm. It was the marked hand.

"Is it possible to *smell* dark-elven magic?" I wondered.

"Some breeds of dogs have up to 300 million scent receptors in their noses," Sigrid said, "and can detect odors in the parts per trillion."

"Did that answer my question?" I whispered to Val.

Rocket woofed.

"I think so." Val pointed her sword down the unknown tunnel. "We'll check it out."

Sigrid put a leash on Rocket so he couldn't surge too far ahead. I didn't know whether to be encouraged or not that the dog smelled something dark elven. It might only be dirty underwear that had been left behind when the inhabitants cleared out.

"Do you feel that?" Val whispered, picking up her pace.

"No." I grimaced at the reminder that my senses were no longer able to detect as much as they had a few days before.

Val didn't explain further, but her knuckles grew relaxed on her sword, and a glazed look came over her eyes.

"Uh oh," I muttered and hurried, making sure she didn't outpace me. Just in case...

When we rounded a bend, a glowing purple artifact resting on the floor in the middle of the tunnel came into view. It appeared identical to the other, identical and beautiful as its light created patterns on the ancient stone walls.

"Hell," I whispered.

Eyes even glassier, Val lowered her sword and ran toward the artifact, her hand outstretched.

8

TERRIFIED THAT VAL WOULD BE MARKED AND SUFFER MY FATE, I sprinted down the tunnel after her. Had she been running full-out toward the artifact, I never would have caught her, not with her longer legs, but she was shambling more like a zombie than an Olympic sprinter. I leaped onto her back, hoping to tackle her and knock her sword out of her hands.

She wasn't expecting it and reacted slowly, her mind under the sway of the artifact's magical compulsion. I succeeded in knocking her to the ground, but when I tried to pull her sword out of her hand, her instincts kicked in. She rolled onto her back, trying to buck me free.

I dodged a punch that would have plastered my nose to my cheek and managed to pin her arm so she couldn't swing her sword at me. She snatched for the thong on her neck, the cat charm, and bellowed for Sindari to join her.

Crap. What if *he* was mesmerized and wanted to touch the artifact too?

Behind us, Rocket barked. Sigrid shouted for Val to wake up

and not give in. Like Willard, Sigrid, as a mundane human, wasn't affected by the artifact's pull. If only I knew how that could help us.

Val attempted to head-butt me. I whipped my own head back in time to avoid it, but she used my distraction to partially free herself from my hold.

With a snarl, she flipped to her hands and knees. I thought she would try to lunge to her feet and get away. Instead, she jerked an elbow back toward me. I attempted to avoid it without releasing her, but it caught me in the solar plexus, stunning me. Val surged upward, getting one foot under her, and lunged closer to the artifact.

Though I couldn't draw in a breath, I refused to let go. I caught her shoulder, pulling her back again.

Silver mist coalesced in front of Val, Sindari's form appearing within it. Right away, he saw the fight and crouched, prepared to leap onto me. My spasming chest muscles let me draw in a shaky breath, enough to speak.

"Don't let her get to that artifact!" I knew that Sindari understood English; I didn't know if he would listen to me. "It's made by dark elves and will curse—"

Val threw another elbow. This time, I managed to twist enough to take it in the side instead of the solar plexus. With more strength than Val looked like she had, the elbow hammered me, knocking me sideways. Val lunged away as my shoulder struck the wall.

"Damn it." I crouched to spring, not prepared to give up.

But Sindari sprang first.

I jerked my hammer up to block his fangs and claws, but he wasn't targeting me. He plowed into Val, hundreds of pounds of tiger slamming into her chest.

Her startled squawk as she tumbled backward, her sword

flying from her grip, promised she hadn't expected it. It only took her a second to react and try to roll away from him, but his weight settled onto her like an anvil.

"Get off me, Sindari!" Val roared, her gaze jerking from him toward the artifact. A longing hand stretched toward it.

Unconcerned by her shout, Sindari gazed blandly at me. *Dark-elven artifacts are most insidious.*

"Tell me about it." I showed him the mark on my palm.

That is unfortunate.

No kidding.

"Keep Val pinned so she isn't cursed by it too. I'll..." What *would* I do?

The artifact rested unconcerned in the tunnel, pulsing its soft purple light. Even though it didn't have a magical pull over me now that the other one had left its mark, I caught myself looking at it, mesmerized by its beauty.

I shook my head and turned to check on Sigrid and Rocket.

She had him by the collar, her eyes wide.

"Is she all right?" Sigrid whispered, pointing at Val.

"Uhm."

Despite the impossibility of heaving hundreds of pounds of tiger off, Val kept squirming, shoving at Sindari. Sweat bathed her face, and she panted from her efforts. Though her sword was out of reach, she might have drawn the pistol in her thigh holster. She didn't try. Maybe Sindari had been an ally for long enough that, even in a mentally altered state, she wouldn't consider hurting him. That hadn't kept her from swinging her sword at *me*.

"Sindari, I'm going to shave you while you're sleeping," Val bellowed.

Apparently, she *did* consider threats acceptable even for good allies.

"I think she's okay." I smoothed my rumpled clothes. "But one of us needs to get that artifact out of her reach. Hang on." I fished out my phone, relieved our wrestling hadn't cracked the screen, and checked the reception. Two bars. Hopefully, that would be enough.

I called Willard, figuring she would be awake, even though it was eight on a Sunday morning. It did ring more than I expected, and I worried the call would go to voice mail.

"Yes, Puletasi?" Willard asked, her voice dry.

I hoped she hadn't been in the middle of sexy times with her lion-shifter friend. "We need another iron box, ma'am."

"I believe you can have such chests delivered the same day from Amazon."

"Uh, I thought yours might be better. Doesn't it need to be *solid* iron to insulate against magic?" I described the new artifact we'd found.

Willard sighed. "I'll be there as soon as I can. Where are you?"

"We started on a dock near Gas Works Park. Now we're underground somewhere south of Lake Union. I think."

"Lovely." Willard hung up.

"She's on her way," I told Sigrid and Sindari.

Rocket barked.

"I'll take the artifact deeper in the tunnels so you can collect Val and head back. It wasn't until we were a hundred yards or so away from it that the pull kicked in, so she ought to be fine once I move it. And then I'll... either follow you and go for a swim or find another way out." The latter sounded much more appealing. I wasn't a great swimmer even when I wasn't carrying a big war hammer.

"You're sure she'll come with us?" Sigrid asked.

The still-struggling Val turned her head and spat, trying to evict silver tiger fur from her tongue. Sindari had her almost completely smothered with his body.

"If she doesn't, Sindari will insist," I said.

Yes, he said.

I waved to them and plucked up the artifact. When it buzzed indignantly against my skin, flashing angrily, I wished I had Willard's rubber gloves and barbecue tongs.

"Well, you can't do much else to me, can you?" Hoping that was true, I headed deeper into the tunnel, the flashing purple light illuminating the way.

Before rounding a bend, I glanced back, catching a worried expression on Sigrid's face. Yeah, I wasn't sure it was a good idea for me to explore down here alone either. If I didn't find a promising way out soon, I would turn around and follow them out —at a distance.

The artifact was likely placed in that location because there is something ahead worth guarding, Sorka said.

What are the chances that it's the answer to all my problems? We hadn't yet found the answer to even *one* of my problems, and I hated to leave before searching further.

Unfortunately, the pulsing artifact in my hand was dusty. It might have been there since before Val had originally battled the dark elves down here.

A rockfall in the tunnel ahead almost forced me to turn around before I'd gone far, but enough space remained at the top for me to crawl over it. A few rats scurried away from the light and my grunts of effort. The last time I'd seen rats, they'd been a prelude to finding that skeleton.

Trying not to think about that, I continued over more rockfalls and paused in an intersection, the tunnel to the left freshly bricked in. I rested my hand on it, not detecting any magic. Again, it looked like humans had built it. Maybe they'd worried that if they deliberately collapsed all the tunnels down here, it would cause damage to the streets and buildings above. They'd simply made sure people couldn't access the half-destroyed dark-elf warren.

"If we knock this down, we might find a way up."

There is magic down the opposite passageway, Sorka said.

I didn't sense it. All I could detect was the artifact in my grip.

"Does that mean you object to hammering down a brick wall?" Despite the question, I headed down the tunnel she'd indicated.

To assist you in escaping a dark-elf lair, I will hammer such a wall without complaint.

"That's good of you. Thanks."

The tunnel slanted downward, and puddles soon dotted the cracked stone floor. Algae and who knew what grime coated the walls. The puddles transformed into an inch of water covering the ground, with more trickling somewhere ahead.

A rat plopped out of a hole in the wall and startled me when it splashed down by my feet. It swam away, tail swishing behind it.

I was on the verge of turning around when the tunnel widened, a faint golden light visible ahead. Finally, my weakened senses detected magic. It felt like a few artifacts rather than any living beings.

"I suppose it's too much to hope one of them can provide the antidote to you." I eyed the purple artifact in my grip, half tempted to bash it against the wall to destroy it.

That would be one way to make sure neither Val nor anyone else was cursed. But it emanated enough power that I worried about an explosion, one that might bring the ceiling down on me. And whatever buildings existed above it. As the occasional rumble of traffic overhead reminded me, I was under the city.

Water dribbled out of gaps in the ancient mortar of the brick walls, and I wondered if I'd turned toward Puget Sound. By now, I'd lost all sense of direction. I slowed my pace as the golden glow intensified, aware that there might be other dangers, even if the artifact in my hands no longer had a pull on me.

The trickling noise grew louder as my tunnel ended abruptly in a waterfall that flowed over the edge and into an arched cavern. I found myself on a ledge, overlooking what had turned into a lake, with rubble and numerous stone rectangles visible in the water. Were the rectangles tables? Sarcophagi? I couldn't tell.

On the far side of the flooded cavern, a golden skull sat atop a half-submerged dais. Its glow highlighted a garish mural of albino-skinned elves in black robes wielding knives and cutting into victims—*human* victims—as a smoky entity with red eyes and horns looked down upon them.

The devil? No, the dark elves had a different religion, one where they worshipped demons.

"Not much of a difference," I muttered.

Along the wall to either side of the dais, human skeletons hung, magical metal stakes through their ankles and wrists, pinning them above the lake. I shuddered, certain those stakes had been driven in when the victims had been alive. Gooseflesh rose along my arms, and I wanted to hurl the artifact into the lake and sprint back the way I'd come.

Do you sense anything that might help me with my problem, Sorka? I spotted a few magical items near the dais that could have done anything. Had my power not been muted, I might have been able to figure out what the enchantments on them were for, but trying only gave me a headache.

I am not familiar enough with dark-elven magic to intelligently guess what the artifacts do. But perhaps it would be worth collecting them so that the human military leader can have them studied.

I'm not touching anything else without knowing what it does. I fished out my phone to take pictures. Willard could have her people zoom in and study the artifacts that way.

Understandable.

Water lapped at tomes in a bookcase along a side wall, all but the top shelf submerged. Another suggestion that this place had been abandoned some time ago. If any dark elves were around, they would have rescued what were probably valuable books from their waterlogged fate.

Those aren't magical, right? I didn't sense anything around the bookcase.

They are not.

They're probably all too water-damaged to read, but... maybe there's something useful.

Overcoming my reluctance to go into what my brain had dubbed the sacrifice chamber, I set the artifact down to climb down from the ledge, suffering water in the face as it continued to flow out of the tunnel. The lake came up to my thighs. I waded over to the bookcase and pulled two tomes off the top shelf. A quick peek at a book that had been underwater verified that the ink was no longer legible. The two from the top had warped pages, with the ink fuzzy, but the words might still be readable—to someone who knew the language.

Back home, I had a trinket my mother had given me that allowed me to read other languages, but I hadn't thought to bring it along. Willard's people would probably be better educated about the ramblings of dark elves, anyway.

Carrying the books over my head, I returned to the waterfall and tossed Sorka into the tunnel above so that I could climb awkwardly with my prizes. Fortunately, the old walls were lumpy and irregular, offering handholds. One handhold crumbled and fell away, and I almost lost the books and pitched back into the lake.

"These better have something useful in them," I said, panting as I finally made it back to the tunnel and grabbed Sorka and the artifact again.

I will hope your mission was successful, especially since you threw me into inches of water to rust.

"You're way too well enchanted to rust. Think of it as a bath."

Hammers do not bathe.

With my arms full of dark-elven paraphernalia and an indignant hammer, I headed back toward the intersection and the brick wall, hoping that it did indeed lead to a way out.

9

Soggy and exhausted, I sat in the back seat of an Uber, the driver throwing curious glances at me and my weird booty. I was relieved when the towering tanks of Gas Works Park came into view. After breaking not only one but *two* brick walls and a stormwater drain grate in a street, I'd come up behind a tavern in Queen Anne. Since I'd had zero interest in schlepping on foot back to the park, the Uber had been most logical.

Matti? Val spoke into my mind, sounding like she was back to her usual calm and rational self. *You're not coming from the direction I expected. I take it you didn't swim across the lake.*

That sounded even less appealing than walking for miles carrying a bunch of dark-elf crap.

The artifact? Or did you find something else?

Some books, and I do have the artifact. I left everything else, including the creepy gold skull, down there. As it is, my Uber driver keeps looking at me like he's sure he's picked up a looter.

That probably has more to do with your giant war hammer than anything you found underground.

Possibly. I'm just glad the guy doesn't have any magical ancestors. I was worried I'd get a quarter-elf or someone else who would jump me for the artifact.

Yes, people who do that are tedious, aren't they?

People without tigers to pin them down, yes. Uhm, is Willard there? With the car slowing to a stop, and the grassy park and Lake Union now in view, I worried Val and I would replay the same scenario if Willard hadn't yet arrived with an iron chest.

Yeah, she's heading over to meet you. I'm staying on the dock and hopefully out of that thing's range until she clams it up in her box.

Okay, good.

When I stepped out of the car, the driver took off in such a hurry that the tires squealed and left black marks. "He *definitely* thought I was a looter."

As if an evil glowing artifact would have come out of the window display of a boutique shop in Queen Anne.

Spotting Willard, I lifted a hand and waited for her to come to me. I could see Val, Rocket, and her mom on the dock we'd used, the submarine floating in the water.

Zav is on the way with Sarrlevi, Val added. *He says they may have a lead.*

A dark-elf lair that hasn't *been abandoned?* After seeing what dark elves did in their lairs, I dreaded the idea of finding one that was still in use. I now had a better idea about why Sarrlevi had been so wary when we'd first met Arwen. If we found a legitimate dark elf, how would I convince such a person to help me?

"Brute force," I decided, patting my hammer as Willard approached.

"I do so love it when my operatives fondle their weapons as I walk up," Willard said.

"Just thinking about bashing in dark-elf heads." I eyed her with some surprise as I took in her outfit. "Is that a dress, ma'am? I didn't think..." I trailed off, deciding it might be insulting to imply I wouldn't have guessed she owned anything like that. The few times I'd seen Willard out of her Army uniform, which fit her so well she might have been born in it, she'd been wearing exercise clothes.

"It's a skirt. I was at church, praying for the souls of my deadly-weapon-wielding operatives, especially the ones dating assassins."

"He's a noble now."

"So I've heard." Had Willard's voice been any drier, her mouth would have spat sparks. Shaking her head, she pulled an iron chest similar to the other one out of a bag and opened the lid.

It was probably only in my imagination that Val sighed into my mind once the artifact was sealed inside.

"We haven't found anyone with much expertise on dark-elven devices," Willard said. "Has Zoltan had any luck?"

"I don't think so, but my mom's people are taking a look at it, the last I heard."

"Dark elves don't live on their world, do they?"

"No."

Willard didn't say that didn't bode well for them being able to help, but she might have been thinking it.

"Maybe these will assist with the research." I handed her the books, though I had no idea what subject matter they covered. It would be nothing but dumb luck if the two that hadn't been destroyed happened to hold useful information.

Willard accepted them and flipped through the pages, alternately considering them and looking at me. "Did you get any sleep last night, Puletasi? You look like shit."

"Not much." I showed her my hand. "This never stops itching, and..." I shrugged, reluctant to voice my fears, as if that would make them more real. "I think it's doing more than simply taking away my powers."

She grimaced in sympathy. "We'll find a solution."

"Sure."

"But probably not in this book." Willard held up a drawing of...

"Is that a trussed turkey?" I asked.

"I think you found a cookbook."

"The natural thing to keep on the shelf in your sacrifice room."

"From what I know about dark elves, *most* rooms are for sacrifices. They're a twisted and evil people."

I thought again of Arwen, wondering how she'd come to exist. My mom and dad had fallen in love, and, from what Val had told me, her father and mother had also been in love, or at least enjoying a passionate summer fling. It was hard to imagine such a scenario with a human and a dark elf. What had Sigrid said about Arwen's father? That he had PTSD because he'd been captured by them? Had he also been forced to have sex with one of them? I couldn't imagine *why* since dark elves had to find humans inferior, but I doubted the man had wanted anything to do with them. Poor guy. Poor Arwen.

"I hope you find resolution for your problem quickly," Willard added as Val, Sigrid, and Rocket joined us.

"That means she has work she needs handled but doesn't feel she can assign us while we're distracted," Val told me.

Willard frowned at her.

"Am I wrong?" Val asked.

"You're presumptuous."

"But not wrong."

"No."

"I thought so."

"Yetis have come down from the mountains and are stealing livestock from farms near Carnation and Fall City," Willard said. "They must think they're living in high cotton after having to hunt deer and elk all fall."

"In high what?" I asked.

"It's a Southern saying," Val explained. "The proper response is, Colonel, if the creek don't rise, we'll be there lickety-split."

Judging by Willard's expression, that was *not* the proper response. "Does your dragon still appreciate your wit?"

"He adores it."

"It's good that you found him."

Val smirked. "As he frequently assures me."

I sensed Zavryd flying in from the north but couldn't tell if any adoring was going on or if Sarrlevi was with him.

"Just handle Puletasi's problem," Willard said. "I can send some of the soldiers from my office out to hunt down the yetis."

"Do you need tracking assistance?" Sigrid asked.

Rocket wagged his tail and leaned against Willard's nice skirt, dusting it with golden-retriever fur.

"I've got trackers, and yetis aren't known for their subtlety—" Willard grimaced, "—as the photos one of the farmers sent to my office attest, but I'll let you know if we need to call in the big guns."

"That's my mom." Val winked at Sigrid and flexed her biceps.

"The dragon may be the *only* one who appreciates her wit," Sigrid said, which prompted Willard to nod at her.

Did your subterranean explorations reveal anything useful? Sarrlevi asked, confirming that he was with Zavryd.

I eyed the cookbook, though Willard had closed it and was flipping through the other tome now. *I don't think so. Val said you guys might have found something?*

He hesitated. *It's a dubious lead but worth investigating since we have few others.*

Yeah. I tried but failed not to sound glum.

There are supposedly some dark-elven artifacts in the forests north of your metropolis, in a small lair that the goblins living in the area leave alone, refusing to recycle and repurpose the nefarious devices contained within. They are also certain that a dark-elf priest visits the lair during new moons to perform rituals. He's said to be waiting for the return of his people. Whether this is true or not, I do not know, as the sources are goblins, but a priest may be exactly who could cure your curse.

Goblins?

Yes.

Zavryd flew into view, majestic as his black wings carried him over buildings and toward the park. I could finally see and sense Sarrlevi and lifted a hand toward them.

I will no longer fly with this sword-wielding assassin on my back, Zavryd declared, speaking to all of us. *He attempted to pry my scales free with his deadly blades.*

As I informed you, Sarrlevi said, *I merely sought to remove the pitch adhered to your back. You are the one who brushed those pine trees as you came in to land in a clearing that was too small for your massive bulk, and you yourself admitted that the goblin magic infusing the pitch made it difficult to incinerate.*

My bulk is elegant and perfectly proportioned, not massive. *And if not for you on my back, I could have shape-shifted in the air to easily land without brushing anything. I was being conscientious of my passenger, but never has an elf so gleefully scraped a sword over a dragon's scales without suffering incineration himself.*

As you well know, dragon, I have the power to resist your fire magic, and did I not remove the pitch for you?

You nearly removed my scales!

Val lifted her gaze skyward.

Willard didn't bat an eye as Zavryd glided low over our heads to land a few yards away. Sarrlevi, a sword in hand, sprang free. He landed lightly on the ground, facing Zavryd, as if he expected the dragon to attack. Zavryd *did* whip his head around on his long neck, skewering Sarrlevi with his piercing violet gaze.

"Tell us more about the lead you found, please," I called,

hoping to distract them from their squabble before it turned into a duel. "There's a dark-elf lair up north somewhere?"

"Yes," Sarrlevi said without taking his gaze from Zavryd or lowering his sword.

Zavryd growled, but he looked away, turning his head toward his flank. He nipped at his side—the scales that had been maligned by magical goblin pitch?—then blew steam—or was that smoke?—from his nostrils. Taking his time, he heated and buffed his scales.

"And he says I take too long shaving my legs," Val muttered.

While Zavryd finished attending his scales with the care of a professional manicurist, Sarrlevi came to stand by my side. He noted Willard's skirt and sandals, perhaps finding it odd attire for a human military leader, but he said nothing.

"She was at church praying for my soul," I told him.

"*All* your souls," Willard muttered. "I'll get someone on these books, Puletasi."

"Did you visit the dark-elf lair of the priest yet?" I asked Sarrlevi.

He shook his head. "According to my contact in the town known as Mount Vernon, the priest and lair are difficult to find and we will need a native guide."

"You have contacts on Earth?" Willard asked him.

"I have contacts in many places. I have lived centuries, traveled far and wide, and undertaken missions even on this wild world."

"Oh, I know it," Willard said.

I clasped Sarrlevi's hand. "He's a very useful elf."

"Yes." Sarrlevi returned my hand clasp, not shying away from my marked palm, though I wouldn't have blamed him. It might not be contagious, but I felt like a leper these days. "We came to get you so you can help us locate a native guide," he said.

I touched my chest and raised my eyebrows.

"I believe the forests where the lair exists are now owned by

Mikki the Wrench and populated by the goblins he seeks to protect. The overpowered dragon with me believed we could force our way onto the land and magically coerce the goblins into helping us, but the group we startled in the woods fled, using camouflage to hide from him before we could employ coercion."

Not only that, but they instructed their trees to fling their odious pitch at me. Zavryd, finally done attending his maligned scales, shifted into his human form.

"You brushed those trees on your own," Sarrlevi said, "indifferent to the fact that they radiated magic."

"That is *your* opinion, elf."

Willard cleared her throat. "The lair?"

"Yes," Sarrlevi said. "Since Mataalii is known to Mikki the Wrench and the entire goblin community, we believed we should return with her. Her presence might convince the goblins to come out and speak with us."

"Uh, I'm not sure I'm known to the *entire* goblin community, especially rural goblins fifty miles north of Seattle." I didn't even know if those goblins knew The Wrench had acquired their land and instructed me to build tiny homes on their behalf. "I can try to get them to come out though. Maybe they know about the tiny-home project and have some opinions on what kind of siding and roof styles they would like."

Willard snorted. "The styles made out of recycled beer cans, I'm certain."

"Might as well check it out," Val said. "Mom, will you see if Arwen is at her father's place? She's our only other possible lead."

"I don't think she knows much about her mother's people."

"Even if she just knows where they live, or used to live, that would be something." Val shrugged.

"All right, but you gave me a ride here. I'm not taking a taxi to Duvall."

"I could call my Uber driver back," I offered, "but I'm not sure he would come."

Sigrid looked toward my hammer and the black tire marks in the street but was polite enough not to suggest I looked like a criminal.

"Here. Take my Jeep." Val gave Sigrid the keys. "I'll ride with Zav and come pick it up later."

"Ah, excellent," Zavryd said. "I can visit the hot box of your mother while we are there."

"You have your own sauna now," Val said as an aggrieved expression crossed Sigrid's face. "As I recall, Mom *insisted* that you get one."

"Yes, but I enjoy the serene surroundings of her hot box. She lives adjacent to the wilderness, and I am able to hear birdsong and howling coyotes. Honking horns and the pollution of human conveyance combustion engines are not omnipresent."

"I heard she had goblins out doing repairs on it recently," Val said. "There's probably pitch all over the seats."

"*Yes*," Sigrid hurried to say. "A great deal of pitch. My sauna is going to need a thorough cleaning before it's suitable for use."

"That is most distressing," Zavryd said.

Val twirled a finger in the air toward him. After a sad look toward Sigrid, he shifted back into dragon form.

"I'll let you know what I find out about the books and artifacts." Willard hefted the items before heading to her car. "Keep me apprised on the egregious condition of your mate's scales, Thorvald," she called back over her shoulder. "If you encounter any actual dark elves, he'll need to be in tiptop fighting shape."

Zavryd squinted after her. *The human military leader does not show proper respect to dragons.*

"Sorry, Zav." Val patted him on a scaled forelimb. "Rough day for dragons. Matti, hop on." She started to point to Sarrlevi as well, but Zavryd growled and rippled his lips.

I will not carry the rude and disrespectful elf on my back again.

"Rude?" Sarrlevi asked. "I assisted you with your pitch problem."

I did not ask you to assist me. My mate would have lovingly removed the pitch when I returned to our lair. It was your pathological fastidiousness that drove you to chisel into my scales like a drunken marble sculptor. Zavryd levitated Val and me into the air and toward his back.

"Uhm, Lord Zavryd." I was tired, grumpy, and didn't want to play dragon-elf moderator this morning, but I groped for something to placate him.

Sarrlevi lifted a palm. "I will form a portal and meet you in the vicinity. Having flown over the area, I am familiar enough with it to travel magically to an appropriate destination." Switching to telepathy, he added, *I will also stop at my domicile to see if any messages have come in. I made numerous inquiries regarding dark-elf curses.*

Okay, I replied. *Thank you.*

It is amazing that you could focus on the terrain below when you were so assiduously chiseling my scales. After assuring he had the last word, Zavryd sprang into the air.

I held on, uneasy, as always, about dragon flight.

"Do you get to lovingly remove gunk from his scales often?" I asked Val as we headed north, soon passing over Green Lake.

"Not often. Unless it's something magical, tricky, and really designed to stick, he has the power to remove ninety-nine percent of substances himself. I do have a bottle of CLR just in case."

"Calcium, lime, and rust remover? Does it cover goblin pitch?"

"I'm not sure *anything* covers goblin pitch. Except maybe magical swords."

"I guess Sarrlevi would have used his magical kerchief if it would have been sufficient." Though I had a hunch he might have enjoyed digging into Zavryd's scales with his sword.

"I have no doubt." Val glanced back. "If all else fails, we can try the CLR on your hand."

I eyed my glowing mark glumly, certain that wouldn't work. I doubted a sword would either, unless it was used to remove my hand entirely. That was a drastic last resort that I would prefer not to turn to.

10

As Zavryd's powerful wingbeats took us out of Seattle, past Everett, and toward the smaller towns and farmlands to the north, I realized I hadn't responded to Vintok's text. I was tempted to go on *not* responding to it, but if The Wrench believed I had brushed off our deal, he would be pissed. I had enough to deal with already. Besides, it wouldn't hurt to get permission to visit the goblins on his land.

The lumber is on the way, so I can start soon, I texted Vintok. *Tinja's customized plans are done, but I thought I might get some additional inspiration by speaking to those who will live in the homes. If it's okay with your boss, I'm heading up to the forest where the rural goblins live.*

After sending the text, I wished I had phrased that better. I was going whether it was *okay* or not.

Yes, yes, of course, came the prompt reply. *The Wrench says you're welcome to visit his lands for inspiration, but he suggests you not mention him. He is doing this work in secret, as a gift, and does not wish the goblins to know until the homes arrive. He hasn't informed them that he now owns the land on which they squat.*

I gave the message a thumbs-up, though I wondered if that meant the goblins were afraid of The Wrench and might not appreciate him helping them if they knew about it. Tinja had been wary of him. Gondo too. They'd been concerned I would end up sleeping with the fishes.

"I'm surprised a dark elf would set up camp under a forest in the middle of nowhere," Val said as Zavryd banked to fly away from I-5 and over farmlands and woods. "I assumed they liked being near population centers so they could easily pop up into the streets and kidnap victims to sacrifice."

"Maybe the priest isn't particular about whether his victims are human," I suggested.

"You think he's plucking squirrels and raccoons from the forest to sacrifice to their demons?"

"I don't know a lot about demons and what souls they prefer." Nor did I want to learn. Before this happened, I hadn't had any interest in dark elves at all. "But there are the local goblins."

Val grimaced over her shoulder.

The forest goblins may still be in hiding from our previous visit. Zavryd followed the Stillaguamish River as he flew roughly east. *Plumber Puletasi may need to call out telepathically and ensure them of her good wishes, but I will attempt to locate huts made from detritus that would indicate the location of one of their encampments.*

With my power on the wane, I doubted I *could* call out to anyone telepathically, at least not across much distance.

"Sounds like a plan. We'll keep our eyes and senses open." Val leaned to the right, then stared, something catching her eye. "Are those kangaroos?"

Though my fear of heights always made me reluctant to lean, peer, or otherwise shift from anything but the precise middle of Zavryd's back, I looked. Numerous dogs out in a field barked, but there were indeed furry two-legged creatures on an adjacent property.

A most tasty species of herbivore, Zavryd said, *but they are usually found on your large southern island continent.*

"Australia, yeah." Val pulled out her phone as Zavryd continued past. "Huh, a kangaroo farm. I had no idea that was here. There are tours, and you can also visit with wallabies, wallaroos, lemurs, llamas, peacocks, parrots, and emus."

"Unless there are goblins in the mix," I said, "I'm not interested at this time."

"I'm going to tell Willard about the place." Val stuck her phone back in her pocket and grinned at me. "She can take Dr. Walker on a date. He'll feel right at home."

"Isn't he a marsupial lion shifter? I don't think any of the things in that park want to meet him." I didn't know what a wallaroo was but wagered it was prey instead of predator, like everything else she'd mentioned.

"I expect the park would get very quiet when he walked in."

I hear the firing of your black-powder weapons, Zavryd announced as we left the river and flew northeast.

"Guns?" Val asked. "It's the weekend. I suppose there could be hunters."

"Is it legal to hunt down there?" I remembered The Wrench mentioning that hunters in trucks had preyed upon the goblins before.

"It might be. I think you can get permits to hunt on some private timberlands."

I sense goblins, Zavryd said.

I couldn't yet detect anything or anyone magical, but the distant crack of a weapon carried to us. Zavryd arrowed in that direction.

"Is it legal to hunt *goblins* on timberlands?" I asked.

"There aren't any laws that cover magical beings from other worlds," Val said grimly, "since the government still doesn't acknowledge that they exist."

"While assisting in kidnapping them and stealing their technology," I grumbled.

"I assume you're referring to your mother's ordeal. I doubt anyone is stealing technology from goblins. Though the engineers in the gaming group *did* come up with an innovative design for the toilet-paper dispenser at the Coffee Dragon. Nin was talking about getting it patented."

More gunshots rang out. I finally sensed the goblins Zavryd had mentioned. They were scattered ahead of us in hills checkered with clear-cut land and old- and new-growth trees. Dirt logging roads crisscrossed the area.

The roar of an engine came from one of those roads, and I spotted two trucks climbing toward a ridge. Smaller ATVs created their own paths between the trees, hunters with guns shooting from their seats.

"Are they really after *goblins*?" I asked in horror. Even though The Wrench had said such things happened, I hadn't wanted to believe it.

"It's not the first time we've come across people doing this." Val patted Zavryd's back. "Let's scare the crap out of them and convince them to go elsewhere."

You refer to the human hunters, not the goblins, correct?

"Yeah. We want the goblins to stick around." Val pointed at the truck in the lead as it crested the ridge. "Why don't you give that one the tree treatment?"

"Tree treatment?" I asked as Zavryd tucked his wings and dove toward the vehicles.

Val shared a telepathic image with me of a black Jeep similar to the one she drove somehow smashed high into the branches of a copse of evergreens. *The day I first met Zav.*

Intent on firing into the woods, the hunters didn't sense our approach. Zavryd roared and spread his wings, casting his shadow over the trucks on the road. Using his magic, he slowed to a stop and hung suspended in the air over them.

"*Nice,*" Val crooned as the hunters noticed him, pointing and yelling in alarm. "Just like the Klingon ship above the whaling ship in *Star Trek IV.*"

"I didn't realize how much of a geek you are," I told Val.

"Well, I was married to a super nerd for a while. He made me watch all things Star Trek and Star Wars."

"Is that why the relationship didn't last?"

"Nah. I failed at retiring from being an assassin, and he disapproved of my tendency to go off on missions and try and get myself killed frequently."

"Weird."

"I thought so."

After staring in stunned horror at Zavryd for several long seconds, the hunters turned their rifles toward him and opened fire.

"Get that thing!" one cried.

"What *is* it?"

"A *dinosaur!* It'll be worth a fortune."

Though he raised a magical barrier, and the projectiles never came close, Zavryd roared in fury and indignation. *The gall! The idiocy! The sheer stupidity of a species that cannot recognize a dragon or understand his superiority and how to properly bow down to him.*

The ATV riders wheeled their vehicles back toward the road so they could also open fire on Zavryd. I fingered my hammer, but we were high enough from the ground that I didn't consider jumping down to attack. The humans had only mundane weapons anyway and weren't a threat to Zavryd.

After roaring again, a thunderous sound that drowned out the truck engines and made needles fall from trees, Zavryd opened his great maw. His head snapped downward, and he snatched one of the trucks by the cab. The men inside shouted, dropping their rifles and jumping out, as Zavryd lifted the entire vehicle into the air.

Snarling, his lips rippling around the cab as metal crunched, he shook his head several times, like a wolf putting an end to the rabbit it had caught. Then, his back muscles flexing under us, he flung the truck into the trees.

Perhaps disappointing to Val, it slammed into them, then crashed to the forest floor instead of sticking in the branches. More metal crunched as the truck landed on its side. Broken limbs and needles rained down on the battered vehicle.

I am Lord Zavryd'nokquetal, punisher of those who disobey the laws of the Cosmic Realms by preying upon intelligent species. You shall be vanquished!

"Just vanquish their trucks, please," Val called over the noise.

Your conveyances shall be vanquished!

Roaring again, Zavryd landed in front of the remaining truck on the road. The driver, foolishly still in the cab, floored the accelerator. What did he think? The truck would run Zavryd off the road?

The fender and grill crunched when the truck struck Zavryd's barrier. The people in the ATVs kept firing, but a few of the less stupid ones turned their vehicles around and fled.

Val drew her big pistol. I stared at her, almost grabbing her arm when she lifted it to fire. She wouldn't try to hit human beings, would she? I knew the magical community considered her the *Ruin Bringer,* but I was sure she didn't go out of her way to break laws.

When she fired, it was to take out tires and headlamps, not hit people. As Zavryd snapped down on the truck that had attempted to hit him, men in the bed leaped out, tumbling and rolling into the woods. The driver tried vainly to escape, still gunning the accelerator, but the truck was no longer on the ground, so the wheels only spun in the air.

Val lowered her gun. "Wait until the driver gets out before throwing that one, Zav."

He shook his head again, as if to knock the driver loose. Eyes wide, the guy dropped his gun and tried to unclasp his seat belt. Before he escaped, Zavryd threw the truck after the other one. The driver tumbled out the open window a split second before the vehicle smashed into a huge cedar.

He is out, Zavryd said.

"Thanks," Val said dryly.

The driver survived the fall and sprinted off into the trees. The vrooms of engines filled the forest as a few remaining ATVs navigated around, picking up the men who'd leaped from the trucks, while giving Zavryd a wide berth.

He settled onto the ridge, his tail flicking in irritation as he scowled around. *Dinosaur. Do I look like a dumb small-headed reptile from your planet's primordial past?*

"I believe dinosaurs came somewhat after the primordial times." Val holstered her firearm and slid off Zavryd's back, landing on the road in a crouch.

I scrambled down after her and gazed into the trees, no longer sensing goblins in the area. Not surprisingly, they'd scattered, as alarmed by Zavryd as the hunters.

"It may be hard to find a guide now," I said.

"They're still around," Val said. "I can sense them in the distance."

I grimaced at the reminder that my senses were growing more limited with each passing hour.

"Hello, rural goblins!" Val called. "It's Val and Lord Zavryd'nok-quetal, friends to the goblin clan that settled near Granite Falls last year. Will you come out so we can speak to you? We're friends to all goblins."

Friends? Zavryd bent his neck, his head turning toward his flank. Was he still buffing out the scratches on those scales?

Goblins are an inferior species, barely worth protecting. Dragons are not friends with them.

"Zav, you use the wedding gift they gave us every day of the year."

"Is that the hot tub?" I'd heard most of the details of her wedding by now.

"The hot tub slash sauna slash steam room," she said. "He *adores* it."

It is appropriate for lesser species to make offerings to dragons, Zavryd said. *It indicates respect and proper deference to dragons, not friendship.*

"Well, *I* consider goblins to be friends," Val said loudly, speaking as much for those who might be listening as for Zavryd. "And so does Matti. She even shares her exotic cheeses with her goblin roommate."

The forest fell silent, the roar of engines gone, and no hint of birdsong or even insects buzzing in the aftermath of our skirmish.

When her words didn't convince any goblins to come out, Val scratched her jaw. "Maybe these guys don't know the other goblin clan. I thought they were all pretty connected and shared news and rumors with each other, but this clan could be too remote."

"Too remote?" I asked. "We're only five minutes from the kangaroo-tour place."

"Five minutes by *dragon*. It would have taken a while to get out here by car. Or by goblin foot."

The assassin approaches, Zavryd said.

"He's not who we need," Val said.

"He's a noble now, not an assassin." I looked down the road, spotting Sarrlevi walking up it before my senses detected him. "And I *always* need him." I waved, relieved he'd found us, though his presence might not help convince goblins to come see us.

He is also not properly respectful and deferent to dragons. Zavryd breathed hot air on his scales. He was *definitely* still buffing them. *Never has he brought me a gift.*

"He brings *me* gifts," I said.

"If we wanted a goblin guide to show up," Val said, "maybe we should have brought *them* gifts."

It's Matti Puletasi, I attempted to call telepathically. *Friend to urban goblins. Will you come out and speak with us? I need your opinions on granite versus marble countertops and self-closing drawers.* Reminded that they didn't know about The Wrench or my project, I vaguely added, *I'm doing research for a project, and the opinions of goblins are important.*

Val gazed at me. "You think flattery will work better than gifts?"

"I didn't think to bring cheese, so it's all I've got."

"We may be here a while."

11

"I'm glad you found us." I hugged Sarrlevi while we debated how to convince the goblins in the area to come out of hiding.

"Even if I hadn't had the ability to sense a dragon's aura from afar, the noise and sheer carnage being created by Thorvald's mate would have led me to this place." As Sarrlevi gazed toward the two smashed trucks, an old tree that had been damaged snapped, creaked, and fell. The ground shook as it landed atop one of the vehicles with such force that it nearly split the truck in half.

"Hah," Val said. "Not as good as getting their rides completely stuck in the branches, but that's a fate those hunters deserve. I hope they didn't manage to hit any of the goblins. Zav, why don't you shift into human form so you're less intimidating?"

The goblins will still know that I am a dragon. Despite the words, he did transform, soon standing in the road with us while wearing his silver-trimmed black robe and yellow Crocs.

"Yeah, but you're less scary now." Val looked down his robe to the bright footwear, the holes sporting meat-shaped charms, a few more than the last time I'd seen them. "It's a mystery as to why."

Zavryd followed her gaze. "A dragon's mighty aura is not diminished by his whimsical footwear."

"You don't think so, huh?" Val winked at me.

"Goblin representatives approach." Zavryd looked toward the trees.

Again, I spotted them—two green-skinned females in animal-hide clothing—before I sensed them. They approached warily, darting from tree to tree, though we were all looking at them. They had to know we'd seen them.

"Is that Plumber Puletasi?" one called. "Laborer for Work Leader Tinja from the human city?"

I snorted. "I guess they're not that remote after all."

Val nodded.

"I'm here," I called. "But *Work Leader* Tinja is my intern. She labors for *me*."

The goblins know of a half-dwarf crafter *but not of the great dragon living in the human city?* Zavryd folded his arms over his chest.

"We know of Lord Zavryd'nokquetal, the Ruin Bringer, and the elf assassin Sarrlevi," the speaker said, creeping closer, a necklace of bicycle chains and rusty charms jangling softly with her steps. Her white hair stuck out in clumps that were held by clips made from refrigerator coils. "I am Work Leader Yurka."

"Varlesh Sarrlevi is no longer an assassin," I said, though it probably didn't matter to them. "He's a noble now and good friends with the elven king."

"It would be more appropriate to say that the king *tolerates* me than that we have a friendship," Sarrlevi murmured.

"I doubt these guys will go to Veleshna Var to check on the story."

Yurka stopped twenty feet from the road, resting a hand on a tree, as if she wanted to be able to duck behind it for cover if Zavryd started hurling trucks around again. Despite her wariness, she waved her younger companion toward the road—or maybe the wrecks beyond it. The goblin—an assistant?—lugged a toolbox and bolt cutters.

"We thank you for your assistance with the human invaders," Yurka said. "Several of our clan were injured. The humans hunt our kind frequently for sport."

"Even though there's a new owner of this property now?" I asked before remembering Vintok and The Wrench didn't want the goblins to know about that.

"Owner?" Yurka tilted her head. "How can one own the forest?"

"It's... a human thing," I said. "I'm sorry people have been hunting you. I hope we can put an end to that soon."

Yurka continued to look curiously at me. Or perhaps that expression indicated puzzlement, as if she couldn't imagine a way such things would end? That saddened me, that their people had been hunted so often that they accepted it as a fact of life.

"We seek a guide to lead us to the lair of the dark-elf priest," Zavryd stated, apparently deciding small-talk time was over.

Yurka shrank back, the words *dark elf* inspiring more fear in her eyes than the hunters or even Zavryd had.

"The half-goblin bookmaker who handles the magical community's bets on the horse races spoke of the priest," Sarrlevi said, "and said one of your people would know how to find him."

"A half-goblin bookie is the Earth contact you have?" I murmured.

"As a widely traveled assassin—former assassin—I have *several* Earth contacts. How do you think I originally found you?"

"I'm in the phone book, dude." Admittedly, he'd located me at the house I'd been renovating rather than by calling my number.

"Only a few goblins know of the dark elf," Yurka said. "We stay away from his lair."

"But there *is* a lair?" I leaned forward, my palm itching madly.

"The priest visits it for rituals." Yurka shuddered. "I will contact someone who can give you more information, but you would be best to stay far away from dark elves. Their kind are pure evil. Even more so than humans." She flung a hand toward the truck with a tree atop it, her assistant whistling softly as she used tools to rip chunks of metal off the frame.

"That *is* evil," Val murmured.

"But first you must come to a feast." Yurka lifted her arms in the air. "It is a great honor for our clan to be visited by such renowned friends of goblins."

"Actually, we were planning to fly through Wingstop on the way back," Val said. "No need for a feast, but thank you."

I was inclined to agree, especially since I'd been feeling nauseated off and on all morning. Even a hale stomach would struggle to eat the roadkill that goblins regularly cooked up.

"Your presence *must* be celebrated. I have already told my worker goblins—" Yurka touched her temple, "—and preparations are being made."

"Will there be preparations of *meat*?" Zavryd eyed Val. "Meat that doesn't require the removal of breading or incinerating of *dipping sauces*?" His lip curled.

"The dipping sauces are for me," Val said. "You're not supposed to incinerate them."

The lip curled even further.

"Many kinds of meat," Yurka said. "Very delicious! Also sweets. Twenty-pound cakes!"

"In case the *ten*-pound cakes weren't filling enough," Val murmured.

"I wouldn't mind seeing where they live," I whispered, "so I can take photos for inspiration for when I'm well enough to work on their housing project."

"The high shaman Bukarka will come to the feast," Yurka said. "Then he can show you to the dark-elf lair."

"It looks like you'll get your wish, Matti," Val said.

Sarrlevi touched my hand. *I will scout this area and attempt to locate the lair on my own while you attend the feast.*

"You're abandoning me to the vagaries of goblin society?"

I am certain the dragon can guide you in what is appropriate at a goblin social function.

"*He* thinks goblins exist only to give offerings to dragons."

I will not be far away. We can continue to communicate telepathically if you believe you need my counsel. Or my company.

I do enjoy that. I clasped his hand.

Naturally. Elves are known to be jocose as well as erudite.

And to use haughty vocabulary words to tell people about it.

Sarrlevi kissed me and headed toward the trees, wrapping his camouflaging magic around himself and disappearing.

Yurka jumped and shifted to the other side of the tree she'd stayed near. I didn't think she believed me that Sarrlevi was now a noble and friend to the elf king. Possibly because he continued to skulk around in an assassinly manner.

"Where's he going?" Val asked.

"To be jocose and erudite in the forest by himself," I said.

"Do the trees like that?"

"He's an elf, so I imagine so."

A clattering arose from the forest, and I sensed a magical vehicle approaching. No, I realized, as it came into view. It was an altered ATV, one the goblins must have found and claimed for their people. It had a magical engine and numerous trinkets attached to it, none of which kept it from wobbling as it navigated over roots and fallen branches.

"This way, friends of the goblin community." Yurka pointed at the ATV. "The chariot will take us to the village."

"The chariot, huh?" Val asked.

Zavryd loosed something between a sigh and a growl and glanced skyward, maybe thinking of shifting back into dragon form to fly to their village. But Val swatted his arm and headed toward the ATV.

I followed, leaving the assistant whistling happily as she continued removing choice parts from the wrecked truck. A twinge of nausea came over me as I reached the ATV, and I bent to grip my knees for a moment, sucking in air to steady my stomach.

"You okay, Matti?" Val asked.

"Yeah." I took a few more breaths, the cool forest air extra earthy from a recent rain, then made myself straighten. "Just tamping down my anticipation for the goblin twenty-pound cake."

"Understandable."

As I climbed onto the ATV, a wave of dizziness crept over me, and I lunged to grip the frame before I could fall off.

"Wonderful," I muttered, "a new symptom."

Was it my imagination or did the purple glow on my hand intensify?

I hoped the promised dark-elf priest was in his lair so we could find him. Find him and make him fix me. Otherwise... I didn't know how long I had.

12

VAL'S PHONE RANG AS THE GOBLIN *CHARIOT* NAVIGATED OVER THE lumpy forest terrain, not using any of the cleared logging roads throughout the area. Val and I rode inside with Work Leader Yurka, as well as the goblin driver, his arm bandaged from wrist to elbow with fresh blood staining the wrap.

Despite the injury—a bullet wound from the hunters?—he turned the wheel and gunned the accelerator with glee, reminding me far too much of a go-kart driver in one of Dimitri's video games. We thwacked regularly against branches, the lack of doors and windows meaning we had no protection from evergreen needles that flew off in our faces. More than once, I had to fight down nausea. Since I didn't usually get carsick, I blamed the curse.

A few disgruntled grumbles drifted down from above whenever the ATV lurched. Since the interior was crowded, Zavryd had opted to ride on the roof. More than once, a burst of magic came from him, and a branch that the ATV would have gone under but that would have struck him went up in smoke.

Afternoon sunlight slanted through the trees, hitting Val's phone as she pulled it out, Willard's name on the display. A whisper of hope crept into me. Maybe the books had given her something helpful.

"Hey, Willard." Val put the phone on speaker. "What's up?"

"I found a picture of Puletasi's artifacts in one of these books," Willard said.

"*My* artifacts," I mouthed. As if I wanted to be associated with them.

"One of my linguists is working on translating the text around it," Willard said, "and we're starting to get the gist. The dark elves make them to thwart enemies who want to encroach on their strongholds and sacred places. It's essentially their version of a home-security system."

"Putting a sticker of the artifact on their patio doors wouldn't have been enough to deter their enemies, huh?" Val eyed me. With concern?

I had a death grip on one of the bars that made up the frame of the ATV, needing support as occasional waves of dizziness came over me. How pale did I look?

"Dark elves are more thorough with their home security than humans," Willard said. "The text says the artifact will, as we've discovered, put a curse on any person who touches it. Any *magical-blooded* person. They didn't seem to consider humans a threat."

"If they wanted to deter enemies, why didn't they make the artifacts repel people instead of drawing them in?" Val shuddered, no doubt remembering her brain going on walkabout while she tried to reach the artifacts. She glanced at me—at my hand —again.

"Dark elves don't seem to be into *deterrents*," Willard said. "They prefer to get rid of their enemies more permanently."

"Does that mean there's no chance the curse wears off on its own?" I asked.

Willard hesitated. "It says that there is a period of three days, during which a suitably powerful dark-elf priest can remove the curse, in case the artifact accidentally drew in an ally to their people, but after that, the person is likely to die."

"Great." I closed my eyes and leaned my face against the cool frame, not caring that the bumpy ride meant that my forehead thumped against the metal frequently. Fear trickled through me. I'd suspected death might be a possibility, but I hadn't known for certain. And I'd assumed I would have more time to figure things out.

I was tempted to call out telepathically to Sarrlevi, wishing he were in the ATV, wrapping his comforting arms around me, but he was searching and might find the dark-elf priest. I didn't want to pull him from that. Besides, with my weakening magic, I probably couldn't reach him telepathically.

"We're still looking for the priest," Val said. "You figure out what kind of lair the dark elves had under Ballard?"

"No," Willard said. "Maybe the priest you find can tell you about it."

"I'll be sure to ask what prompted his move from city life to rural living."

"I'll let you know if we learn anything regarding a cure. There's more in the book for us to translate."

"There's a charm in a box on a shelf above my office desk that can translate text," I said, feeling guilty that I hadn't thought to guide Willard to it earlier. Or had Zavryd stop by the house so I could have grabbed it.

"That would have been handy," Willard said dryly.

"It still could be. You're welcome to have someone pick it up while we're..." A fresh bout of queasiness swept over me.

"We've been invited to a goblin feast," Val finished for me.

"I'd say I'm envious that you're relaxing while I'm working, but I've had goblin food."

"Yeah. It's about as relaxing as a mallet to the gut. We won't be long, I hope. Matti isn't looking too good."

I straightened, wanting to deny that, but my stomach lurched again with queasiness. Scowling, I sucked in more deep breaths. At this rate, I would end up puking in the bushes long before the goblins brought me a twenty-pound cake.

"Well, don't let her die," Willard said. "She has that wedding to plan."

"I'm not sure she's that excited by wedding planning. Maybe you should offer to do it for her. You like that kind of thing."

"Planning yours was torturous."

"You run marathons and climb mountains. You're into torture."

"And I associate with you. Your assessment may be accurate." Willard hung up before Val could make a rebuttal.

Metal glinted ahead, the first of the goblin huts coming into view.

"We'll find a nice dark elf to fix you." Val patted me on the shoulder. "Or a horrible one that we'll make play nice."

After a few final bumps and lurches, the ATV rolled to a stop. Goblins peered at us from behind trees and the wobbly walls of their huts, most made from rusty corrugated metal, street signs, and window blinds. Some were little more than lean-tos; none looked like they would withstand a stiff wind, much less gun-happy poachers roaring down on the village.

As I looked bleakly around, the sun setting and casting long shadows from the trees, a desire to build the goblins decent homes washed over me. This time, it had nothing to do with my deal with The Wrench. I just wanted to help these people. Numerous goblins wore bandages, their clothing little more than rags or hides. They all looked beleaguered.

That didn't keep them from, after several wary looks toward Zavryd on top of the ATV, scurrying out to throw wood on cook fires. Several already had unidentifiable skinned animals turning on spits. Ragged blankets were spread in a level clearing, a couple of goblins sweeping needles out of the area with brooms made from branches. A rickety folding table held earthenware jugs.

When I stepped down from the ATV, the dizziness and queasiness combined to send me tottering toward a bunch of ferns. Waving an apologetic hand to the goblins—and everyone else who had to witness me being sick—I bent forward and threw up. It had been inevitable. Maybe I should have jumped off the ATV before reaching the village.

As my stomach twisted itself in knots in its efforts to eject everything I'd eaten that day, I grew aware of a presence at my side. A gentle hand came to rest on my back. Glad he'd come, even if I didn't want him to see me weak and sick, I did my best not to throw up on Sarrlevi's boots.

They were elegant, tasseled, free of dirt, and had probably been made by a gnome artisan hammering leather by hand in a remote mountain village where the knowledge of cobbling was passed down from father to son.

How did you know? Sarrlevi asked softly into my mind.

Just a hunch. They look expensive. I stepped back from my mess, relieved it had disappeared between the fern fronds, though that might only make it more difficult for the broom goblins to clean.

When I lifted an arm to wipe my mouth with my sleeve, Sarrlevi stopped me by extending his magical cleaning kerchief. I hesitated, thinking of all the gross things I'd seen it wipe up, everything from the blood of his enemies to eggs spattered on my door to months of grime on my old truck's dashboard. But it was as white and pristine as always, faint magic emanating from it, and I accepted it and wiped it over my mouth.

A faint refreshing floral scent clung to it, and I wiped the rest of my face and pressed it against my cheek, finding it soothing.

Do you steep this in flowers in between uses? I envisioned it stored in a sachet full of dried lavender buds.

It's part of the magic. Sarrlevi stepped closer, wrapping his arm around me.

I leaned gratefully against his chest, ignoring the goblins looking on and Val explaining to them that I wasn't contagious, just cursed by a dark elf. If only I had something as benign as the flu.

I thought you were hunting for the priest. I closed my eyes, glad he was with me.

I was going to, but I saw you struggle to get on the goblin conveyance and realized you were more ill than I'd believed. I ran alongside in case you got worse.

Thank you, but you could have let us know, and we would have given you a ride. Not that there'd been much room.

On top with the dragon and his ego?

We would have found a way.

Few of these goblins have auras of any significance. Sarrlevi was studying the village—its residents—while he supported me. *The shaman the work leader spoke of may not be that powerful.*

Does he need to be powerful to lead us to a dark-elf lair?

Perhaps not, but one wonders if he'll be able to find it. Dark elves use their magic to protect their lairs.

Don't I know it.

Zavryd stalked around the village, making the goblins nervous as they prepared the feast. The scents of roasting meat filled the clearing, along with the fumes of something bubbling in a cauldron that managed to bring to mind both maple syrup and paint thinner. At least, with my vomiting done for the moment, I didn't feel queasy.

That might change if you consume some of the food, Sarrlevi said, reading my thoughts.

I'll know it's the feast and not the curse if everyone is over here decorating the ferns.

I judge the likelihood of that result to be high. At least for Thorvald.

Dragons eat all manner of raw meat; I imagine they can stomach anything.

Half-elven stomachs are more delicate. You'll want to make sure your hoity-toity boots are out of the way.

Instead of replying, Sarrlevi looked toward a hill, a trail meandering up it past vegetation that two goats were noshing on. *I sense a slightly more powerful goblin in a cave in that direction. Their shaman perhaps.*

A pair of goblin girls no more than two and a half feet tall headed toward us, carrying trays full of sliced meats and... was that cheese? They were accompanied by a slightly taller boy wearing glasses made from a hodgepodge of recycled aluminum. He carried a large magnifying glass and seemed to be collecting fallen leaves to study.

"Are you really an *elf*?" the boy asked Sarrlevi curiously.

"Yes," Sarrlevi said. "Have you not seen my kind before?"

"They don't come here." The boy looked toward the dragon. "Neither do *they*," he whispered in awe. "But my mother said not to pester a dragon." He looked back to Sarrlevi. Actually, he gazed raptly at Sarrlevi. "Do your ears tickle when the wind blows over the tips? Mine do. Did you know that ears are key to balance? For goblins and humans and elves too. We have something called the vestibular system, fluid-filled loops that respond to the rotation of the head. Did you know that elves were once servants to dragons and may have been granted some of their power by their overlords? Did you know the Earth sun is a star? A yellow dwarf."

Sarrlevi looked at me. I wasn't sure I'd seen him at a loss for words before. This must be his first geeky goblin kid.

"It is not appropriate to pester dragons," Sarrlevi told the boy, "but it is also not appropriate to pester *elves*."

"Oh," the goblin said, his facing falling.

I elbowed him. "Be cool."

"Be what?"

"You're not an assassin anymore, right? Your attitude doesn't need to be so aloof and dangerous. As a noble, aren't you supposed to be an ambassador for your people?"

"My people are aloof with lesser species. My attitude is appropriate."

"Well, how about this? As a future *father,* maybe you should learn how to be chill with kids. Talk to them. Humor them. Maybe you could even *play* with one."

The boy's face brightened. "I have a ball. I'll get it!"

Sarrlevi opened his mouth, an objection probably springing to his lips, but after regarding me for a moment, he only said, "Do so," to the boy.

I wasn't sure he would have agreed to *play* if I hadn't been pale, sickly, and pathetic looking, but I leaned against him as the boy let out a whoop and ran off to retrieve his ball.

"Cheese or salami?" The girls offered their trays.

The salt-encrusted slices of meat were congealed and had a greenish tint, making me positive the goblins didn't have a refrigerator. Maybe, if The Wrench agreed to finance it, I could add solar panels to a few of the tiny homes so they could have appliances.

"The cheese doesn't look too bad," I murmured, though I worried that my queasiness might return if I ate something. Still, the girls were gazing earnestly at me, so I took a sample. "Do you know what kind of animal the milk came from?"

"We made that batch from goat milk," the boy said, returning with a ball with bites taken out of it and white fur stuck to dried mud adorning it. It made me recall the field of dogs we'd passed over on the way out here.

"Oh, goat cheese is pretty normal." I selected a piece and nibbled at the corner. It was more pungent and salty than expected.

"*Mostly* goat milk," the boy amended, pushing up his glasses.

"My momma says we have to make use of what the land gives us. Did you know it's possible to milk weasels?"

"Uh." I eyed the cheese and slowed my chewing on the piece in my mouth. It wasn't *horrible*, but it lacked the smooth creaminess of so many of the delicious varieties Sarrlevi brought me.

His eyes glinted with humor. Maybe he wondered if I wanted to tell the boy that it wasn't appropriate to pester half-dwarves either.

"It's good," I said, forcing a smile for the kids. "Thanks."

"Perhaps," Sarrlevi murmured, "I should remove my boots if I'm going to remain in the vicinity of these ferns."

"Probably," I said, relieved when the girls headed to Val and— more warily—Zavryd with their trays.

The boy stayed, lifting the ball hopefully toward Sarrlevi.

Sarrlevi eyed it with distaste. At first, I thought he'd changed his mind, deciding that *playing,* especially with a child from a lesser species, was beneath him. Then he gently took his kerchief from my grasp and held his hand out for the ball. The boy tossed it to him. Sarrlevi started to catch it but must have decided that having its grime touch his fingertips would be loathsome, for he used his levitation magic to float it in the air instead.

The boy clapped in delight. Goblins didn't have much in the way of powerful magic.

I watched in bemusement as the magical kerchief scrubbed the ball vigorously, and flakes of mud and dog fur wafted to the ground. Once he'd satisfactorily sanitized the toy, Sarrlevi plucked it out of the air and tossed it to the boy. Grinning, the goblin spun a pirouette before catching it.

"My vestibular system is very good," the boy blurted.

"Clearly." Sarrlevi didn't seem to know how to muster perk or cheer appropriate for a child, but he *did* toss the ball back and forth with the kid while adult goblins came by with trays, offering more food and saying the main feast would be ready soon.

Twilight was darkening the forest when Sarrlevi spoke to me again, opting for telepathy.

The shaman comes. He nodded toward the hill.

Work Leader Yurka guided a bald goblin with a gnarled staff down the trail. She beckoned me with a wave.

I intended to leave Sarrlevi with the boy—if we were going to have kids, practicing fatherhood would be good for him—but he informed his playmate that he had to depart and returned the ball. The kid took it to one of the fires and examined it with his magnifying glass, maybe wondering how the kerchief had worked so effectively. Did it leave magical enzymes on what it cleaned? I had no idea.

"I bet that one will be a work leader one day," I said. "Or maybe he'll want to attend a human university and stay in Tinja's urban goblin sanctuary."

Val must have also spotted Yurka and the shaman approaching. She met me, and we headed toward them together. Zavryd was crouching by one of the fires, a buxom female goblin flirting with him while handing him skewers of meat. Whether he could *identify* the meat, I didn't know.

"Are you bothered by another woman hitting on and feeding your man?" I asked Val.

"Nope," she said.

"Are you sure? She's cute."

"I'm okay too."

"It's good that you're confident in your own appeal."

"Yup." She thumped me on the shoulder.

What did that mean? That *I* should be confident in *my* appeal? Probably.

We met Yurka and the shaman outside the village, the firelight not reaching them, but a polished knob atop the shaman's staff glowed a faint red. When he rested a hand on it, it brightened enough to illuminate the ground around us.

"You wish to see the chamber of the dark elf?" the shaman asked in a raspy voice.

"I wish to see the dark elf," I said. "I'm not super excited about his chamber."

The shaman shuddered, his staff shaking. "You will forgive me if I hope he is not there. Only for a friend of goblins would I take you close to his lair. The chamber and the land around it are haunted by those who were tortured there before their awful passing."

"We used to hear their screams as they died," Yurka said. "Some time has passed since those screams filled the nights, but we have not forgotten them."

I grimaced. Normally, I wouldn't want to visit a place like they were describing, but I needed a dark elf, damn it. And I needed him or her to be home.

"*How* much time?" Val asked.

"During the summer drought, there were screams," Yurka said.

"That's more recent than the places in the city at least," Val told me.

"Yeah."

"Come." The shaman lifted his staff. "I will go as close as it is safe for our kind. For *any* kind." The long look he gave me before starting up the hill promised I didn't want to visit this place.

But it wasn't as if I had a choice.

13

LIGHTNING STREAKED DOWN FROM THE NIGHT SKY AND STRUCK LAND somewhere ahead. Startled, I jumped, almost tripping over a root. There weren't any clouds in the sky, and the lightning had been a creepy orange instead of a natural white.

The shaman leading us didn't pause, simply shambling between the trees at a slow pace, thumping his staff on the ground with each step. We'd left behind the trail and were picking our way through undergrowth. As they'd implied, I doubted the goblins came in this direction often.

"That was some eerie-ass lightning," Val said.

"Eerie-ass?" Sarrlevi, who walked at my side, offering support whenever I wobbled, asked softly.

"Weird," I told him.

"It was magical."

"As in dark-elf magical?"

"Perhaps. I sense its power lingering in the air, and there is something magical ahead near where it struck. Or where it was drawn to strike, perhaps."

"The lightning comes every night," the shaman said. "It powers the chamber."

"Powers it to do what?" I asked.

"Sometimes, those who enter are changed. But usually, great power grasps them and twists them and eventually kills them, after many torturous hours during which their screams echo across the forest."

"Changed how?"

The shaman did not look back as he answered. "Changed to better serve the dark elves."

I exchanged dubious looks with Sarrlevi and Val.

"Maybe we should have asked Zavryd to come with us," I said.

"He's not far away if we get into trouble," Val said.

"Was he too busy gorging himself on meat offerings to go for a walk right now?"

"He can fly over here quickly if need be."

"That was a yes, right?"

"Yeah." She smirked. "The goblins are giving him some rotisserie roadkill that has a mouthwatering tartness that he says is most delectable."

"I didn't have a similar experience with their cheese."

"Well, you're sick. Your taste buds are probably affected."

"Yes, that must have been the problem."

"*I* will protect you sufficiently if there's danger," Sarrlevi said.

"Thank you." I bumped my arm against his. Usually, I wouldn't have worried, being confident that I could defend myself, but a bone-wearying fatigue had crept into me. Walking through the forest and carrying Sorka over my shoulder was atypically burdensome.

Lightning branched through the sky again, striking down in the same spot. No hint of smoke suggested a tree had been hit and caught fire, but my skin crawled at the electricity—or magic?—in the air. It reminded me of the research station in Dun Kroth with the Stonehenge-like construct that had attracted lightning.

We crested a hill, and our guide stopped. He pointed past a gully of blackened stumps without any vegetation growing around them and toward another hill. More stumps ringed a towering jumble of boulders at the top.

Areas devoid of greenery were rare in rainy Western Washington, and I wondered if the dark-elven magic seeped toxins into the ground.

When the lightning came again, it struck the boulders. They glowed orange, as if absorbing the energy, then returned to normal.

While the light lasted, we could see bones scattered around the top of the hill. There weren't any intact skeletons, but so many bones lay in the dirt that I believed they might have started out as skeletons. Then been torn apart by scavenging animals? One of numerous skulls had tusks, but most appeared human. I shivered.

"There's a lot of magic emanating from that jumble of rocks," Val said.

Was there? It was too far away for me to sense.

"Yes," Sarrlevi said. "Dark-elven magic."

"That's what we came for." Val nodded at me.

"I believe we're looking for a *dark elf*," I said, "not his left-behind magical stuff."

"Well, if a priest made this place, maybe he's inside. Or left a forwarding address."

"Let's hope."

"I do not sense a dark elf," Sarrlevi said, "but a great deal of magic is coming from the boulders and the ground—or perhaps a cave—underneath it. It is possible a living being is inside, his aura dwarfed by the rest of the magic."

"Let's hope," I repeated, though I worried this would end up being a waste of time. The goblins had said they hadn't heard screams for months.

"I will go no farther." The shaman thumped his staff to the ground. "Most of those who've passed this way before have died. I will not risk myself."

"Most," Val said. "But some others changed, you said, right? Changed into what?"

"Loyal servants of the dark elves."

Val shared an exasperated look with me.

Yeah, he was being vague.

"I shall hope you find what you seek and that fate doesn't befall you." The shaman turned, his gaze lingering on my glowing palm, then headed back the way he'd come.

I couldn't blame him for not wanting to go closer. The place was creepy.

"I will go ahead," Sarrlevi told me. "You may remain here, and I will let you know if I locate anything useful."

My fatigue tempted me to agree and to take a nap propped against one of the stumps, but I shook my head. "I don't want you to die of torture *or* be changed into a minion. I'll come too. In case a good bashing from Sorka will keep that from happening."

"I have my own magical weapons with which to *bash* things."

"I don't recommend that," Val said. "Since you arranged it, you may remember how much trouble I got in from bashing a fae artifact, and they're not as evil as dark elves."

Val and Sarrlevi gazed coolly at each other at the reminder that they'd started out as enemies.

"Let's all go and get this over with." Not waiting for agreement, I headed into the gully.

Sarrlevi trotted to catch up. He didn't reach out a hand to stop me, though he gave me a look that managed to be both concerned and baleful as he passed by to take the lead. Val only looked worried when she caught up, walking beside me.

The lightning flashed again, once more striking the boulders, turning them orange while making the air crackle with creepy energy.

"Wonder what happens if the lightning strikes while we're under there," Val said.

"The chamber probably gets toasty," I said.

Without being asked, Sorka wrapped a barrier around me, extending it to include Val. Sarrlevi was too far ahead to include, but he could summon his own barrier.

"My hammer thinks we're walking into danger," I said.

"That's a safe assumption." Val eyed the top half of a rib cage with part of the spine and a skull still attached.

It didn't have tusks, but the head was too large to be human. Had it belonged to an ogre? Or troll?

Sarrlevi reached the jumble of boulders at the top of the hill first, wrapping magical protection around himself as he walked around them. About twenty feet across, the pile rose more than twice his height.

"There's not a door," he said as we joined him. "Not a *visible* one."

"Hang on." I pulled out Mom's charm for finding hidden entrances.

Sarrlevi knelt and touched the ground. "There are scrapes in the earth here. One of these boulders may be moveable."

Standing in front of the spot, I activated the charm. It warmed in my hand, something it hadn't done before. Maybe it was my imagination but a sense of uncertainty came from it. As if it wanted to know if I was *positive* I wished to unveil what was here.

"Show us, please," I whispered.

Sarrlevi, no doubt reading my thoughts, stepped closer to me, our barriers bumping, and gripped one of his swords.

A blue outline formed around one of the boulders on the bottom. It looked like moving it would cause the whole pile to fall, but I trusted the charm was showing me a door. Too bad it didn't show me how to open it. The boulder didn't have a handy latch or knob.

I grabbed it, the barrier morphing to allow me to stick my hands through, and was going to try to pull, but as soon as I touched the warm rock, orange light flashed. Energy surged from the boulder and struck my barrier. I stumbled back. Even though Sorka's magic protected me, the light left me blinking.

Sarrlevi tried to grab me to steady me, but the barrier kept allies from touching me too. I waved that I was fine.

"I'll attempt to open it." Warily, he reached forward with his sword and prodded the boulder.

It didn't react to the magical blade. He started to slide it into a crack—to use it as a pry bar?—but paused and reached out to touch the boulder with his hand.

"Careful." I winced, certain it would lash out at him too.

Surprisingly, it didn't react to his touch.

Val leaned forward and prodded it. No reaction.

"We can go in, but Matti can't?" Val asked.

"It might have reacted to her mark." Sarrlevi nodded at my hand. "Since she's been cursed by a dark-elven artifact, their magic may recognize her as an enemy."

"Oh, sure. *I'm* the enemy."

Sarrlevi gripped the boulder and tried to pull it, but it didn't budge. Again, he placed his sword in the crack, this time murmuring something in Elven. Power surged from him and into his sword. It brightened, and when he leaned against it, its magic flared, and the boulder shifted. He grabbed it, pulled it outward, and warm orange light flowed out of a nook too small to be considered a cave. But there was a trapdoor in the bottom, a trap-door made from bones, a raft of them tied together with twine. Or... maybe that was dried intestine or something equally morbid. I shuddered.

The orange light seeped up from below, shining through gaps between the bones.

"How cozy and inviting," Val muttered and eyed the sky.

For the moment, the lightning had ceased. Sarrlevi murmured something and swept his power into the space.

"I do not sense booby traps." Sounding surprised, he looked toward Val and me. Asking if *we* felt anything?

Though his power was greater than ours, I tried to examine the area with my senses. That prompted a headache to blossom.

Val rubbed one of her charms, then shrugged. "I don't either."

"The priest may *want* people to visit," Sarrlevi said.

"So they can be changed into minions?" I asked.

"Providing they're not marked as enemies." Sarrlevi stepped warily inside, both swords in his hands now and his defenses wrapped around him.

When no power lashed out at him, he knelt and lifted the trapdoor. The orange light shining on his face and pointed ears made him look demonic, and the shaman's words about people changing made me shift uneasily. Maybe I should have insisted on leading. It wasn't as if life could get much worse for me.

I was about to step inside and suggest that when Sarrlevi jumped down.

Wincing, I hurried after him. Just because the entrance wasn't booby trapped didn't mean the rest of the place wasn't.

Val knelt beside me, and we peered down. Sarrlevi crouched on a stone floor below, gazing about him.

"It's something of a laboratory with magical devices, some quite large, and—" Sarrlevi pointed, "—there's writing on a wall."

"I'm coming in." A laboratory sounded promising. Maybe a tool or device inside could lift curses.

When I swung down, my barrier narrowing so I could fit through the trapdoor, dizziness struck me. I would have landed on my ass instead of my feet if Sarrlevi hadn't reached out and steadied me. Thankfully, Sorka let him.

A grinding noise came from above us.

"Shit." Val lunged out of view.

A clank sounded, and the grinding halted.

"Please tell me the boulder door didn't close," I said.

"It tried to," Val called down. "I've got my sword jammed between it and the next boulder to wedge it open."

"Stay up there," Sarrlevi called, "to ensure we're not trapped."

"That's why Willard pays me the big money. To act as a human doorstop."

"You are half-elven," he pointed out.

"Fine, a *mongrel* doorstop."

"I am unable to read the writing." Sarrlevi faced what looked like a stanza of poetry or song lyrics written in an elegant but alien language in rusty brown on a flat stone wall.

Blood, I realized. Of course. Why be normal and use paint or ink when you could be a weirdo cultist and write in blood?

"It could be instructions on how to use the equipment." His gaze shifted to one of two translucent oval pods that hovered an inch above the floor and nearly reached the ceiling. They looked like high-tech shower cubicles.

Even with my senses failing, I could detect the great magic emanating from them. Whatever one did inside, I doubted it had anything to do with bathing.

"Probably nothing to do with my mark or removing it," I said, though I couldn't help but imagine stepping into one of the pods and having it scour off all the sweat, grime, and magical marks on my skin. Wishful thinking.

"That is unlikely. Unfortunately." Sarrlevi looked sadly at me. "It may be worth translating the text."

"Yeah." I didn't know if Willard had gone to retrieve my charm, but she had linguists, regardless. As I took a photo with my phone,

I realized it didn't have a signal. "Val, have you got reception up there?"

"One sec."

A faint orange flash came from the nook above. More lightning?

"Ow," Val said, though she didn't sound alarmed. "That tingles mightily if you're inside when it strikes. I think it fried all my arm hair." She paused. "Maybe other hair too."

"Zavryd might not be as into you if you're bald."

"But I wouldn't have to shave for a while. That would be a plus." Her voice grew more distant. "Okay, I've got reception as long as I'm outside the boulder pile."

"Will you let me borrow your phone to take a photo that you can send to Willard and her translator?"

Not arguing, Val appeared above the trapdoor and tossed her phone to me.

I took photos not only of the writing but of the pods and a bunch of other magical equipment around the chamber. Maybe Willard's people would have ideas about what the things did.

Sarrlevi, being careful not to touch anything, was walking about, examining everything. Devices glowed from countertops, and a bookcase held numerous small magical knickknacks.

Using his sword, he eased open one of three drawers in what I wanted to call a credenza but that didn't hold anything as benign as dinnerware. Its corners and style brought Gothic design to mind. *Ugly* Gothic design.

"I hope there aren't any of the security artifacts down here." I couldn't imagine being able to stop Sarrlevi if we stumbled upon one in a drawer, and it magically compelled him the way it had Val.

After taking the photos, I tossed her phone back up to her, hoping Willard's translation person was available to work on a Sunday night. She stepped outside to send the images.

"There are scrolls in this one." Sarrlevi had opened the last of the drawers and risked fishing them out.

I kept expecting a booby trap to trigger. Even if the priest *wanted* people to come to his laboratory, it was hard to imagine he would be cool with tourists rooting through his drawers.

"Val?" I called up as Sarrlevi unrolled one of the scrolls. "There's some more writing down here. Do you want to lower your phone again, and I'll take more photos for Willard?"

She didn't answer. How far had she been forced to move from the boulders to find enough reception to send a text?

"Val?" I called more loudly.

A *crack* came from above, followed by a loud grinding. The boulder shifted back into place as the bone trapdoor clattered shut.

"Hell."

14

SARRLEVI SPUN TOWARD THE NOW-CLOSED TRAPDOOR, HIS WEAPONS raised, but he spoke calmly. "The bones have an application of magic, but we should be able to break through them and get out. And we moved the boulder before, so we'll be able to move it again."

It sounded logical, and I wanted to believe he was right and stay calm myself. That didn't keep the desire to unleash my temper from surging through me. I hefted Sorka, barely restraining from smashing everything in the laboratory to pieces. Only the knowledge that powerful magical artifacts tended to explode when they were destroyed kept me from swinging. From swinging at *them* anyway. Since I didn't think there was anything magical about the stone floor, I snarled and slammed Sorka into it. Multiple times.

Shards of rock flew as I loosed my rage, gouging an impressive hole in the stone. My fatigue made the temper tantrum shorter than usual, and I pulled myself together, slumping against the ugly credenza.

"I am fortunate my barrier is up," Sarrlevi said dryly, eyeing shards of stone on the ground around his feet.

"You should always raise it when I'm in a bad mood." I scowled at the trapdoor.

"I thought you might be pleased to escape your neighbor's watchful eye and spend time alone with me."

"This isn't a cozy romantic spot, and I puked an hour ago. I doubt my breath would be appealing for a make-out session."

Sarrlevi contemplated me, then pulled his kerchief out of a pocket and offered it.

"What? You want me to swab out my mouth?"

"It cleans *everything*." His humor promised he wasn't that concerned about being locked down here.

I sighed, walked over, and leaned against him. "Thank you for being... better than me."

Sarrlevi wrapped his arms around me. "I am not that."

His grip tightened, and I got the sense that he *was* concerned. Maybe not about being trapped but about me.

"After centuries of obnoxious plotting," he whispered, resting his chin atop my head, "why *now* have all the dark elves disappeared?"

"It sounds like Val and her dragon allies sent them packing after defeating their last plot. But there have to be some around somewhere, licking their wounds."

"Even those who had encampments on other worlds are scarce now. Trust me; I asked." Sarrlevi squeezed me again, as if he was afraid to let me go.

No, he was afraid to lose me. After his perusal of the laboratory, he must have concluded that we would find nothing useful here.

I swallowed, not wanting to think about failing. About *dying*.

"Elves have never been a fecund species," he said, "and the

dark elves are even less so. Their disdain for other intelligent beings and their heinous religious beliefs have made them so they were hunted and chased off many worlds completely."

"We'll find some of them." It was strange to be the one reassuring him.

"Yes." Sarrlevi pressed his face into my hair for a long moment, then loosened his grip, but he didn't drop the hug completely. He seemed reluctant to do so.

I eyed the scrolls he'd dug out. "Are those magical?"

I didn't think so, but I didn't trust my senses to determine that anymore.

"No."

When Sarrlevi released me, I walked over, switching my plan of taking photos to unrolling the scrolls and flattening them so I could fold them and stuff them in my pocket. Petty theft wasn't as satisfying as hitting things, but it made me feel better. Besides, wouldn't it be easier for a translator to read the originals than photos?

Light flared from the wall with the writing, and I raised my hammer. No, it didn't come from the wall but those two pods. They pulsed as if in invitation.

"Right, we'll jump right in."

Sarrlevi did not, instead walking to stand under the trapdoor. He summoned magic to thrust against the bones. At first, they held, their power combatting his, but with a grunt, he applied more force.

Something snapped, as if he'd broken a hinge. Good. I wanted to break this whole vile place.

Before he could jump or levitate himself out, the pods pulsed again, and an image formed in the air between them. It was an albino-skinned dark elf in a black cloak with a hood pulled over his eyes and locks of long white hair flowing past his shoulders.

The deep shadows from the hood made it hard to see his features, but he had a strong jaw and was probably handsome, much like a surface elf. Handsome but evil.

The writing on the wall was visible through him, making it clear this was an illusion. An illusion or the magical equivalent of a holographic recording?

He started speaking in the dark-elven tongue. I whipped out my phone and hit record on the camera.

The dark elf didn't speak for long, finishing by spreading his arms toward each of the pods. If he smiled under the hood, I couldn't tell, but he sounded friendly. Inviting. *Please, friends, step into my nice cozy little pods...*

Sarrlevi said something in Elven. A question. Maybe, since the two peoples had evolved on the same world, he thought the priest would understand.

The dark elf lowered his arms and started speaking again, but it wasn't an answer. He was repeating what he'd said before. A recording, as I'd suspected.

Sarrlevi must have suspected it too because he didn't appear surprised. He flicked his sword dismissively toward the figure, then levitated himself partway through the trapdoor.

"The boulder shifted back into place," he said.

"I figured. Val's sword isn't lying on the ground in pieces, is it?" I doubted a boulder could have broken her magical Dwarven blade and crossed my fingers that would prove true.

"It is not. I sense her outside, and I also sense Zavryd approaching." Sarrlevi floated up into the nook, then peered back down at me, holding up a finger. "I will force the boulder open again. Do not smash anything magical and dangerous."

"Is it okay to smash the floor a little more? It would look good with more holes in it."

"If your Dwarven blood compels you to."

I didn't know if I could blame my temper solely on my Dwarven blood, but I gave him a thumbs-up.

While he worked on the boulder, I walked slowly around the room with my hand raised, as if my cursed palm might do something to indicate which device would be helpful in fixing it. There wasn't any dust in the laboratory, making me wonder if there would be any point in getting a tracker up here to see if the dark-elf priest had been by lately. Maybe he lived somewhere in the forest and commuted to work.

"Right," I muttered.

My senses didn't detect Zavryd until he was almost on top of the jumble of boulders, presumably back in his dragon form.

A grinding sound came from above, Sarrlevi's magic, I thought, but I couldn't be certain.

I have arrived to rescue the inept elf from the trap he has foolishly walked into, Zavryd announced telepathically.

I rolled my eyes, hoping Sarrlevi *had* opened the boulder by himself. I highly doubted he'd needed rescuing.

Sarrlevi bent over the trapdoor, waved toward me, and his levitation magic swirled down to carry me toward him. Disappointment flooded me. I'd wanted so badly to find an answer here. All I could do was hope the scrolls or wall writing held useful information.

I doubted it though. There hadn't been a security artifact here. This place probably had nothing to do with that type of magic.

We found Val standing on the hillside about twenty feet from the entrance with her phone to her ear. Zavryd perched atop the boulder pile and looked smugly down at Sarrlevi as we stepped out.

"We escaped the modest trap without your assistance, dragon," Sarrlevi told him. "Had you truly wished to be helpful, you would have accompanied us here from the beginning instead of gorging yourself on goblin-scavenged carcasses."

I was replenishing my reserves in case the need to go into battle arose.

"The only thing you were battling was how many skewers of meat you could shove in your mouth."

Zavryd's eyes flared violet. *Watch yourself, elf. I tolerate your impudence since you are the mate of my mate's friend, but I will challenge you to a duel if you irritate me, and I will not hold back.*

"I'll duel you any time you wish." Sarrlevi's hands tightened around his sword hilts, though I knew his irritation was with the situation and not the always-pompous Zavryd. Maybe he should also have gouged a few holes out of the floor.

I bumped his arm. "You're right. You're not better than me."

Sarrlevi snorted softly, sheathed his swords, and wrapped an arm around my shoulder.

"Yeah, I'm waiting to hear back from Willard—specifically her translator," Val was saying.

Not certain who she was talking to, I stepped closer. She nodded to me and put her phone on speaker.

"I'll let you know if we learn anything," she continued. "I take it you haven't found anything to help Dimitri yet?"

I winced, feeling self-centered because I hadn't thought of him all day. He was in as much trouble as I—if not more, since he'd been double marked.

"Not for lack of trying, dear robber," Zoltan said.

"He's tried *everything*," came Dimitri's voice from the background. "Even things I *knew* wouldn't work. Who's ever heard of *exfoliating* a curse away?"

"You said you would permit me to experiment on you without complaint," Zoltan told him.

"That's bull. I didn't say *anything* about complaining. Complaining is all I've got left."

"We will find a solution."

"Meanwhile, my hand is more raw and painful than when we

started. It feels like a tractor with a brush-cutter attachment ran over it fifty times."

"I barely touched your palm with my tools."

"Don't forget about the *acid*."

"Ah, yes. It is unfortunate that even a magical acid was insufficient for removing the mark."

"Save me, Val," Dimitri said, his voice plaintive. "*Please.*"

"We're trying," she said. "Hang in there."

"I guess I'm glad I didn't stick around for Zoltan to experiment on," I said after she hung up.

"I am fortunate that the vampire did not spray me with acid when he experimented on *me*," Sarrlevi said.

"He just injected weird stuff in your veins while I stroked your head."

Val's phone rang again. "Hey, Willard. Good news?"

"I hope none of your more impulsive allies sprang into the pods in that photo," Willard said.

"Nope. We know better than that." Val looked at Sarrlevi and me, her eyebrows rising.

I nodded.

"Good," Willard said. "Here's the translation of the writing on the wall. *Leave your inferior species behind, enter here into the treatment chamber, retain your power while being converted by its magical caress, and embrace your new heritage as you go forth as an elf of the night and serve* Yeshelee."

"And Yeshelee is what?" Val asked.

"One of the primary demons the dark elves worship."

"Lovely."

"That doesn't sound like anything that can cure my curse," I said.

Val shook her head bleakly.

"I don't think so," Willard said. "Sorry. Do you have any more leads?"

"Just Arwen," Val said. "Mom sent over directions to her father's farm. We can check there next."

"I don't think that shy, introverted girl is going to know how to remove dark-elven curses," Willard said.

"I wouldn't think so, but she may know where we can *find* some dark elves. I know where to find regular elves, after all."

"*Regular* elves live on their home world. *Everyone* knows where to find them."

"Most people on Earth don't even know they exist," Val said.

I sighed and stepped away, their arguing making me tired. Tireder. Or maybe it was simply our ongoing failure to find anything useful.

Sarrlevi had turned back toward the boulder pile. The one that acted as a door had ground back shut, the blue outline that had marked it gone. For some reason, he was gazing contemplatively at it.

Remembering the scrolls I'd folded and stuffed in my pocket, I handed them to Val. She could take photos and send them along to Willard or give them to her in person. By now, I doubted grabbing dark-elven literature wherever I found it would lead to anything, but maybe I would be proven wrong.

"What's up?" I asked, joining Sarrlevi. "You're not taunting Zavryd about duels, are you?"

Sarrlevi lifted his gaze to where the black-scaled dragon perched atop the boulders. "No. I am considering the translation."

"It sounds like it can turn a person into a dark elf. Is that possible? I've never heard of such magic."

"Nor have I, but I am not a scientist."

"Even if that were possible, why would dark elves *want* to turn other species into their own kind? Don't they look down on everyone else? It even said that. *Inferior* species."

"They do, but as I said, they are not fecund. Their population has been dwindling for centuries, if not thousands of years.

Perhaps, the priest—or is he a scientist?—believed he found a way to increase their numbers."

"It doesn't work, though, right?" I waved toward the bones scattered around the hill. "If these people—orcs, trolls, and who knows what else—came here, hoping to be changed, they ended up dead." I couldn't imagine why anyone would *want* to be turned into a dark elf. Maybe, when the priest was here, he had the power to lure people from other races out to his laboratory. Presumably, he didn't bother with the goblins, not thinking they would make decent dark elves.

"It may *sometimes* work," Sarrlevi mused. "The goblin shaman implied that, did he not? Some die a torturous death, but others are changed. Changed into a dark elf? That must be what he meant."

"Uh, I guess. But this isn't going to help us." I hesitated. "Unless you think I should step into one of those pods and try to get turned into a dark elf in the hope that the mark goes away because the curse isn't meant for their own kind."

"*No.*" Sarrlevi spun toward me, his eyes widening.

I stepped back, startled by his intensity.

"No," he said more softly. "It is too dangerous. Even if the curse would not remain on a dark elf, there is no certainty that the change would work on you." He waved toward the skeletons.

"I know." If I was facing death anyway, it wouldn't *matter* if the change failed, but if it worked, would I be willing to live as a dark elf? My family and friends wouldn't be happy if I turned into an albino demon-worshipper. And what if my whole attitude changed and I became someone who wanted to hurt them because *they* weren't dark elves? The thought was horrifying. "There's nothing to contemplate then, right? Let's go visit Arwen."

"Very well," Sarrlevi said, but he turned back toward the boulders. Contemplatively. "The translation implied that one would keep his power, that it would simply be altered. Instead of elven magic, one would have *dark* elven magic."

I blinked slowly, realizing he wasn't thinking about the pods for me but for himself.

"*Why?*" I gripped his arm.

"I might then be able to remove the curse and cure you," he said softly, looking down at my hand, the hand seeping its purple glow into the night. "I have *power* but not the kind of power needed for this."

I tightened my grip on his arm. "Don't even think about it, dude. You're not going to get yourself killed *or* transformed into a dark elf on my behalf."

He lifted his gaze to mine but didn't reply.

"I won't let you risk your life or turn into something evil."

A mulish glint in his eyes was my only response.

"Damn it, Varlesh. Stop *thinking* about it." Groping for some unassailable logic to throw at him, I said, "Look. Even if it worked and turned you into a dark elf, just like you're thinking, wouldn't it have to alter your mind too? Make you like one of them? Then you wouldn't care about curing me or care for me at all. You'd probably want to throw me on an altar and sacrifice me."

"I would not stop caring for you because my skin lost its color."

"You *know* there's more to it than that. If it would change your appearance and your magic, it would have to change the core of you too. Come on. Don't be obtuse."

"Zav," Val called up to the dragon. "I may need you to destroy this place and those pods."

Because of the vileness of dark elves?

"Because Sarrlevi sounds like he has a really stupid plan in mind."

She probably hadn't caught everything, but she'd finished her call and must have gotten the gist. Sarrlevi looked coolly over at her.

I squeezed his arm. "Come on, Varlesh. I appreciate you caring and trying to make a selfless sacrifice and all that, but let's not do anything drastic yet, okay? I've got plenty of time. Time for us to hunt down a real dark elf."

"Ten minutes ago, you were contemplating using my kerchief to clean vomitus remains from your mouth," he said, as if that indicated impending death.

"Just bad breath, thanks. I left the *vomitus* in the ferns. And I'm feeling much better now. Look." I lifted Sorka overhead and attempted to appear perky. "We've got plenty of time."

His narrowed eyes promised he didn't believe my perkiness was real. He looked up at Zavryd. "Leave this place intact for now, dragon. I will not do anything prematurely, but I insist that the option remain."

Zavryd rose on all fours. *You will not presume to command me, elf. I—*

The night sky flashed bright orange, and a bolt of lightning streaked down, striking the boulders under Zavryd.

From the startled—pained?—screech he emitted, it was possible it caught his tail as well. Either way, he leaped twenty feet into the air, flapped his wings in fury, and used his great dragon power to obliterate the boulder pile.

Sarrlevi wrapped a barrier around Val and me as we scurried away from the hilltop, rocks flying everywhere. Pieces larger than my head slammed down all around, some landing all the way in the trees on the far side of the gully.

"That makes my temper tantrum in the chamber seem mild," I said.

I detest dark-elven magic, Zavryd announced. *Come. Let us question the mongrel tracker about the location of a dark-elf lair with dark elves present.*

Before any of us could object, Zavryd's magic swept under us, levitating us into the air. Not only Val and me, but Sarrlevi as well.

Zavryd deposited all three of us on his back and flew off, heading south.

Smoke wafted from his tail. The lightning *had* gotten him.

As we flew away, Sarrlevi gazed behind us. The boulder pile had been annihilated, but the hilltop continued to glow a faint orange, and I sensed that magic remained.

15

MY NAUSEA RETURNED WHILE WE WERE FLYING SOUTH, THE CITY lights of Lake Stevens and Snohomish visible below us. Zavryd's powerful wingbeats were smooth, and the cool autumn air smelled refreshing, of impending rain, so I couldn't blame the flight for my sickness. I was on the verge of asking if Zavryd could land so I could find another batch of ferns when a telepathic voice spoke into my mind.

Nika? Mom asked. *You are not in your home.*

No, I'm out looking for a living dark elf who can cure me, and I'm also trying not to vomit on a dragon.

The dragon will appreciate that.

My fellow passengers too. What's up? I couldn't keep from sounding painfully hopeful when I added, *Did you learn anything that could help me?*

Our research into the artifact has not uncovered a way to lift the malady, but I've brought a dwarven priest who specializes in curses and blessings.

Dark-elven curses? I couldn't imagine dark elves had blessings. It didn't sound like they had gods in their religion, and I couldn't envision *demons* blessing anyone, no matter how fine the sacrifices.

She does know something about them. She isn't certain she can lift a dark-elven curse, especially one that a dragon could not remove. I told her to try anyway, and she will, but her plan is to give you a dwarven blessing in the hope of counteracting the damaging magic of the curse.

Will that work?

Mom hesitated. *I believe it will give us more time to find a solution for you.*

More time before I die.

I have been asking all the elders I could find with expertise on the matter, and they believe that's a possibility, but the blessing will help. Mom hesitated again. *I am certain.*

She didn't *sound* certain, but it was worth trying. How long could it take anyway? I imagined a dwarven priest resting a hand on my head, saying a few words, and a magical light shining down from the heavens to enrobe me.

"Five, ten minutes tops," I muttered.

Sarrlevi and Val looked at me.

I shared what Mom had said, finishing with, "Does Zavryd mind if we stop at home first?"

"That might be a good idea." Val nodded. "Mom said Arwen's father isn't expecting her back until tomorrow. I thought he might be a decent resource and know where to find dark elves, since he presumably had relations of some kind with one once, but it would be better to speak with both of them about the matter. I'm also not sure how wise it is to show up on the farm of someone with PTSD after dark and uninvited."

A dragon shows up wherever he wishes, whenever he wishes, Zavryd announced.

"Should I tell your mate I'm on the verge of being sick again and would prefer to do it at home in my bathroom than on his back?" I asked.

This dragon wishes to return promptly to his lair, Zavryd said.

Val patted him on the back. "Don't worry, Zav. Sarrlevi is happy to help clean off your scales if they're begrimed again."

"Perhaps not *happy*," Sarrlevi murmured.

Zavryd not only changed direction to fly toward our homes in Green Lake, but he picked up speed. I couldn't blame him. After telling Mom we were coming, I placed a hand on my stomach and inhaled deeply, willing my queasiness to subside—or at least not get any worse.

Sarrlevi, who sat behind me on Zavryd's back, rested a hand on my waist. *Your mother will have the power and connections to have found the best among her people. I believe this will help.*

I hope so. When we finally find a dark elf, I want to make sure I have the strength to smash him in the head a few times before strangling him and forcing him to cure me.

That is an interesting method of extracting assistance.

Don't tell me you haven't employed it.

Not with smashing.

But with strangling. I know *that's an assassin thing.*

Occasionally. Sarrlevi rested his face against the back of my head. *Perhaps the dwarf blessing will override the dark-elven curse and cure you.*

Mom said it would probably only buy time.

With time, we can find a solution. There are dark elves left somewhere.

I hope so. Had the pod chamber not been visited relatively recently, I might have suspected their kind had all slunk away in defeat after Val thwarted their plan the year before and had left Earth forever.

They would not have bothered placing those artifacts to guard their lairs if they hadn't planned to come back, Sarrlevi assured me. *Even if Earth is not ideal to those with power, since there's so little native magic in the ground here, other aspects of it do make it appealing. Because humans are inept at finding those with magical blood, it is a simple matter to hide here.*

I suppose that's true. I haven't once seen a police car slow down so the driver could eyeball you.

Because I camouflage myself from your authorities. And their eyeballs are inferior.

You're so haughty.

Yes. He kissed the back of my head.

As Zavryd soared toward Green Lake, the water and surrounding park a dark oasis framed by streetlights, I leaned back into Sarrlevi's arms, willing some of his strength to seep into me. Tired, I almost dozed off until Tinja contacted me with alarm in her telepathic voice.

Matti, your home has been invaded by dwarves!

It's my mom, I replied.

She is with them, yes, and that is why I was not immediately concerned when I sensed their presence, but then they entered uninvited, and I heard all manner of thumping and banging.

There's a priest with them. They may be preparing for a ceremony. I had no idea what kind of *ceremony* would involve thumping and banging, but dwarves weren't known for serenity, so it didn't seem out of left field.

I looked through the back window, and most of them are in the kitchen, peering in the cabinets and pushing things around. This cannot be a ceremony, Matti. I believe it is what humans call a home invasion! Shall I retrieve the goblinator?

That's not necessary. I'm almost home, and I'll find out what they're looking for.

I might have asked my mother, but Zavryd was already descending, heading for the street between our houses. He spread his wings, slowing for his landing, but surprised me by wrapping me in magic before his talons touched down.

My stomach lurched with queasiness as he levitated me swiftly toward my front door. It opened ahead of me, and I floated inside.

My mother stood in the living room and gaped at me, the high priest Lankobar and a female I didn't recognize with her, while numerous other dwarves—her bodyguards?—peered out from the kitchen.

Before I could do more than lift a hand, Zavryd thrust me into the closest bathroom. His power released me in front of the toilet, and with a final whisper of magic, he shut the door behind me.

I gather the dragon was alarmed by the thought of you being ill on his back, Mother said into my mind.

I think so. I opened the bathroom window for fresh air and gripped the sink, debating if I needed to be sick or not.

When you are ready, we will begin with the blessings.

Okay. I didn't hear any thumping. My abrupt arrival must have stopped the home invasion, though I could sense Tinja on the back porch, still peering through the window. *Were your people looking for something, Mom? Does the priest need ingredients for the blessing?*

My limited experience with such things didn't suggest they involved bubbling cauldrons full of eye of newt and toe of frog, but that was on Earth. Who knew what dwarven ceremonies involved?

No. The last time we visited, you said for my bodyguards to make themselves at home. They are doing so, seeking more of the sweet nutty shards they enjoyed previously.

Oh. Grandma hasn't brought down any more peanut brittle. It still boggled my mind that the dwarves enjoyed the dessert that everyone else chipped their teeth on. *I can ask her to make some so I have it on hand next time you visit.*

Lovely. One must keep one's bodyguards happy. That ensures they're more likely to risk themselves to save you if a threat presents itself.

Yes, I understand peanut brittle is well known to have the power to win loyalty. I sensed Sarrlevi coming into my house. Presumably, Zavryd hadn't magically thrust him off his back at top speed.

You okay, Matti? Val asked from her front yard. *Do you want me to see if Zoltan has an appropriate concoction?*

I imagined Zoltan's vast indignation at being asked to make something as pedestrian as an anti-nausea formula.

That's okay.

There's Dimitri's Maalox too.

I'd never had the stuff and was only vaguely aware that it helped with indigestion. If only my problems stemmed from the fishy—*weaselly*—goblin cheese. *No, thanks.*

Okay. Holler if you need anything.

When I stepped out of the bathroom, I found Sarrlevi waiting to offer assistance if I needed it. I paused to hug him, appreciating his support.

Lankobar said something tart in Dwarven. I'd picked up a few more words during my visits to Dun Kroth but not enough to get the gist. I rubbed the translation charm in my pocket and debated if I wanted to ask him to repeat himself.

"He says it's wonderful that you've found true love, no matter the species of the male who cares for you," Mom said.

Lankobar squinted at her. She squinted back at him.

"Yes," he said gruffly. "When are you going to give her a real Dwarven name, Your Highness?"

"I believe she likes her human one. Matti," Mom said, instead of using her nickname for me, "this is High Priestess Keylaka." She nodded to the female dwarf, a boulder of a woman with thinning white hair and a face creased with age. Her aura was as powerful as my mother's—something even my failing senses couldn't miss, not when they were this close.

I eyed her hopefully. Maybe she *could* help.

"This will be a draining ceremony," Keylaka said in a raspy voice. "She will lie on a bed for it."

I'd been hoping it would be the *opposite* of draining.

"This way, High Priestess," Sarrlevi said more politely than usual. He gestured toward the stairs, then levitated me up the stairs ahead of him.

I can still walk, I told him a little tartly.

Of course you can, but it is not necessary for you to do so when I am here.

You're not trying to outdo Zavryd, are you? I asked as he navigated me into the bedroom.

I am assisting you because I care deeply about you and wish you to be as unburdened as possible, not *because I'm worried about you leaving vomitus on me.*

Not even on the fancy boots? Those tassels can't be easy to clean.

I can clean anything.

You truly are a master of the art. Perhaps, for your next career, you could open a maid service. Monied people on Earth pay top dollar to have their bathtub rings scoured by others. I shared an image of him in the Hollywood version of a French maid's uniform with lots of leg on display.

I am pleased that the curse has not stolen your wit. Sarrlevi followed me into the bedroom, Mom and the high priestess trailing after him.

You'd miss my teasing terribly if it disappeared.

I would. He helped me take off my shoes and lie on the bed.

"That is the elf who is an assassin?" Keylaka asked my mom. "He does not act like a hardened killer."

"I understand he's a noble now," my mother said.

"He also does not act like a noble."

Sarrlevi's eyes narrowed slightly, and I trusted he would have given the priestess a baleful look if he hadn't wanted her to fix me.

Do you wish me to stay? he asked me silently. *Or go downstairs and protect your kitchen from the plundering fingers of dwarves?*

Stay. I rested a hand on his. *They can plunder all they want, as long as I... get better.*

Sarrlevi climbed into bed, propping himself against the headboard, and found a position where he could hold my hand. Keylaka hesitated, looking at Mom. And asking something telepathically? Like if she could kick out Sarrlevi?

I gripped his hand and scowled.

"Begin," Sarrlevi ordered the priestess.

"*Now* he's acting like a noble," Keylaka said with a harrumph, but she didn't object further.

She opened a satchel and drew out a few items, resting them on the nightstand, though she also placed a glowing green gemstone in my free hand. Since it was cool and soothing against my itchy palm, and it and the other items all radiated magic, I didn't complain. Keylaka wrapped her gnarled hand around mine as I held the gem, then closed her eyes and started murmuring to herself.

Whatever she said, my translation charm didn't pick up on it. I closed my own eyes, leaned my head into my pillows, and tried to relax, though it was hard not to feel like I was tilted back in a dentist's chair with pain on the horizon.

Power poured into me, brusque and unappealing, nothing like Sarrlevi's gentle caresses. It wasn't painful, but it was, as she had promised, draining.

At first, it flowed through my whole body, and then it centered on my hand, making it throb and ache, despite the soothing stone in my grip. I willed my flagging power to help, to drive the curse away.

My body and hand tingled with magic, hers and mine. At one point, my mother added some of her own power, as if by sheer brute force, we could bring enough magical strength to bear to defeat the curse. Since Zavryd hadn't been able to heal me, I doubted that was true, but as exhaustion crept into me, sleep—or maybe unconsciousness—threatening, I willed it to be so. I was reluctant to let myself fall asleep though, the fear that this wouldn't work high in my mind. What if I didn't wake up?

I *had* to wake up again. And get better. Those goblins needed homes, and I had so much left that I wanted to do in life. I'd only just found love, and I wanted to keep experiencing it, being with Sarrlevi and having a family with him. Teaching him how to loosen up and play ball with kids. I didn't want to miss that.

Rest, Mataalii, Sarrlevi whispered. *You will waken. I will ensure it.*

He couldn't ensure that, I knew, but the words made me feel better, and I let myself go, sleep overtaking me.

16

T<small>HE GRAY LIGHT OF A RAINY MORNING FILTERED THROUGH THE</small> window when I woke curled against Sarrlevi, using his arm for my pillow. After the memories of the previous day washed over me, I assessed my body. Though I couldn't say I was bursting with energy and ready to jump out of bed, I didn't feel nauseated, my eyes weren't gritty, and when I lifted my head to look around, I wasn't dizzy.

Hope crept into me—until my gaze landed on my hand pressed flat against Sarrlevi's side. I lifted it and slumped. The purple knotted design still glowed on my palm. It itched less, but it hadn't faded.

Sarrlevi brushed the side of my head with his fingers. "The priestess wasn't able to remove the curse, but she said her blessing should give you increased stamina and vitality for a time. Under normal circumstances, it would last for months. In your case, it might be weeks, but it should counteract the curse to some extent."

"Okay." I'd hoped for more, but if this meant I had more time to hunt down dark elves, at least it was something. "Thanks for staying with me."

My senses told me most of the dwarves remained in the house, some in the guest bedrooms, some downstairs. The priest and priestess were gone, maybe called back to their home world. None of the dwarves were in the kitchen now, though I sensed Tinja there.

"Your roommate brought her weapon over to defend you while you rest and also protect the contents of your cabinets," Sarrlevi said.

I groaned. "She didn't threaten to shoot my mom's bodyguards, did she?"

"She bravely stood up to them, saying you would need sustenance when you woke. I believe the dwarves brought their own food and it was only the addictive dessert you gave them last time that had them so assiduously delving into your supplies."

"Like junkies looking for a stash. Who knew Grandma's peanut brittle could affect anyone that way?"

While Sarrlevi puzzled out my slang, I grabbed my phone off the nightstand. The dwarven artifacts were gone, and someone—Sarrlevi, I assumed—had plugged it in to charge. A text from Val waited for me.

Let us know when you're feeling well enough to go see Arwen. Sarrlevi and Tinja threatened bodily harm if I came over to wake you. Even though I have an anti-nausea medication from Zoltan. He's been giving it to Dimitri.

Too impatient to type out a text when I still had enough power to use telepathy, I blurted to Val, *How is Dimitri doing? I should have asked my mom to send the priestess over to see him.*

They are here now. The priestess blessed him, similarly to you, and she and the priest are discussing dark-elven magic and the artifact with Zoltan.

Oh, good. Give me a minute to pee and brush my teeth, and I'll be ready to go.

Good. The anti-nausea formula is on your porch swing. There are several doses.

I'm feeling better after the blessing.

Nonetheless, Zav insists *that you take the medicine before climbing on his back.*

I sighed. *Fine.*

Sarrlevi, not privy to the telepathic conversation, raised his eyebrows.

"Zavryd is a pain in the butt," I explained.

"Naturally. He is a dragon."

As I hurried through my morning ablutions, a dwarven portal formed in the street. I sensed Mom going outside to meet whoever was coming, so maybe she expected it. Toothbrush dangling from my mouth, I peered through a window.

Three dwarves I didn't know well hopped out. I'd seen one of them before. He'd been carrying a clipboard and trying to usher my mom off to her princess duties. They conversed quietly on the sidewalk.

By the time I finished dressing and headed downstairs with Sarrlevi, another portal was forming. I peeked into the kitchen and found Tinja snoring as she lay propped against the pantry door, her cannon-like goblinator cradled in her arms.

"An effective home defender," Sarrlevi observed.

"There's still cheese in the cheese grotto—" I waved at the bamboo box on the counter, "—so she must have done something right."

"I tucked that in there this morning. I picked it up yesterday before returning, assuming that your cursed taste buds would accept only the most palatable of sustenances."

"That was thoughtful of you. My taste buds thank you." I wasn't hungry, though, and walked to the door to meet my mother as she came back inside. Her usually affable face was grim. "You have to go?" I guessed.

She hesitated. "If you need me to stay, I will."

"What's happening on Dun Kroth?" I debated if I wanted to ask her to stay. As comforting as it was to have her around, she couldn't fix me, and we shouldn't get into much trouble going to visit a farm.

"The trouble is on Veleshna Var. Since the meeting where King Eireth was nearly assassinated—" Mom nodded at us, knowing about how we'd crashed the party to help prevent that, "—the elves and dwarves have agreed to hunt for the half-dragons together, but they are proving elusive. I believe I told you there are four, including Starblade, that have been freed from their stasis-chamber prisons."

"Yeah."

I was surprised everyone was getting worked up over so few of them. Did four half-dragons truly represent a threat? When there were full-blooded dragons all over the Cosmic Realms?

"They *do* represent a threat," Mom said, following my thoughts, "because of their power and because they have—what is the human term?—chips on their shoulders. Nor do they feel bound by the laws of the Dragon Council. They could raise armies to send against our people. My father has asked me to come home and enchant armor that will help our warriors defend themselves. Those who hunt the half-dragons have means of tracking them and have heard rumors about where they've been seen. When an inevitable confrontation occurs, our people must have every advantage possible."

Though I didn't say anything, I couldn't help but feel sympathetic toward Starblade since he'd helped me free Sarrlevi's mom as well as my mother and father. He might be an asshole who'd once killed thousands, but... I didn't know if I would have achieved my goals without him.

Mom pursed her lips in disapproval at my thoughts.

"Where are some of the places they are believed to be hiding?" Sarrlevi asked. "You said Veleshna Var?"

"That is one of the worlds where they have been seen," Mom said. "I am not certain about the others. If I return, I might be able to learn that information."

"Do you think the half-dark elf is with them?" I'd shared the information Mom had given me about the half-dragons with Sarrlevi earlier and looked at him now, wondering if he'd asked about their location because he believed the dark-elven female might be able to lift my curse. *If* she'd been raised to know about their magic, maybe she could. Would she be easier to find than the dark-elf priest?

"From what I have heard, they are all together." Mom hesitated. Since she'd been the one to tell me about the half-dark elf, she had to know what we were thinking. "If I learn the location, I'll send word back to you. Maybe you could find a way to strike a deal with them before the attack, but... I fear she will not help you. *She* will not feel indebted to you the way Starblade did. He was the one to free her."

"But I freed him, resulting in him being able to free her. She should love me."

Mom held a finger to her lips. "Don't speak loudly about that. Many, including Lankobar, are still bitter that you were responsible for that."

"Lankobar can kiss my ass."

Sarrlevi had heard the expression a number of times by now, but that didn't keep him from looking down at my backside. "I would not allow that," he murmured.

"There are other enchanters back home." Mom gripped my hands. "If you believe I can be of help here, I will stay with you. Sarrlevi said there is a dark elf you can visit?"

"A *half*-dark elf who was probably raised as a human. From

what I've seen, she thinks she's more surface elf than dark elf. I'm mostly hoping she knows where her dark-elf mother is hanging out these days. Or *any* of those people."

Mom nodded. "A true dark-elf priest raised in their culture and with their knowledge of magic would be the ideal person to lift the curse."

I had a feeling she didn't want me trying to wheel and deal with the half-dragons. If the dwarves and elves were about to start a war with them, that was understandable. But I would keep it as an option.

"Thanks for the help, Mom, but I don't know that there's anything more you can do here right now."

Sarrlevi nodded in agreement, his eyes closed to thoughtful slits. If he was considering searching for the female half-dragon, he might believe that would be easier to do without any dwarves or elves trailing along.

Mom hesitated, maybe not agreeing that she couldn't do more to help, but Lankobar and Keylaka returned, asking if she was ready. The portal remained outside, one of the other dwarves keeping it open for them.

"I will come back soon to check on you," Mom said firmly.

I nodded and hugged her. "Thanks."

Once the dwarves were gone, Zavryd and Val came out of their house.

"Let's go see if Arwen can help us," I told Sarrlevi, then grabbed cheese and protein bars from the kitchen.

On the porch swing, I found not only several vials of a green liquid—the anti-nausea medication, presumably—but bottles of Maalox and Pepto Bismol, two bags of lemon-ginger lozenges, two containers of pills with prescription labels filled out to people I didn't know, and a pamphlet touting the benefits of bland diets.

"Do you think Val brought all this over?" I asked. "Or Zavryd?"

"That dragon is overly uptight about his scales remaining in a pristine state," Sarrlevi said.

"Yeah, I think it was him too."

Val might have snagged the formulas from Zoltan and even picked up the bottles from the store, but I couldn't imagine her rummaging in strangers' medicine cabinets and stealing their prescription drugs.

"Such an odd neighbor," I added.

"I did inform you that moving in across from a dragon was a dubious choice."

"Here on Earth, we just say *I told you so*."

"Yes."

17

"ARE YOU *SURE* THAT'S THE RIGHT ADDRESS?" I ASKED VAL AS Zavryd banked and descended toward a wild-looking property along a stream.

Val, Sarrlevi, and I rode on his back, with Tinja also along, her eyes wide as she flew for the first time on a dragon. Saying she wanted to recruit some of the rural goblins known to live in the area, she had talked Val into finagling her an invitation.

"It's hard to direct a dragon by GPS," Val said, holding up her phone as she telepathically communicated with Zavryd, "as he doesn't do left and right and follow streets, but it *looks* like we're in the right place."

I glanced back at Sarrlevi, though it wasn't as if he'd been here before and would know. Only Sigrid, who hadn't come along, was familiar with the place.

"It looks like a goblin village," Tinja said, peering down, "wild and natural."

"It's supposed to be a *farm*," Val said. "I suppose Mom's directions could have led us astray. They left a lot to be desired."

"I thought she gave you an address," I said.

"She said it's called Wild Berry Creek and Honey and sent the name of the street and how many turns you take from her house to get there. Apparently, if we see two silos, we've gone too far. Mom can *use* computers, but she doesn't own one or a smartphone, so those are the kinds of directions you get from her."

Silos are great cylinders for storing grains, yes? Zavryd asked.

"Yes," Val said.

He flicked a wing toward the south, where two such structures were visible near other buildings surrounded by fields adjacent to a river. *That* property looked much more like a farm.

"I looked up Wild Berry Creek, and they don't have a website," Val said as Zavryd descended toward a gravel road. "It's possible Arwen's dad is as anti-modern-tech as my mom."

"You'd think a business would want to be found," I said.

"From what I've seen of Arwen, *she* doesn't want to be found often," Val said. "Maybe her dad is the same way. It could be a hobby farm. Or maybe they only deliver or sell at farmers markets."

"Maybe they forage in the woods like goblins and sell what they discover," Tinja said.

"Fewer people do that than you'd think," Val said, "though I suppose there are those who hunt for mushrooms. Mom took some classes with Rocket, and he can sniff out truffles in the woods."

"No wonder he's her best friend and gets to sleep with her," I said.

"He does have valuable skills. You could teach him to be the ring bearer at your wedding. Wouldn't a golden retriever be cute carrying your jewelry up the aisle?"

I looked back at Sarrlevi and whispered, "Suggestions like these are why eloping sounds so appealing."

"I am amenable," he said.

"You could have a goblin wedding." Tinja lifted her arms. "I could even marry you."

"I didn't know you were a priest," I told her as I leaned against Sarrlevi, fantasies of being married without fuss, perhaps by a justice of the peace, lingering in my mind. "Or would it be a shaman?"

"I am neither, but goblin work leaders can also wed dedicated foraging partners, and now that I have been designated as such, the power is mine. You would enjoy a goblin wedding. The ceremony is very short and simple, and then the feasting goes on all night."

"I've heard dragon mating ceremonies are similar," Sarrlevi murmured.

"You've really been designated a work leader, Tinja?" I reached back and clasped her hand to congratulate her. "I didn't realize that. I thought your people were just calling you that because you work hard and they like you." A lot of the male goblins, in particular, liked her.

"That is how work leaders become work leaders. It is all organic. Others are drawn to be guided by and do work with some goblins, and those goblins naturally take charge. Then you start getting invitations for you and your clan to come to the jamborees." She smiled a little shyly. "I recently received my first one."

"That's great news." I hesitated. "The jamboree won't be hosted in your tiny home or my backyard, will it?"

"Oh, no, but I have been invited to suggest an *urban* location. It will be the perfect opportunity for me to recruit for my sanctuary. I am going to suggest the great bathing lake."

"You mean Green Lake?" I envisioned the hordes of people that skated, bicycled, walked, and jogged there in between hosting barbecues, birthday parties, and yoga on the lawn. "That should prove interesting."

"Yes," Tinja said brightly.

The pothole-filled gravel road wasn't wide, and Zavryd nearly took out a parked tractor with his tail when he landed. He *did* utterly destroy a newspaper box. Since the tractor looked like it was being used to level the road and add more gravel, it was good for the neighborhood that he didn't demolish it.

"This isn't a county-maintained road, I'm guessing." I squinted at a for-sale sign farther down.

"Is this the kind of neighborhood that gets you excited?" Val slid off Zavryd's back. "What are you going to work on when your curse is lifted and after you finish the tiny-home project?"

"I haven't thought that far ahead." I also slid off, glad my stomach had cooperated on the ride over and that I wasn't queasy. Though I had, per Zavryd's insistence, taken several items from the collection he'd left on my porch, I'd only sucked on one of the lozenges. "Since I haven't started any of those homes yet, it's going to take a while."

"Mataalii has expressed an interest in producing and raising offspring," Sarrlevi announced.

I blinked and looked at him. "That's not so much a project as a lifelong endeavor."

"That may be started whenever you are ready." He nodded at me.

"You must have had fun playing ball with that kid."

"The youth had surprising intelligence for a goblin."

Tinja cleared her throat. "Some goblins are *very* intelligent. I will admit that not all of my rural brethren suitably apply themselves."

Thinking of the Coffee Dragon goblin gamers, I said, "Not all of your *urban* brethren apply themselves either."

"That is true. I am only providing a sanctuary for those who wish to improve themselves and eke out an admirable place in this predominantly human world. Oh, are there still crab apples on that tree?" Tinja wandered to the side of the road. "What a delightful find this late in the year."

Sarrlevi squinted at the tree, which did indeed have numerous small apples hanging from its branches. Surprisingly, its leaves hadn't yet fallen, and were those raspberry bushes offering fruit behind it?

"There's a sign." Val pointed up the road and trotted over to take a look.

"There is dark-elven magic clinging to that tree," Sarrlevi said quietly. "To many of the trees and shrubs."

My first thought was to be alarmed, but we had come here *looking* for a dark elf. A half-dark elf at least. Hope blossomed. Assuming Arwen had been responsible, maybe she *did* know something about her heritage and where her mother's people might be found.

"*Dark-elven* magic?" Tinja asked in a squeaky voice, staring in horror at an apple she'd already bitten into. "Does that mean these fruits are poisoned? That they'll kill me?"

"No," I said, though I couldn't know for certain. "Arwen is helpful. She wouldn't do that." I looked at Sarrlevi, hoping for verification. The dwarven blessing might have given me some extra stamina, but it hadn't done anything to return my waning power and weakening senses.

I believe the magic is making the trees fruit longer than typical, Zavryd said, *while protecting them from frost.*

"I was not aware that dark-elven power could do that," Sarrlevi said. "Their people are not known for extending and enhancing life of any kind."

Tinja eyed the apple, not appearing reassured by their comments. She set the rest of it in the crook of the tree for an animal to find.

"This is it." Val pointed at the sign and waved for us to join her.

The driveway for the property was so overgrown, with high

grass sprouting from the gravel and with branches stretching in from either side, that one could have easily driven—or flown by it. The paint on the wooden sign was faded with moss growing on one side and half hiding the farm's name.

"I'm guessing they don't host a corn maze or offer U-Pick sessions," I said.

"Lord Zavryd'nokquetal," Tinja said. "While Matti and the others seek out the tracker, will you fly me approximately four more miles to the east? That is the location of the rural village I wish to visit."

I am not a goblin taxi, Zavryd said.

"I believe they will insist on preparing a feast for you," Tinja said. "To be visited by—and not eaten by—a dragon is a great honor for goblins."

I will fly you to this location. Zavryd levitated Tinja onto his back and promised Val he would return soon.

"Does he have a hard time enforcing the Cosmic Realms laws for his mother," I asked, "when he has to spend so much time eating?"

"She makes him work a lot," Val said as she, Sarrlevi, and I headed up the driveway. "He enjoys relaxing and just hanging out when he's here on Earth with me. In fact, we're not that far from my mom's place outside of Duvall. She'd better hope that story we gave about magical goblin pitch all over her sauna will keep him from visiting."

"Is it not a great honor for her when he visits?"

"Not that she's mentioned."

"Halt." Sarrlevi caught Val and me by the arms, then pointed to the grass-carpeted driveway ahead of us. "Magical traps."

I couldn't sense anything, but Val said, "I see one now. Mom didn't mention *traps*."

"When was the last time she was here?" I asked.

"Not that long ago." Val scratched her jaw.

"We will levitate over it, but be wary." Sarrlevi released us and drew a sword. "It appears that the landowner does not wish guests."

He floated Val and me into the air. Only when the trap was inches under me did I sense a hint of magic. I couldn't detect it in the bushes and trees at all, though we passed numerous varieties that were still fruiting. In addition, chanterelle mushrooms peeked up from nooks between their roots. Tiny red berries clung to leafy undergrowth along the driveway. Something edible?

Through the trees and past a clearing of beehives, an old manufactured home came into view with vegetation on the roof. Not the typical moss that infested *many* roofs in the Pacific Northwest but something leafy that grew out of soil rather than shingles. More clumps of small berries dotted the foliage.

"Looks like a Hobbit house," Val said.

"If Hobbits lived in trailers," I muttered.

"There are more traps around the area," Sarrlevi said as we floated over another magical spot in the driveway.

"They're definitely not into visitors here," I said.

"Too bad." Val shrugged. "We can't go anywhere until our ride gets back."

"That is untrue." Sarrlevi twitched a finger to remind her that he could make portals.

Yes, but where else would we go? To the elven world to look for the half-dragons? The half-dragons that all the dwarves and elves were hunting?

A pained yowl sounded in the distance.

An animal? A person? The foliage muffled the sound, and I couldn't tell.

Sarrlevi halted our forward progress and wrapped a barrier around us. "I sense... I believe you call them yetis. They are only slightly magical creatures, brought to this world by ogres. They are a favorite prey of their kind."

"Willard did say there are yetis in this area. We're supposed to evict them when we're done dealing with our dark-elf problem." Val peered into the distance, but we couldn't see anything through the trees. "Unless Arwen's father's property is really large, I don't think they're on it."

The yowl came again.

"Don't come any closer," a gruff male voice spoke from a door that had been closed a few seconds earlier.

A shirtless man in his fifties stood on the porch, pointing a rifle at us. He wore camo pants and boots, and a leather band tied back his wild salt-and-pepper hair. Faded tattoos ran down his arms, leather cuffs banded his wrists, and he wouldn't have looked out of place in the biker clubs in town.

"This guy is a farmer?" Val whispered, perhaps thinking similarly.

"I don't think there's a dress code for harvesting berries," I said.

"Guess not."

His rifle didn't seem to be magical, but I didn't trust my senses to tell me that, instead relying on Sarrlevi's indifferent expression. Val didn't appear worried either.

"The farm is closed for the year," the man said. "And visitors aren't welcome in the off-season."

Something told me visitors were *never* welcome.

The yowl came again, and the man twitched, half-turning his rifle in that direction before jerking it back toward us.

"Are you Patrick?" Val asked. "We came to see Arwen, not buy from the farm, though we may owe you for an apple our friend munched on. I'm Sigrid's daughter."

"Why are you looking for Arwen?" The man—Patrick—peered not at me or Val but at Sarrlevi, his gaze lingering on the sword he held. "She's done nothing wrong. She obeys the human laws and helps our authorities track criminals. She's a good girl."

"I know that," I offered, pressing Sarrlevi's sword arm down.

"She helped me track down some bad guys who kidnapped my parents. I really appreciated that."

"Elves don't appreciate their night kin." Patrick's eyes remained locked on Sarrlevi.

Sarrlevi lifted his chin. "A dark elf or *half*-dark elf is no kin of mine."

"You're not helping, dude," I whispered.

An explosion ripped through the air, startling us all.

"The traps!" Patrick snarled. "Those bastards can't leave well enough alone."

After a suspicious glance at us, he leaped over the porch railing and ran down a trail heading in the direction of the explosion.

"Do we... follow him?" I asked uncertainly.

"Two of the yetis have approached the area," Sarrlevi said.

"Let's help him." Val attempted to turn to follow Patrick, but she still levitated, thanks to Sarrlevi's magic, and gave him an exasperated look. "Maybe he'll be more inclined to talk to us then."

Probably worried about more booby traps, Sarrlevi didn't lower us to the ground, but he did levitate us after Patrick. He'd already disappeared through the brush. Since he was human and didn't have a magical aura, we couldn't track him once the trail branched and presented other options. The yetis, however, we could sense. Sarrlevi cut through a berry patch to take us straight toward them.

We smelled them before we saw the ten-foot-tall shaggy white beasts, blood coating their fur as they crouched beside a stream. Some of the blood might have been theirs, but the head of a pig lay on the ground nearby, so it might have come from a kill. When I'd encountered yetis before, they hadn't been that aggressive toward humans, but these wore tiny shell necklaces half hidden by their shaggy fur. Magical necklaces?

I didn't see evidence of an explosion and didn't think we'd

come out in the right spot. Gunfire rang out farther upstream, verifying my belief. With bushes growing thick along the banks, and bends in the waterway, we couldn't see the shooter, but I assumed it was Arwen's father.

The two yetis whirled toward the gunfire, snarling and lifting their claws. One called out, half query, half roar. When I'd faced the creatures before, I hadn't gotten the impression that they had a language, but they did communicate to some extent. An alarmed cry—another yeti?—came from farther up the bush-choked stream.

"Return to the mountains," Val told them, drawing her pistol. "Those in the magical community who prey on humans or their livestock aren't tolerated."

One of the yetis turned toward her, arms raised, claws extended, and roared.

"This is your only warning," she yelled.

Did she expect them to understand? We'd scared yetis away before without having to fight, but these had a wild—maybe a *crazy*—glint in their eyes.

"Leave now, or we'll shoot," Val said, a final warning.

After roaring again, the yeti charged across the stream toward us. Val fired at the same time as Sarrlevi hurled a dagger. Both weapons found its chest.

The other yeti ran upstream, away from us and toward Arwen's father.

I threw my hammer as Val shifted her aim toward it. Sorka took the creature in the head as Val's bullets hammered into its back.

Though we hit the creature numerous times, it kept running. As Sarrlevi levitated his dagger back into his hand, he blasted the fleeing yeti with magic. It flew forward, face-planting in the stream, but it didn't stay down. When more gunfire rang out, it charged off in that direction again.

I wanted to hurry after it, since I worried Patrick didn't have the weapons needed to fight yetis, but the first one shook off its injuries and ran toward us again. Val fired three more times, finishing her clip, then sheathed her pistol and reached for her sword.

But Sarrlevi released our levitation spell and sprang past her with his blades out. He engaged the yeti before Val could.

Trusting they could handle that one, I ran after the one heading toward Patrick. A roar thundered from upstream, a reminder that he already had another one he had to deal with.

I hefted my hammer, but the yeti charged around a boulder, disappearing from my view. Snarling, I willed my legs to greater speed, relying on the dwarven blessing to override the curse and give me the strength I knew I should have.

Another explosion ripped through the air, this one close enough that the ground shook beneath me, making me stumble. Something landed in the stream scant feet ahead of me. A furry white leg—detached from the rest of the body.

"Ew," I growled, then caught sight of the now one-legged creature. Despite the grievous injury, it crawled forward, trying to join the yeti battling Patrick.

I surged ahead until Patrick came into sight. His foe had either knocked his rifle from his hands, or he'd run out of ammo and cast it aside. Either way, he now faced a ten-foot-tall powerful beast with nothing but a serrated dagger. He ducked, his wild hair flying, as the yeti slashed claws at his head.

Since the injured one was getting close to him, I threw my hammer at it first. Once more, Sorka cracked into the back of its head. Bone split, my hammer crushing into its skull.

This time, the blow was enough to stop the yeti. Patrick glanced over as it collapsed fully onto the ground, an arm dangling into the stream. I barked the command for Sorka to return.

The yeti that Patrick faced slashed at him again with its claws. Once more, he was quick enough to dodge, but his heel caught on the uneven stream bank, and he tottered for a second before regaining his balance. The creature leaped, trying to take advantage.

Sorka flew into my grip, but I feared I would be too late to throw the hammer again.

A blast of power came from behind me, whispering past as it knocked into the yeti. The beast flew ten feet and smashed into a tree.

Patrick recovered his balance, his blade at the ready again, but one of Sarrlevi's throwing daggers found the yeti's throat first. It pitched sideways and landed on another hidden explosive. It blew to pieces, more than a leg coming off, and I grimaced at the grisly sight.

We started to lower our weapons, but Sarrlevi pointed his sword in warning two seconds before a great crashing came from across the stream.

Another yeti staggered through the brush, white furry arms flailing, its big head shaking. It also wore a necklace.

Patrick snatched up his rifle as Val, Sarrlevi, and I readied our weapons. But the yeti didn't make it to us. With a gurgling roar, it pitched face-first into the stream, revealing half a dozen arrows sticking out of its back and one thrusting from its skull.

The yeti twitched several times, then lay still.

18

"THE HALF-DARK ELF COMES," SARRLEVI SAID.

Patrick glanced at him, frowned, then called, "Arwen?" into the brush.

"Yes," came her reply. "I'm coming. Are you all right?"

He eyed us, as if we were the ones who'd tried to rip his head off. "I think so."

With no more yetis stomping through the area, we lowered our weapons.

"You say you're friends of Sigrid's?" Patrick asked.

"She's my mother," Val said.

He looked down at her boots.

"The weird barefoot thing is just her," Val said. "It doesn't run in the family."

"Huh."

"I'm going to call Willard," Val said. "I think these might be the yetis she was going to send Matti and me out to hunt down. They've been killing livestock around here, right?"

Patrick grunted.

"Were those necklaces driving them to do it?" I waved toward the shells on thongs around the yetis' necks. They looked like something one would buy three-for-five-dollars from a tourist shop in Long Beach, but each yeti wore one.

"They are magical," Sarrlevi said.

He removed one of the necklaces and considered it. My dulled senses couldn't tell what it did, and I sighed. Though I tried to tell myself that I'd only been learning enchanting for a few months, and before that, I hadn't been able to sense much about magical artifacts either, it didn't make me feel better.

"How many yetis did you want Matti and me to find, Willard?" Val asked over the phone. "And are you willing to send the corpse mobile to pick up their bodies? I doubt the homeowner here wants to keep them." She raised her eyebrows toward Patrick.

"We burned the last one, then added the ashes to the compost." Patrick nodded toward a nearby persimmon tree, the fruit still on the branches and ready to harvest. Maybe yeti compost helped extend the growing season as much as magic.

"Ew," Val said, "are you supposed to compost dead animals?"

Patrick shrugged. "Many tribes that once lived in this area buried dead fish to fertilize their garden beds. Nutrients should be returned to the earth when the living no longer need them. We use everything here on the farm."

"Am I or am I not sending a corporal to pick up the yeti corpses?" came Willard's voice over the phone.

"I guess not," Val said.

Sarrlevi was gazing into the brush across the stream. Only then did I realize that Arwen had arrived. She watched us warily, her bow in hand, her red-blonde hair swept back in a ponytail with a few twigs and leaves sticking out of it.

Patrick nodded to her but didn't beckon her over.

"Any idea what has the yetis stealing animals from farmers?" Willard asked. "They usually stay in the mountains."

"This." Sarrlevi lifted the necklace he'd been examining.

"Goblin magic?" Val stretched a hand toward it. "It's kind of pretty, but it's weak magic, isn't it?"

"It is, in fact, gnomish magic designed to look like goblin magic that does very little, but I've seen these for sale in Cosmic Realms flea markets and pawn shops. As vendors wishing to hawk them to me have promised, there are two enchantments on them, one to convince those with weak mental defenses that the trinkets are beautiful and should be worn—"

Val lowered her hand and frowned at him.

"—and the other to make the wearers susceptible to suggestion from those with the power to use magical coercion. Yetis aren't intelligent enough to understand language, but they can perform moderately complex tasks if given a series of telepathic commands." Sarrlevi looked toward me.

"I'll take your word for it. I can't tell one enchantment from another right now."

He nodded with sympathy toward me.

"At least I'm not nauseated this morning," I said, trying to look on the bright side.

"I don't see how you could be after that gift basket Zav levitated over," Val said.

"I'm not sure you can call it a *gift* basket when it contains other people's stolen prescription drugs," I said.

"Thorvald?" came Willard's voice over the phone. "Unpack that for me, will you? I couldn't catch it all."

"Zav, concerned that Matti would upchuck on his back, sent her every anti-nausea medication available from the grocery store, Zoltan's laboratory, and the neighbor's medicine cabinet."

"I couldn't catch everything pertinent to the *yetis*," Willard clarified.

"Ah. Sarrlevi says someone handing out gnomish shell necklaces is behind the yetis attacking. He's seen them before in the Cosmic Realms. At pawn shops."

"Good to know those exist on every world," Willard said. "I will grudgingly thank him for the information."

"His centuries of experience traveling out there make him kind of useful," Val said.

"*Many* things make me useful," Sarrlevi said.

I walked over and clasped his hand, in part to back up his claim, and in part to make him appear less threatening to Arwen. She remained across the stream and kept eyeing him—and the sword that remained in his other hand. I doubted Val and I were the ones worrying her.

Will you sheathe that, please? I whispered telepathically.

Sarrlevi gazed sadly down at me.

What?

Nothing.

Am I losing my ability to project my words telepathically? I guessed.

When we'd met, I hadn't been able to do that either, and he'd still read my mind. Then, I simply hadn't known how. Now, I probably lacked the power to.

We will find a solution, he said.

That sounded like a *yes.*

Sarrlevi squeezed my hand, then released it so he could draw his kerchief and clean the blood off his sword and dagger.

I shuddered at the reminder that he'd offered to let me scrub my mouth out with that kerchief. Yuck. I didn't care how much magic sanitized it between uses.

One wonders if his sword feels equally disgusted, Sorka said, *knowing the kerchief was used to clean your vomitus and is now bathing its blade.*

I doubt his sword is as easily offended as you.

Hm.

Val hung up and put her phone away. "Willard said to prioritize fixing you up, Matti, but if we happen to find whoever's sending yetis down here and why, she would like to know."

"Uhm." Arwen lifted her bow diffidently. "Because the yetis have been disturbing farmers in the area, I tracked one back to its lair." She pointed the bow toward the east, into the foothills of the Cascades. "I found a cave with goblin beds in it, a few magical trinkets, and more necklaces like that."

"Good work, Arwen," Patrick said. "What do the goblins want? Part of the stolen livestock for themselves?"

"I'm not certain. They fled when I approached." Her voice lowered, almost inaudible, as she added, "As many who can sense my heritage do."

"They probably fled," Val said, "because they were up to no good. This reminds me of a mission I had in Idaho last year. The goblins over there wanted the lakeside resort town of Harrison for themselves and convinced Sasquatches to make trouble and scare away the people living there."

"This is good farmland that we've worked on improving for decades," Patrick said. "Yetis would not scare us away."

"You're atypical though, Father," Arwen said. "The Donovans were talking about selling if nothing was done and complaining that it would be hard to get a good price if heads of livestock were left scattered about their land when potential buyers came out."

"Funny how such things bring down property values," Val said.

"I can show you the cave, if you'd like," Arwen offered.

"We actually came on another matter." Val extended her hand toward me.

Arwen looked curiously at me, and I showed her my glowing palm. She shrank back, as if the magic might leap out and bite her. No, as if she *recognized* the magic—and didn't like anything about it.

Me too, girl, I thought.

"You are cursed?" Arwen asked.

"Apparently. I don't suppose you know anything about curses and how to lift them?" I smiled hopefully, though I doubted someone who used her magic to keep persimmons ripe knew much about traditional dark-elven spells.

"I know a little about curses—did you touch a *slewvethna* artifact?—but nothing about lifting them, no. You would need a powerful dark-elf priest."

"Any chance you know where we could find one?" I asked.

Arwen shrank back again, looking like she wanted to disappear into the trees. Maybe her dad wasn't the only one with PTSD.

Patrick was the one to answer. "There aren't any around here anymore. Haven't been for decades."

"Are you sure?" Val asked quietly, watching Arwen instead of him.

"Positive," he said coolly. "Listen, we appreciate your help with the yetis, but we don't entertain. I'll get you a jar of honey, and you can see yourselves out."

"Honey?" Val mouthed.

"Arwen?" I would have questioned her telepathically, but I worried she wouldn't hear me. "I'm going to die if I don't get help."

Sarrlevi winced. Nobody had wanted to say it, but he didn't deny it...

"Do you have any idea where we could find a priest?" I asked. "We had a lead up near Arlington and found a chamber full of pods that are supposed to turn people into dark elves, but the priest that built the place or at least looked over it wasn't home."

Arwen looked toward her father, who shook his head, as if to say she didn't need to talk to us, but then her gaze settled on my palm.

"I have encountered that priest," she said softly. "Last year."

Patrick frowned at her. "You didn't say anything about that."

"I know. I... Matti, will you speak with me alone?"

"Sure." I didn't know if she didn't want her father to hear what she had to say or was nervous talking in front of a number of people, but I hopped across the stream.

Patrick's grip tightened on his rifle, and Sarrlevi stepped toward him, but Patrick didn't raise the weapon. His instincts probably told him to protect his daughter.

Be wary, Sarrlevi spoke into my mind as I followed Arwen down a narrow trail.

Of her dad? Or her?

She *is the one with a dark-elf heritage.*

I think he's *the one more likely to fill me full of holes.*

Call me if you need assistance.

I think we'll be fine.

Arwen didn't go far before stopping and facing me, keeping several feet between us.

A fan of personal space myself, I didn't mind and nodded to her. "Anything you could tell me about him or where to find someone who could lift the curse would be great."

"I understand. I did not want my father to worry about me."

I almost asked how old she was but decided there was probably no age at which a parent didn't worry about a child when it came to dark elves.

"That priest... I know him. Verdavin. He came looking for me last summer. Most of his people left the area after the collapse of their Seattle lair and the defeating of their volcano scheme. You know about those things?"

"I know that Val and her dragon mate had a lot to do with their woes."

Arwen nodded. "That is what I've heard too. I was worried to meet her. Even her mother... Well, I met Sigrid before learning she was the mother of the *Ruin Bringer.*"

"I was worried about meeting Val for the first time too."

"Why? *You* are not a half-blood from a despicable and hated species." Anguish and bitterness twisted her lips.

"She sounded like trouble."

"Yes. I have heard that about you too."

"That's accurate then." I smiled, though I was antsy to get the information I needed. "What did the priest want? Did he say where he stays when he's not at his underground laboratory?"

"He did not. Verdavin wanted to procreate with me, and he tried to use his magic to convince me that *I* wanted that too." Arwen grimaced.

"Ass."

"Yes. Since there are so few of his people left, he wishes to propagate the species. Normally, they would not be interested in someone with mixed blood, and he made it clear that three-quarters dark-elven offspring wouldn't be ideal, but he believed that since I am half human, I would be more fertile and could have *many* babies for him."

"Gee, wouldn't that have been an honor." I would have offered her a hug or a comforting pat, but she continued to keep her distance.

"Maybe *some* of them would have sufficient power to be useful, he said." Arwen shook her head. "I have sometimes wondered about... finding a mate, but not a dark elf. Not one who uses his magic against me and wants me for *breeding* purposes."

"Yeah, I avoid those guys on Tinder too." I hesitated, not wanting to press her when she was disturbed, but my palm itched, reminding me that the dwarven blessing would only buy me so much time.

"You are with the elf, aren't you? Mates?"

"Yes."

"I've longed so much to meet their people, to learn from them.

I love nature and have tried to find books to teach myself their magic, but it is not easy when you are not... A dark elf isn't the same as a surface elf."

"A lot of them are haughty pricks. You're not missing much."

Her expression promised she disagreed.

"Do you have any idea where I could find the priest now?" I asked.

"I do not. I am aware of the laboratory you mentioned, but, as I said, it is not his home. I do not know where he lives when he is not working there. I have heard... Well, there's a rumor. The goblins to the east of here mentioned it."

"The goblins that might be responsible for the yetis invading farms and eating pigs?"

"If they are, I'm sure that's only *some* of them. Most goblins don't make trouble aside from scavenging things left outside on people's property. Sixteen broken-down cars and trucks have gone missing in the last year from the Derringer property."

"I'll bet the neighbors weren't upset about that."

"No," Arwen said. "The goblins said they heard from their cousins in Seattle that half-dragons that were a part of an experiment centuries ago were recently released from prisons."

"Uh." I shouldn't have been surprised that random Earth goblins had found out about that, since they found out about everything, but I didn't know what to say.

"I'd always heard that dragons couldn't have offspring with any of the other intelligent species, so I didn't put much stock in the rumor, but one of the half-dragons is supposed to also be half dark elven. A *female*. If that's true... Well, the priest is single-minded, and, for his purposes, a half-dragon would be better than a half-human." Arwen waved at herself. "One of the goblins thought he'd gone out into the Cosmic Realms to look for her. He is, of course, powerful enough to make portals." Her expression turned wistful again. "If I could do that, I would want to see the elven home world. I know they would never agree to let me into their cities and would probably drive me away, but even if I could see those forests and that world for a short time, it would be wonderful. Dark elves originated on Veleshna Var too. Did you know? Long ago."

"I figured." A part of me was tempted to offer to take her there using my mother's portal generator, but I wasn't that welcome on Veleshna Var myself. If Sarrlevi's reaction to Arwen was anything to go by, the elves might shoot *me* if I showed up with a dark-elf mongrel. "My mom thinks the half-dragons might be holed up on Veleshna Var."

"Your mother is human?"

"No, that's my dad. The same as you, I guess. Mom's a dwarf, one of the people Val brought you out to the Olympic Peninsula to help track."

"Oh, right. I remember."

"She lives on Dun Kroth now, but she and I visit. I am—uhm, before this curse, I *was* learning enchanting from her."

"That's amazing. I can't imagine— I mean, from what little I remember of my mother, I can't imagine wanting to learn anything from her. She was awful. I'm not sure if she's alive or not. I think she was with those in the volcano."

"Oh." That meant Val might have killed or helped kill Arwen's mother? I grimaced. "Thanks for the information."

"You're welcome. Don't tell my father about the priest, okay? He gets weird about men—males of any species—coming around. He'd probably try to track down the priest, and that wouldn't turn out well for him. I can't let him be hurt."

"I won't say anything."

Arwen led me back to the stream, but Val, Sarrlevi, and Patrick had left the area. I followed Arwen back to the house and found them in front of the porch, Val with multiple jars of jam and honey in her arms.

Patrick must have decided he'd been social for long enough because he'd disappeared. The scent of smoke came from somewhere behind the house. Maybe he was throwing wood into his fire pit, getting ready to torch yetis for compost. The thought made me eye the jam uneasily and imagine the dubious fertilizers that might have been sprinkled around the berry bushes.

"Zav is questioning the goblins who may be behind the yeti scheme," Val said, "and then he'll be by to pick us up."

"Does he work for Willard too?" I asked.

"He assists me when it moves him to do so, but he would never lower himself to *work for* or seek the employment of a lesser species."

"So only his mom gets to boss him around."

"That's right." Val offered me two jars, one of honey and one of jam. "For you. Your fastidious elf wouldn't touch them."

"They are sticky." Sarrlevi looked at me as I accepted the gifts. *Did you learn anything useful?*

The dark-elf priest might be hitting on the half-dragon female as we speak.

Sarrlevi gazed blankly at me.

Which could be useful, because it would imply they're located in the same place. I wiped my hand because the honey jar *was* a touch sticky. Arwen's father either didn't have a professional bottling setup or he'd given us the less desirable stock left over at the end of farmers-market season.

We do not know where the half-dragons are.

Not yet, no, but we could look on Veleshna Var. That would be home for them, right?

Perhaps. But it is a large world with many places that such powerful individuals could hide. They can camouflage themselves as easily as I can—even more effectively, I am certain.

My mom implied there's a way to track them. I shrugged.

I can return to Veleshna Var and see if there has been word of them there, but unless the information of their whereabouts has reached my mother, it is unlikely anyone would tell me. Despite my official status as a noble elf lord, I have not yet been invited to salons, meetings, or other gatherings where gossip would be passed among the attendees.

Salons? I imagined three elves sipping tea while balancing on a tree branch and having their hair done.

A salon, as in an assemblage of notable people at the home of a prominent person.

Ah. I smirked, the image of curlers in the elves' hair persisting. *The cool kids aren't letting you play with them yet, huh?*

Sarrlevi sighed at me.

Don't sweat it. I swatted him on the chest. *I didn't get invited to salons in high school either.*

I will create a portal to Veleshna Var and see if I can learn anything.

Good. Thanks. Here, the jam jar isn't sticky. Give it to an elf you're hoping will befriend you.

Sarrlevi eyed it skeptically.

Look, lingonberries. It's exotic fare from a wild world. The snooty elves in the capital ought to eat it up. "Right, Val?" I asked aloud.

She hadn't been privy to our telepathic conversation but saw me offering Sarrlevi the jam and backed me up. "Right."

"Very well." Sarrlevi accepted the jar and made a portal, but he hugged me before leaving. *I will return soon. Rest, and do not work yourself overmuch.*

Is that your way of saying you sense the dwarven blessing is already wearing off?

He hesitated, but all he said was, *It should last for some time.*

That didn't keep him from giving me a long look over his shoulder as he strode toward the portal.

"What did I agree with?" Val asked as he disappeared.

"That lingonberry jam is exotic Earth fare and haughty elves will love it."

"Arwen said it comes from the berries they cultivate on the roof of their 1973 trailer." Val waved toward the manufactured home.

"*Exotic*," I assured her.

19

Zavryd stopped at Willard's office on the way home to drop off four goblins that had confessed to being involved in the yeti scheme, buying the necklaces and convincing the creatures to munch on livestock to scare farmers into leaving their land. Apparently, the area the goblins had claimed for themselves was prone to flooding every year, and they wanted something more desirable but didn't have the funds to pay for it.

"What will Willard do to them?" I asked after the drop-off, with Zavryd flying Val and me back to Green Lake. Tinja had stayed outside of town with the goblin clan to continue speaking to them about the delights of city living and educating oneself in the human manner. If she'd succeeded in recruiting any of them to stay in her sanctuary, I didn't know.

"Threaten to send them back to their home world or possibly coerce them into working for her as informants," Val said.

"Is that how she ended up with Gondo?"

"How'd you guess?"

"He seems like someone who would be involved in schemes."

"That describes *most* goblins."

Zavryd coasted over the houses and trees of our neighborhood, gliding toward our street.

A portal was recently formed, he announced, *and an unfamiliar mongrel female waits in the area.*

"I'm sure if she's planning to make trouble," Val said, "your arrival will scare her into good behavior. That worked with the goblins, after all. I doubt they would have confessed their scheme to Tinja or me, but it sounds like they nearly wet themselves in their eagerness to come clean when you plopped down in the middle of them."

Not responding to that, Zavryd said, *The mongrel is half dwarven.*

His head turned enough for a single violet eye to regard me. Implying what? That someone with dwarven blood *had* to be trouble?

"What's the other half?" Though my weakened senses couldn't pick out anyone yet, I had a guess about who this was.

She is also half-elven.

"Sounds like Nesheeva from the Assassins' Guild," I said.

"Not here to take a shot at you, I hope," Val said.

"Probably looking to chat with Sarrlevi. I *shouldn't* have assassins after me anymore."

Zavryd landed on Val's rooftop, his head pointing toward my house. Nesheeva, wearing all black, including her leather armor, leaned against the signpost on the corner with a sword hilt jutting over her shoulder and throwing axes in a hip sheath. She looked like she'd come for a fight, not a chat, and I second-guessed myself.

Zavryd levitated Val and me to their front yard, keeping us within his wards instead of dropping me in the street where I might have to defend myself.

What happened to you? Nesheeva asked bluntly, ignoring Val, though she did bow toward Zavryd.

Dark-elven curse. I assumed she didn't refer to the honey stuck to my palm.

Your aura is diminished.

So I've heard. If you're looking for Sarrlevi, he's gone to the elven home world.

I did come to deliver a message to him. Nesheeva cocked her head. *Did he leave because of your diminished magical abilities?*

No, he left to bribe snooty elves for information with jam.

She blinked a couple of times.

What's your message? I can give it to him when he comes back.

Nesheeva considered me again. Deciding if she could trust me with her precious message? Or if I was worthy to receive it? Or if I'd lied and Sarrlevi wouldn't really be back?

I scowled at her.

Nesheeva smirked, indifferent to my ire. *There's a new prestige hunt. I'm thinking of asking him to join me in collecting the reward.*

He's not an assassin anymore.

Val must have decided I wouldn't get in trouble talking to Nesheeva from her yard, because she headed up to her porch. Zavryd shifted into his human form and hopped down from the roof to join her.

Yes, I heard about his retirement. And that he's an elf noble now. Nesheeva's smirk widened. *Did you talk him into accepting that? I can't imagine he cared about kissing up to King Eireth.*

His mother did. I didn't point out that Sarrlevi had missed his homeland and hadn't objected too vehemently to his retirement.

I guess that's not surprising. I bet he's already bored. Either way, the king wouldn't care if he hunted these particular targets, I'm sure.

There's more than one? I didn't comment on the boredom possibility, since I worried Sarrlevi *would* grow restless without challenging work that he could engage in.

Four.

You may need more than one ally to go after them then. I assume the prey is challenging?

Very challenging. Her smirk shifted to a grimace. *I almost didn't agree to make them the prestige hunt, as I already lost enough dues from assassins who died coming after you, but... one does not refuse dragons when they wish to hire you.*

I wouldn't have guessed dragons hired assassins.

Rarely. They're seeking the targets themselves and hope to avoid paying. The elves and dwarves are also seeking these targets.

With a sinking sensation, I realized who the assassins had to be after. *The half-dragon Starblade and the others he freed from stasis chambers?*

Yes. I heard you had something to do with that.

Inadvertently.

Well, the dragons think those four are abominations and want them dead. The dwarves worry they'll return to attacking their world and also want them dealt with. The elves are being pressured into helping the other intelligent species find them since one of their kind originally created them. Half-dragons may be powerful, but there aren't many of them, and they're not going to be able to survive so many people hunting them.

Do you know where they are? If I asked her to keep her assassins away until I found the dark-elf priest, she would only scoff, but maybe she would let a clue slip.

Not yet, but I will.

I'll give Sarrlevi your message when he returns. I don't suppose you know any dark elves? Are there any who are assassins in your guild?

There are not, and I haven't seen a dark elf in a long time. I would happily accept them as members if they applied. They're powerful and like to creep around at night. That makes them ideal assassins.

Nesheeva stepped away from the signpost, formed a portal, and bowed to me before leaping through it.

I headed toward my house, thinking of Sarrlevi's suggestion

that I rest. It was good advice, but I had to figure out where those half-dragons were—before everyone else did. Even if the dark-elf priest wasn't with them right now, if he'd visited the female half-dragon, she might know where he'd gone. Or, as I'd considered before, she might have the power herself to cure me.

Not sure how long my search would take, I gathered a few supplies in the kitchen, snorting at a fresh batch of peanut brittle that had arrived, probably via my sister, while I'd been gone. Someone must have told Grandma how popular it was in these parts.

I added some to my pack, thinking of visiting Dun Kroth. By now, Mom might have learned of the half-dragons' location. If she hadn't, she might be willing to help me research that information.

Even if they'd been raised on the elven home world, the half-dragons had been the dwarves' mortal enemies, and Starblade had been incarcerated on Dun Kroth. There ought to be some records on him there, maybe a clue that would help me guess where he was hiding now.

I was beginning to feel bad that I'd let Starblade go, however accidentally, for more reasons than before. When the dwarves had told me he might be a threat to their people, I'd regretted my actions. But now... I regretted that everyone was hunting those guys down. Starblade had *helped* me. As criminals, maybe they deserved to be hunted, but everything they'd done had been centuries earlier during a war. Had their crimes truly been heinous? Or had it only been that they'd been the generals on the other side? It didn't sound like the elves particularly wanted them hunted down and were going along with it because of pressure from the dwarves and now the dragons.

In my office, I pulled down the portal generator, but I stared at the box before opening it. If I could figure out where on Veleshna Var they were hiding, I could go directly there. But I had only been a few places on the elven world and knew little of it. I also didn't know if they were there. Wouldn't it be better for them to hide out on a wild world?

But when Sarrlevi had been exiled, he'd missed his homeland. I remembered him leaning his forehead against a tree on Veleshna Var and basking in its aura or scent or whatever exuded serenity to elves.

Maybe after so many centuries imprisoned on another world, Starblade felt the same way. Maybe he'd wanted to go home.

"Home to a specific place?" I murmured. Where had he grown up and been trained? He had to have been a boy before he'd been a warrior.

The elves probably knew where he'd been born, but if I asked them, they might think to check that place themselves. If the dwarves knew or Mom could find out, she might give me a head start before telling her people.

"Mom, it is." Armed with peanut brittle, I activated the portal generator.

20

MOM, AS I FOUND OUT SHORTLY AFTER ARRIVING IN THE CAPITAL CITY on Dun Kroth, wasn't home. That would make things more difficult, but I had my translation charm and had also picked up the trinket that could decipher written languages. Between those items, I ought to be able to do my own research. If I knew where to look. Did Dun Kroth have the equivalent of a public library?

"Would you like to go to your room in the royal quarters and wait for your mother?" asked the guard who always insisted on escorting me from the gate into the city for *my* protection, not, she assured me, because the dwarves still eyed me suspiciously when I wandered around alone.

I was hoping to learn about dark elves from the perspective of your —our—people, I replied telepathically since she didn't understand English or have a translation charm. I doubted she would help me research the half-dragon war criminals. Besides, I'd already shown her my hand when she had, like everyone else, asked what the hell was wrong with my aura. *Is there a library I could visit?*

"Yes, we have many libraries, but you will not find more than cursory information on dark elves and the way they attack enemies in them." She frowned at my hand—sympathetically, I thought.

Earth libraries don't even have cursory information. Humans don't acknowledge the existence of dark elves. Or any other magical beings.

"It is bizarre that such an ignorant species rose to dominance on that wild world."

Yeah, chimps or dolphins probably would have been more open-minded if they'd ended up in charge.

Not surprisingly, that earned me a blank look. I doubted dwarven libraries had *any* information on them.

"It is likely that dragons will eventually impose their rule over your world and force the natives to learn about the Cosmic Realms—and how best to serve dragon-kind."

Our world leaders look forward to that day.

"Do you wish to study in one of the public libraries or the private one in the royal quarters? As your mother's daughter, you should be allowed access to it." She pursed her lips. "All might be of limited use to you since you've yet to learn our language. You will not be able to *telepathically* read our books."

"I've got tools for that." I patted my pocket, wishing I *did* understand the language. Mom had been teaching me a few words here and there, but our lessons had focused more on enchanting than learning Dwarven.

The guard grunted with disapproval.

On the way up a set of stairs in the royal quarters, I tripped before catching myself on the wall. After the busy morning, fatigue was catching up with me. The mark on my hand throbbed, and I imagined the dark-elven magic battling the dwarven blessing, slowly wearing it down.

"Just need a little more time," I whispered.

The guard looked at me with atypical concern. "I will inform your mother that you're here as soon as she returns. She went with King Ironhelm to a meeting."

A meeting about hunting down those half-dragons? I kept myself from grimacing and thanked her.

After showing me into the library, the walls carved from salt, with the stone and wooden bookcases freestanding, she pointed out the section on intelligent species of the Cosmic Realms, then stood back a few feet and nodded for me to begin. With her watching? That hadn't been the plan.

I brought a gift for my mother and her bodyguards, something they enjoyed the last time they were on Earth. Since they're not here, maybe you'd like to have some? I would hate for you to be bored and hungry while you're stuck watching me. I shrugged off my pack and dug out the container of peanut brittle.

At first, she eyed me suspiciously, but then she said, "Do you refer to the sweet candy shards? Mukmor mentioned them."

If that's one of Mom's bodyguards who raided my kitchen, then yes.

"Mukmor raids *many* kitchens. He has a love for food, especially sweets."

I offered her the container. *You're welcome to try them and share with other dwarves that might like them.*

Especially if she would leave the library to do so...

After removing the lid, she sniffed before taking out a piece. The rock-hard peanut brittle didn't give way to her first tentative bite, but then she chomped down with jaws like a Doberman pinscher. A piece broke off with a loud snap.

After a few thoughtful chews, the guard smiled. "It *is* wonderful. And with such intriguing texture!"

Yeah, the texture of glass shards grinding in one's mouth. I still couldn't believe the dwarves liked my grandmother's loathsome dessert.

Feel free to share, I repeated, waving at the box and not-so-subtly toward the door. If I'd had my power, I might have tried magically coercing her.

After the guard took another bite, she considered the rest of the peanut brittle, and said, "Yes. Perhaps I will put this some-where safe."

Somewhere safe? Like her room? Maybe she wasn't the sharing type.

"I will return if you need me," she said.

Okay. I gave her a thumbs-up, though the gesture probably didn't mean anything to dwarves.

Or maybe it meant something crude because she gave me a startled look. "Earth culture must be strange."

Since she also headed for the door, I didn't object to the statement.

Standing in front of the Other Intelligent Species section, I waited a minute before running off to search the rest of the library. I hoped the guard's home was outside the royal quarters, and she would be gone a while. And that she wouldn't send someone else to watch me.

Fortunately, nobody else showed up. The guard was either too distracted noshing peanut brittle to assign someone else, or she didn't believe I would be a threat to the books.

"Not unless I lose my temper and start swinging my hammer." Not planning on that, I activated the charm that would allow me to read the Dwarven language.

I would object vehemently to the destruction of books, Sorka informed me.

Don't worry. I've never beaten up a book. Not even a bookcase, unless it was a built-in made from cheap plywood and I was replacing it with something better.

Hm.

Everyone knows bookcases should be solid wood and have gargoyle or dragon corbels.

Gargoyles? Why not hammers?

Hammers don't lend themselves to corbels.

Harrumph.

After perusing the shelves in front of me, I took a slow amble around the library to make sure there wasn't anyone inside spying on me. Then I searched in earnest for information on the elf-dwarf war. Something that would have been easier if I'd known what they'd called it. Had anyone said? I couldn't remember.

"One bonus to a dwarven library is that none of the books are on shelves too high for me to reach," I murmured, finding a history section where I skimmed titles such as *The Golden Pre-Dragon Era, The Orc War, The Period of Isolation, Dragon Invasion Epoch*, and *The Campaigns of General Throndak*. Elves didn't come up much, at least not in the titles, though I chanced across *The Elven Interlude* and pulled the square tome out to skim. If the library was an indication, dwarves favored square books to rectangular ones.

"We like our books like our men," a familiar voice said from behind me. "Short and stout."

"Mom." I fumbled the book, almost dropping it as a surge of guilt swept over me. Would she care about what I was *really* researching? And where had she come from? I hadn't heard or sensed her, though the latter wasn't that surprising these days.

Smiling sadly, Mom glanced at my hand and hugged me. "The blessing is already fading, isn't it?"

Her voice was thick with emotion, and it made *me* emotional. For a moment, I could only manage a nod as an answer, tears threatening.

She held the hug longer than I expected, then grasped my hand and willed her power into it. I felt the rush of energy—it almost buzzed with its intensity—but I also felt the dark-elven magic resisting her. The purple knot throbbed angrily, and the usual itching turned to pain.

I would have happily endured it if it would have cured me, but I sensed before Mom finished trying that it wouldn't.

"I'm sorry, *Nika*," she whispered. "It's distressing to have power but not have it be useful. Distressing and atypical. Dark elves are truly vile."

"Because dwarven enchantments don't affect their curses?" I tried to smile, though I also looked away so I could brush the moisture from my eyes before tears fell.

"For *many* reasons." She squeezed my hands before releasing me. "But especially that one."

"Yeah."

"I cannot believe..." She swallowed, and this time, *she* looked away and brushed her eyes. "For so many years, I had only glimpses of you, those which my captors showed me to keep me motivated." Her lips twisted in a bitter grimace. "But at least you were alive and well in the recordings. To finally have been reunited with you, only to..." She shook her head, not voicing *only to lose you,* but I knew she was thinking those words. "How did this happen? You did not say exactly."

"An accident." I laughed without humor. "All those attacks from assassins that I survived only to chance across a dark-elven artifact in a building I was thinking about renting..." I thought but didn't say that it didn't seem fair. People died of accidents all the time or because of surprise illnesses that came too young. I'd dodged more bullets than many.

"It is *not* fair." Mom hugged me again.

I smiled, wondering why I bothered leaving thoughts unvoiced when in the presence of mind readers.

"We haven't had enough time together," she whispered. "But you haven't given up, and I won't either." She wiped her eyes again as she released me. "What quest are you on? Yilta said research on dark elves, but she must have told you our people don't have much on their kind. The libraries on Veleshna Var would contain much more information. Are you permitted to visit their world? Sarrlevi is allowed now, isn't he? Couldn't he take you?"

"I actually came here for a reason."

"Beyond my company?" Mom looked at the book in my hand.

"Yeah. You were the one who gave me the lead on the dark elven half-dragon, and I've since learned a full-blooded dark-elf priest may have sought her out, so I'm trying to find the hideout of the half-dragons."

"You and many people seek to do so. People and *dragons*."

"And assassins, yes. I've heard. Maybe it's foolish to think I can find them when so many others haven't yet, but I thought Starblade might have wanted to go home. I'm trying to figure out where home is for them."

"Veleshna Var."

"A specific location on it. Where they were raised and trained to be warriors and mages—whatever all their upbringing involved." I shrugged. "It's just a hunch, but…"

Again, I remembered how Sarrlevi had leaned against and found peace from the trees of his home world.

"Ah. I see." Mom crooked a finger and led me to a group of spheres on stands.

From across the library, I'd assumed they were globes of various worlds, but she rested her hand on a gray sphere, and it flared to life. The face of a bearded female dwarf appeared above it.

"Where on Veleshna Var were the half-dragon warriors raised?" Mom asked it.

"Oh, is this the dwarven Siri?"

That earned me a puzzled look, reminding me that Mom might know more about humans than most dwarves, but she had spent most of her last three decades on Earth asleep or locked away underground.

"We call it the librarian," she said, then fell silent as the magical hologram replied.

"An experimental clan of half-dragons that the elves sought to turn into powerful soldiers with great ability were birthed between the years 342 and 345 Post Expansion Era. Through magic and science, dragon genetic material was mixed primarily with elven genetic material to spawn beings capable of drawing on the power of both species and with the best attributes of both. The scientist-general who spearheaded the program resided in Sylvan Moor but worked out of his laboratory on Mount Serathyan, a remote location on the larger southern continent of Veleshna Var. It has much volcanic and seismic activity, so he believed interruptions would be few. Many elves did not approve of the project, and it was kept secret from the dragons and much of the elven populace."

I scratched my jaw, having a hard time imagining an elf—or anyone—being drawn back to a home that was basking in sulfuric fumes and surrounded by volcanos. Maybe the area wasn't that bad and had forestlands surrounding the peaks, but... "Can it give a picture of the place?"

Mom commanded the dwarven Siri to do so.

A map displayed, showing a forested area but also a lot of bare black rock. As if this were the equivalent of an encyclopedia entry, photos also appeared.

I watched dubiously. The pictures didn't appear as inhospitable as the red-skied area around the Dun Kroth volcano base, but between a gray haze in the sky and a lot of craggy and forbidding black rock, I didn't think it held much of the lush vegetation and natural beauty that elves enjoyed.

"You believe they would go back there?" Mom also sounded dubious.

"I don't know. Maybe not."

"Their people would have thought to check there, regardless. If we know where the half-dragons were raised, it's common knowledge."

"Did they go anywhere else for training?" I envisioned the half-dragon kids being like Boy Scouts taken into the wilderness for survival exercises. Or, in their case, maybe it had been *war* exercises.

Mom asked, but the answer came back as unknown.

"Is there anywhere on that continent or near it where aspiring elf warriors in general are taken for wilderness training? Or where young elves of that time period were taken for any reason?"

Mom's expression suggested she didn't think the line of questioning would lead anywhere, but she didn't object to relaying my query to the holographic librarian.

"In the past, elven warriors wishing to prove their worth trained and hunted on the Frozen Taiga of Loylora. The magical *daiyeesha* are formidable animals native to the area, with the ability to shift into different dimensions to avoid attacks and position themselves to pounce on their prey. To lead a team to find and slay one was considered proof of command ability as well as martial prowess."

"That was in the past?" I asked. "It's not done today?"

"Due to the number of young elves who died hunting the *daiyeesha,* as well as their dwindling population numbers, the Taiga was turned into a nature preserve. Hunting is no longer permitted there."

Mom raised her eyebrows.

A nature preserve that didn't get a lot of visitors sounded like a promising hiding spot.

"Do you have pictures of the area?" I asked.

Again, the librarian showed a map, this one dominated by whites and greens, and then pictures of frozen lakes, snow-smothered forests, and vast grasslands stretching away from mountains. The wintry aspect made the area appear harsh, but it was also beautiful, especially in an evening photo that showed purple-red light from the setting sun gleaming off the snow. I could see elves appreciating it, especially hardened elves who didn't mind tough living. And those mountains might be filled with caves—caves that people might hide in. Normal elves might not naturally hole up underground, but dragons *liked* caves, so maybe these guys would contemplate such a lair.

The final imagery, a recording of a few seconds, showed one of the *daiyeesha* loping across a frozen tundra, the muscles of the feline-like creature rippling under its glossy fur. It could have been a cross between a saber-toothed tiger and a snow leopard. It disappeared as it came close to a herd of shaggy elk-like herbivores digging at grass under the snow, only to reappear within their midst, slashing and biting and taking down one of the animals for dinner.

I nodded to myself, and Mom lifted her eyebrows.

"Like I said, it's just a hunch, but that's where I want to look for the half-dragons."

"I believe the preserve is quite large," Mom said.

"I want to check those mountains. I saw a cave in one photo."

"A cave? Elves build their homes in the trees."

"Half-*dragon* elves?"

"They may have some different tendencies, but they were raised in elven culture."

"I could start there, at least."

"You may look, of course. The portal should take you there, but the *daiyeesha* alone would be a reason for you not to go by yourself. Especially now." Mom hesitated and looked toward the library door. "I should go with you."

"Will you get in trouble if you do?"

"Not *trouble*. Not precisely. But my father has been leading the push to have the half-dragons recaptured—and, as I said, the dragons want them killed. If I found them, I would be... expected to assist with that. Regardless, I might not be welcome on Veleshna Var right now. Even beyond the issue with the half-dragons, tensions have been elevated between dwarves and elves since my sister kidnapped Sarrlevi's mother. Even though she's gone..."

Mom spread her hands and shrugged. "As I said, tension exists. Our people are supposedly working together to find the half-dragons, but it could be problematic if I were caught in a remote part of Veleshna Var without getting permission from King Eireth first."

"If you asked him for permission, we would be tipping off the elves to where the half-dragons are." Where I *thought* they were based entirely on a hunch, I reminded myself.

That preserve might be completely devoid of half-dragons—and everyone else except the animals that lived there.

"I will come anyway." Mom nodded firmly. "You are my daughter, and you need my help."

"I don't want to be responsible for starting a war between elves and dwarves—or getting the dragons pissed at you."

"That will not happen."

Was she truly confident in that? Or trying to talk herself into believing it?

"It's okay, Mom. I do appreciate the offer, but I think it would be better for me to go with Sarrlevi."

She opened her mouth, an objection on her lips.

"Because he's an elf, and the half-dragons shouldn't immediately want to attack him, not because he's more useful than you are."

"If the Assassins' Guild has declared the half-dragons their prestige hunt, they may know that Sarrlevi is an assassin—and a threat."

"He's a *retired* assassin. The half-dragons shouldn't automatically worry that he's after them." I hoped.

"He has only been retired for two weeks."

"Closer to three now."

"*Nika*..." She said my nickname as a sigh.

"Just let me go in with Sarrlevi, Mom. If we don't find them right away, I'll come back, and we can try something else."

"You are a most stubborn daughter."

"Sarrlevi says it's my dwarven blood that makes me so."

"Possibly true." Mom hugged me.

"Thanks for wanting to help, Mom. At any cost."

After wiping her eyes again, she turned toward the door.

I remembered another concern that had been on my mind. "Wait, Mom?"

"Yes?"

"If this doesn't work out and I don't make it—"

She opened her mouth, and I could tell she wanted to protest the idea, but I held up a hand, and she let me continue.

"—will you finish a project that I took on before this started?" I explained the goblins being hunted and my promise to build and enchant tiny homes for their village, homes that would be difficult for poachers or anyone else to find.

"*Twenty* homes? So few."

"They're tiny homes, and I'm sure Abbas and Tinja will help build them. It's mostly the enchanting that I need you for."

She smiled sadly. "It's all right. Of course, I will do this. I will help *regardless*. We have not discussed how to hide dwellings, have we? That would be more ideal for your domicile than having weapons all over the premises, yes? Weapons that are not legal in the human city."

"They're hidden by elven vines."

She snorted. "An enchantment would be *far* superior. We'll make it happen when you're better."

"Thanks." I hugged her again.

"Show me the area where the goblins live—in your thoughts—so I can find them to install the homes."

I did, and she nodded and patted me. "All right." As she released me and headed for the door, she added, "Be safe."

"Somehow, I doubt that's in the cards," I murmured to myself, eyeing the image that lingered in the air above the sphere, the deadly creature eating its meal in the snow. It wasn't even the most dangerous thing we would have to worry about encountering. The half-dragon Starblade might have helped me once, but he hadn't been warm and friendly about it. I doubted he wanted to see me again.

21

"WHAT DO YOU MEAN YOU DON'T WANT ME TO COME ALONG?" VAL asked. "Sindari can kick the butts of those elven cats, and we can help you find half-dragons skulking around, no problem. Me and Zav." She pointed toward the backyard, where he was relaxing in his goblin-pitch-free sauna.

We were in Val's basement as I explained the mission to Dimitri, who'd been alternating between sleeping in his room and being experimented on by Zoltan these past couple of days. The glowing marks on his palms promised that nothing had come of the experiments.

"I think the more people we bring, the more likely they'll view it as an invasion force and treat us as hostile," I said. "We *especially* can't bring Zavryd. His people want to *kill* the half-dragons. The elves and dwarves only want to lock them up again." At least, that was the impression I'd gotten from my mother. It was possible they also wouldn't mind the half-dragons being killed and out of their hair forever.

"Something I'm *sure* those guys will be amenable to."

"We just want their help." I pointed to Dmitri and myself.

Maybe I shouldn't have mentioned my plans to Val—I'd suspected she would, as the loyal friend she was, offer to come along—but I'd had to come to her house to get Dimitri. If I managed to talk the half-dragons into helping, I doubted they would be willing to come back to Seattle to cure him at his bedside. Had we needed Starblade, I might have believed that a possibility, since he'd traveled to Earth before, but the female half-dragon was an unknown to me.

"You don't think they'll be willing to help if you bring a friend with a big sword and a bigger tiger along?" Val asked.

"One who's known to be the mate of a dragon?" I raised my eyebrows.

"I doubt people who, up until a couple of months ago, had been sleeping in stasis chambers for centuries have heard about Zav and me."

"You did invite a great many people and dragons to your wedding," Zoltan put in.

He'd been frowning since I'd come downstairs and told him I needed to take his patient away, and he didn't stop frowning for his interjection.

"Not people who've been chatting up half-dragon war criminals, I'm sure," Val said.

"Maybe, but haven't you said that those with magical blood can sense Zavryd's aura on you and tell that you're mates?" I'd never been sensitive enough to determine anything like that, but she'd said it had come up often when she first started hanging around with Zavryd—even before they'd been a couple.

"Other *dragons*."

"Well, these are half-dragons. They're powerful too."

Val sighed. "Matti. You can't get yourself killed. And you can't get my roommate killed either."

"Didn't you say you'd enjoy having more pantry space if he

didn't make it?" I smiled, but it wasn't much of a joke. Besides, I had no intention of getting Dimitri killed.

"I've rethought that. I'd miss his five hundred a month in rent. It covers the appetizers for Zav's meals."

"I'm touched by how much my life means to you, Val," Dimitri said.

He had bags under his eyes and hadn't contributed much to the conversation—the argument—other than to look wistful whenever I spoke of the curse being lifted.

Val's response was to swat him on the shoulder. She was even worse at showing affection than I was.

"When do we leave, Matti?" Dimitri pushed himself from a chair to his feet. "And what should I bring?"

"Cold-weather clothing and whatever weapons you have."

"Weapons?"

"Dimitri is a big guy but not a big fighter," Val said.

He nodded. "I make art, not war."

I'd assumed he wasn't a trained warrior, but I hadn't realized he objected outright to fighting. "You know there's a skeleton wielding a scythe on your shirt, right?"

"That doesn't mean I'm a bruiser. This is my favorite band."

"Well, put a sweatshirt on over that. And a sweater. And a parka. The part of the world we're going to looks cold."

Zoltan shook his head. "It is not a good idea to take Dimitri to such place. Or to another world at all, especially when he is in a delicate state."

"Maybe you can send along some potions to keep him from catching a cold," I said.

"*Potions?*" Zoltan gave me an exasperated look, which he soon turned on Val. "Dear robber, how is it that you and your neighbor have not learned more about alchemy? As I've told you before, I am not a witch with a broom, cackling and stirring burbling goo in a cauldron over open flames. I make scientifically and magically precise *formulations*."

"I didn't say anything." Val stepped aside so Dimitri could head toward the door.

I was glad *he* didn't object to coming, even if his doctor did. Zoltan's protest surprised me until I realized he might care about Dimitri. Who would have thought such an aloof, pompous, and overcharging-for-his-services vampire could have feelings for a mostly normal human?

"You have used similar—similarly *ignorant*—terminology before. All of you should spend more time reading books." Zoltan shot me a particularly dark look before pulling vials out of his cabinets.

I suspected it had more to do with me taking his patient away than concern about the execrable state of my education.

Val led me out of the basement, leaving Zoltan muttering as he chose *formulations* to send with Dimitri. We stopped on the patio, and she gripped my shoulder.

Night had fallen, but the landscaping lights were enough to see the grim set to her face. Would she make another entreaty to come along? Should I let her?

If not for Val's link to Zavryd, I would have welcomed her company, but with the citizens of three worlds hunting the half-dragons, they *had* to be on edge. Even taking Sarrlevi might be risky, since they must be feeling that the elves had turned on them, but I couldn't imagine going on this quest without him, not in my current state.

"I understand your reasoning," Val said, "but I'm worried that those half-dragons will see you coming and kill you outright."

"You haven't met Starblade. He helped me before. Probably because of my charm."

Val glanced at Sorka.

"Not *that* charm," I said, though I acknowledged that dwarves were more known for bashing people over the head to get their way than winning friends and influencing people through schmoozing. "And I helped him, so he ought to be predisposed to like me."

I didn't mention that Starblade had conveyed that we were even now.

"Isn't it the help of the one that's partially dark elven that you need?" Val asked.

"Yeah, but Starblade let *her* out of prison, just as I let him out, so she should like me too. It's a chain of liking." Even though I'd voiced that argument before, it didn't sound much more convincing now than it had then.

"Uh huh."

"I probably don't even need her, other than to ask her where the dark-elf priest went after she rejected his suggestion that they boink often and have enough offspring to repopulate their species." Somehow, I knew she'd rejected his offer without ever having met her or the priest.

Val blinked. "*That's* what he was going to see her about?"

"Arwen thought so. It's what he propositioned *her* with."

Val's lip curled.

I rubbed my gritty eyes, aware of the fatigue creeping into me again. It had been a long day, and I wanted a good night's sleep, not to go on a quest. Of course, if Sarrlevi didn't return soon, I might have nothing to do but get that night's sleep. I'd been surprised when he hadn't been here when I'd returned from Dun Kroth. Had he found useful information on Veleshna Var? Was he even now seeking out the half-dragons by himself?

As much as I would be delighted if he found Starblade and convinced him to bring his dark-elven ally to my bedside to cure me—and Dimitri—I worried about Sarrlevi searching for them alone. Though Starblade had met him before, and they'd destroyed that furnace guardian together, I didn't know how much love the half-dragon felt for him. And if Starblade had heard about the Assassins' Guild hunt...

Thumps sounded in the house, Dimitri banging around in drawers and cabinets, looking for cold-weather gear that was rarely needed in temperate Seattle.

I pulled myself from my thoughts. "If Mikki the Wrench shows up, will you let him know that he'll get his tiny homes, no matter what? My mom agreed to finish the project in case... you know."

Val scowled at me. "Is that really the main concern on your mind, now?"

"It's *a* concern. I hate the idea of going and leaving a project unfinished, an important project."

"All right. Don't get yourself killed though. Now that I have a neighbor who isn't concerned by the odd things that happen in this house, I don't want to lose her."

The basement door opened, and Zoltan walked out in a white lab coat with red-tinted goggles covering his eyes.

"Odd, you say," I murmured as he handed me a couple of vials with instructions on when to give them to Dimitri.

"Here is an analgesic to soothe the mark on his palm. You may use it as well."

"Thanks." I accepted what looked like a tube of Bengay, then looked again toward my house. *Varlesh?* Though my telepathic ability was waning, I tried to project my thoughts outward, hoping he was close enough to hear me. *You're not waiting over there, are you?*

I didn't get an answer.

"Val? Can you reach out telepathically and see if Sarrlevi is in the area? I've been... losing my magic." I grimaced, hating to admit that, though everyone who could sense auras seemed to have figured it out.

"Sure, were you expecting him back tonight?" Val squinted toward the dark sky as she shouted telepathically.

"Earlier, actually. He was going to see if the elves knew anything and would tell him. Since he's not invited to salons regularly, he didn't think they would."

"Uh, all right." After a pause, Val shook her head. "I suppose you could ask Zav to try. His range is a lot greater than mine. But if Sarrlevi was on Earth, he'd be here with you, wouldn't he? It's not like he flies off to hunt buffalo in Wyoming."

"Zavryd does that?"

"Yeah, but not, since I've expressly forbidden it, within the boundaries of Yellowstone."

It took me a moment to process the imagery that brought up and pick out her question. "Varlesh wouldn't be hunting buffalo, no. He has some contacts in the area, but if he's not back on Veleshna Var, he could be—" A jolt of fear blasted me as the memory of orange lightning striking that pile of boulders popped into my mind. "Hell, he *better* not have gone back up there." I gripped Val's arm. "Do you think Zavryd could reach him if he's up near Arlington?"

"Where the priest's lab is? Why would he have gone back there?"

"No good reason," I said grimly, then released her and ran to the sauna. I would ask Zavryd myself.

If Sarrlevi didn't answer him—and I had no trouble imagining him ignoring a telepathic call from a dragon—I would need a ride up there. I had to be sure Sarrlevi wasn't contemplating something horrible. Something that could *kill* him.

"He's usually naked in there," Val called in warning as I grabbed the handle to the sauna door.

"I don't care." Raising my voice, I did call, "Lord Zavryd?" before opening the door and looking in.

After catching an eyeful of her naked mate and empty bamboo skewers scattered all over the bench and floor, I jerked my gaze up.

"You presume to interrupt a dragon during his relaxation period?" Zavryd demanded.

"Sorry, sorry, but it's an emergency. Can you try to reach Sarrlevi? And if he doesn't answer, can you fly me up to the dark-elf laboratory? Please? I'll order you more of whatever that is —*was*." I waved at the skewers without looking down.

Zavryd was in human form—a dragon wouldn't fit in a sauna —but the rumble of discontent sounded like a growl. I leaned back out and shut the door. Maybe I should have waited and had Val ask him.

She stepped up beside me, a finger raised. "He'll do it. Just give him a minute." She eyed me. "I hope you weren't too disturbed by his nudity."

"No, it was fine. I mostly saw bamboo skewers. I'm used to a fastidious boyfriend."

"Oh, Zav is fastidious too. He incinerates his mess when he's done eating. Cleans everything that way. It's even better than UV light, he tells me." Val must have been speaking telepathically with Zavryd because she soon added, "He didn't get a response to his call, and he's willing to fly you back up there."

"Thanks." I fished out my phone. "What do I have to order him? That was take-out food, I gather." I doubted Val threaded the meat she made for her mate onto bamboo skewers.

"Kebabs and gyro meat—since he's discovered Mediterranean seasonings, he's eaten almost nothing but Greek food—but I'll handle it." Val pushed my phone down. "Like I said, Dimitri's rent money pays for the appetizers around here."

"How many skewers of meat does his five hundred bucks buy you?"

"Fewer than you'd like. Inflation is a bitch." Val stepped back, waving for me to join her, and the sauna door opened.

Still naked, Zavryd strode out. The skewers littering the sauna had disappeared except for the faintest lines of ash where they'd been.

He shifted into his dragon form, barely fitting in the backyard —no wonder he usually landed out front or on the roof—then levitated Val and me onto his back.

"Why do you think Sarrlevi would have gone back there?" Val asked as we flew north into the night.

I sighed. "To nobly sacrifice himself for the possibility of saving my life."

22

THE FORESTLANDS WERE DARK, AND THE EERIE ORANGE LIGHTNING wasn't visible until we flew within a half mile of the barren hill that held the underground laboratory and those pods. With the chilly night air gusting through my hair and Val's braid trying to thwack me in the face, I tightened my grip on Sorka. I wished I'd used the weapon to destroy everything in that chamber the last time we'd been here. Unleashing great magical power by breaking things might have killed me, but that would be better than more innocent people—and Sarrlevi—being lured into those pods to die.

My gut twisted as we flew low over the ground, and the whites of bones came into view. The scattered remains of the boulder pile still glowed orange every time the lightning struck. Zavryd's temper tantrum didn't appear to have affected much. Meaning the pods might still work—as well as they ever had.

"Can you sense Sarrlevi?" I might have dragged Zavryd and Val up here for no reason, for nothing more than a hunch—or unfounded anxiety—but I couldn't regret it. Not if there was a chance Sarrlevi was here.

I cannot, Zavryd replied, *but his camouflaging magic is powerful enough to keep even a dragon from detecting him.*

"Usually, that's a *good* thing. Set me down outside, please. I'll run in and check."

"We might have to do some digging," Val said. "When Zav lashed out at the boulders, they tumbled down to cover that trapdoor."

As I intended.

"Right," Val said. "That tantrum you threw after the lightning struck your tail was premeditated, your aim scientifically precise."

Yes.

As Zavryd rounded the hill to land on the side nearest the trapdoor, I stared. There weren't any boulders covering it. Not only that, but the door was open to the night, the orange light from the laboratory seeping out, as if in invitation.

With great certainty, I knew this wasn't how we left the place. I also knew the *goblins* hadn't been the ones to come up here and mess with things. Scavenging might be in their blood, but the shaman had made it clear their people wouldn't visit the laboratory.

"He's here," I blurted.

Or... had he already been? My gut heaved again at the thought that Sarrlevi might have used one of the pods already, that he might have been transformed into a dark elf. Or, if what appeared to happen often had happened, he might be dead.

After sliding off Zavryd's back, I intended to rush straight in, but Val jumped down and caught my arm.

"Someone else could be in there," she warned.

"I'll be careful." I twisted to pull my arm free, then ran toward the open trapdoor. *Varlesh, if you're down there, don't you dare step into one of those pods.*

When I didn't receive an answer, I started to doubt that he was there. He might ignore Zavryd, but he wouldn't ignore *me*, would he?

Though I wanted to jump down without pausing, in case he'd already stepped into a pod and the process had begun, I made myself kneel and peek through the open trapdoor. Val wasn't far behind me, but she stopped by a boulder and peered into the dark night on all sides of the hill.

An orange flash made me flinch, but it was only the lightning. The eerie-as-heck orange lightning that was only visible to someone close to the hill. It struck down near the trapdoor, and one of the rocks sizzled and glowed, the electric air making my arm hair rise.

I didn't see or sense anyone in the chamber below, but my ability to detect the magical had all but disappeared.

"Varlesh?" I risked calling.

Power wrapped around me, lifting me from the ground and over the doorway.

"Matti," Val blurted as the magic lowered me into the laboratory.

The trapdoor slammed shut behind me.

Before my feet touched down, I had my hammer raised, ready to swing. As I spun in a circle, I half-expected to find the dark-elf priest in the shadows, waiting for me. Or Sarrlevi turned *into* a dark elf.

"I haven't done anything yet," he spoke quietly, not from the shadows but from somewhere near the pods. He didn't sound pleased to see me. Because I'd interrupted him?

"*Yet*?" I demanded. "But you're planning to? Are you *nuts*?"

He stepped closer so I could see through his camouflaging magic and looked me up and down, probably seeing—sensing— my pathetically weak aura. On a desk, a journal lay open to a page of handwritten text. The priest's notes about his experiments? A small trinket that looked like a magnifying glass glowed. A device to allow Sarrlevi to read the language?

"I love you, Mataalii," he said.

"Damn it, Varlesh."

A thud sounded above me, Val's knees hitting the trapdoor as she bent, trying to see through the cracks between the bones. "Matti, is everything okay? Do you need us to break in?"

"Everything is *not* okay, but..." I eyed Sarrlevi as *he* eyed the pods.

Why did I have a feeling he was thinking about pushing me aside and leaping in?

"Don't come down here," I finished, not taking my gaze from him. "Please."

"Are you sure?" Val asked. "I have a dragon, and I'm not afraid to use him."

"Give us a few minutes."

As if he were a wild animal that might bolt, I walked slowly toward Sarrlevi with my palm toward him—the unmarked one. I also positioned myself to block the pods, though if he wanted to get past me, I wasn't deluded enough to believe I could stop him. *Zavryd* could stop him, and I would call out to him and Val if I needed to, but...

"This isn't the answer, Varlesh," I said softly. "You know that. That's why you're hesitating. That's why you haven't done it yet."

"I haven't done it, because I'm reading the priest's notes so I can determine what the success rate is." His tone was dry, but no humor brightened his eyes.

He kept looking at me like I was a terminal patient dying in front of his eyes. I supposed I was, though it didn't feel that hopeless to me, not yet. Maybe it was good that my debilitated senses meant I couldn't tell how bad my own aura looked.

"I don't want to die, only to have *you* die," he said.

"Yeah, let's not do the *Romeo and Juliet* thing, eh?"

"I am not familiar with that reference."

"Once I'm better, we'll rent one of the movies. Though I suppose you, being an educated and book-loving elf, might like to read the original play. If you come with me right now, we can check it out from the library." I forced a smile and waved toward the exit.

The mulish set to his jaw worried me.

"If what I'm reading is accurate," he said, "the transformation works about one third of the time. The priest believes the constitution and innate power of the individual determine whether he or she will survive and be altered. It's unclear whether the deaths are a design flaw of the device or if they are the intended result because he wants to weed out those who would become *weak* dark elves. If those are the determining factors of a successful transformation, I believe I would survive the process."

"To what end, Varlesh?"

He looked at me as if I were daft. "To *cure* you. To remove the curse. If my power no longer has an elven signature but a dark-elven signature, then I ought to be able to lift it. Even if I have to research and find out how those artifacts work first, it ought to be possible at that point."

"If you die, I would still be cursed. If you turn into a *dark elf*, you might not care about me anymore, and I'd still be cursed." I glanced at the trapdoor, wondering if I should call for Val's help— for *Zavryd's* help—but she wasn't kneeling on it anymore. I hoped something hadn't happened to distract them.

"I *would* care," Sarrlevi assured me, then touched something on the desk.

The image of the priest returned, floating between the two pods, his face hooded. It was the same recording that had played before, the dark elf pointing in invitation toward the devices.

"You don't know that," I said. "You don't know *what* you'd be like as a dark elf. How could you? It has to change you, otherwise what use would it be to the priest and their people? It has to be designed to make you into one of them in body *and* in spirit. Or kill you trying."

Whether it succeeded in making people full-on dark elves, I didn't know. Maybe not. Else why would the priest have been harassing Arwen for breeding purposes? But this wasn't a risk I would let Sarrlevi take.

"I do not believe it could make me lose my full sense of self, of who and what I am."

"Come on, Varlesh. My evil aunt's fingernail polish almost made you lose all that. Just think what a whole *pod* could do."

He snorted softly, a faint smile curving his lips, and I thought I was getting through to him. But then he lifted a finger, flicked the trapdoor open, and wrapped his levitation magic around me. Gently but inexorably, it lifted me toward the exit.

"What are you doing? You're *not* jumping into one of those things."

"With luck, I can cure you before I lose my sense of self."

"No. I forbid it, Varlesh." I hefted my hammer, intending to throw it at the closest pod—why were there *two* of them, damn it? —but his magic accelerated, lifting me above the trapdoor before I could throw. I lost sight of the pods—*and* him.

"Zavryd!" I yelled, praying he hadn't gone off to find more *meat.*

But he and Val were waiting on the hillside, watching me.

"Get him out of there," I ordered before remembering one needed to be circumspect with powerful dragons. "*Please* get him out of there. He's trying to do something *stupid.*" I shouted that last word, not caring if Sarrlevi heard me.

I was about to plead further, to promise great offerings of meat on platters, but Zavryd's powerful magic whooshed past me. Even nearly sense-dead, I felt it.

Sarrlevi cursed in Elven, then switched to telepathy. *Let go of me, you scaled behemoth. You weren't able to save Mataalii, but I will.*

She, being a wiser mongrel than you are elf, says that you would be foolish to attempt to do so in this manner, Zavryd replied. *I concur.*

A thud and crash came from the laboratory below. The power that had gripped me released.

More dragon magic whooshed past, but I sensed Sarrlevi using all his power to resist Zavryd's attempt to rip him from the laboratory. No elf was a match for the tremendous strength of a dragon, but he fought hard, roaring with indignation and fury. When I peered through the trapdoor, Sarrlevi was trying to reach the pod, to throw himself in.

With his power no longer restraining me, since all of his focus was on resisting Zavryd, I jumped back into the laboratory. I placed myself between Sarrlevi and the pod. But I needn't have worried. With another whoosh of power, Zavryd pulled Sarrlevi outside.

You overpowered bully! Sarrlevi cried. *I challenge you to a duel.*

"No dueling tonight," Val said. "We have to focus on finding a way to fix Matti and Dimitri."

I have *a way.*

"To get yourself killed or turned into a villain?" Val asked. "Yeah, no kidding. But you were villainous enough as an *elf* assassin. Nobody wants a dark-elf assassin running around the Cosmic Realms killing people."

As they argued, I turned to face the pods and the image of the priest floating between them.

Though I trusted Zavryd could keep Sarrlevi from escaping for the moment, what about tomorrow? If we didn't find the half-dragons on Veleshna Var and couldn't get anyone else to cure us, I would grow worse. Sarrlevi would want to come back. And I couldn't allow that, couldn't allow him to possibly die on my behalf. Or be turned into a dark-elf monster.

"Nobody else should be killed in these things either." I thought of the bones littering the hillside, the people who'd died torturous deaths after stepping into these pods. "Sorka, I need you to protect me in case there's a backlash."

Her barrier wrapped around me, but she said, *Perhaps it would be better to request that the dragon destroy these. From a distance.*

Probably. But he's distracted keeping Sarrlevi restrained. And you know how much I like bashing things.

Whether it's wise to do so or not.

Yup.

It is your dwarven blood.

I have no doubt.

Believing Sorka's barrier, made from the power my mother had infused in the weapon, would be a match for the dark-elven devices, I hefted my hammer. I was tempted to smash the dark elf, but my weapon wouldn't do anything to a recording. Too bad. I longed to flatten the priest's nose.

Instead, I struck what seemed to be the source of magic forming the leftmost pod. The backlash of power that I'd anticipated did not disappoint. It was like a grenade detonating, with white light flashing as energy exploded outward.

Sorka's barrier protected me from it, but the ground rocked under my feet, and furniture toppled or shattered. The journal flew off the desk, hitting the opposite wall. Earth crumbled from the ceiling, chunks of rocks pelting my barrier and the floor.

When the ground stilled and things stopped falling, the husk of the pod remained, but it had gone dark. Beside it, the second continued to glow and pulse in invitation.

"Yeah, right."

The image of the priest had disappeared. It occurred to me that if he found out what I was doing to his laboratory, he wouldn't be inclined to lift my curse.

"If it keeps Sarrlevi and others from being lured to their deaths here, so be it." Using all the energy I had left, I smashed Sorka into the remaining pod.

The second explosion equaled the first, but the results were even more catastrophic. The ceiling caved in, and boulders hammered down all around me.

My heart lurched before I remembered Sorka's barrier would protect me. I gripped her tight, my lifeline.

A boulder that struck the top of the barrier would have caved in my skull, but it bounced off and crashed into already-smashed furniture. More dirt and rocks fell, and I instinctively lifted my hands over my head, visions of being buried alive filling my mind.

Panic crept into me as I imagined being safe in the bubble but, having no way to escape from under tons of earth, suffocating. But Zavryd, Val, and Sarrlevi were outside. They would pull me out.

Even as I had the thought, the rockfall stopped, and power wrapped around my barrier. Zavryd's magic lifted me in my protective bubble, and dirt and rocks sloughed off around me. As I floated upward, I glimpsed the remains of the two pods, both dead now, mostly buried under the collapsed hilltop.

"Good."

When Zavryd settled me next to Val, dirt still falling from my barrier, she said, "You couldn't do the enchanter equivalent of pulling the plug, huh?"

For a moment, I stared dumbfounded as I wondered if I'd buried myself unnecessarily, but I shook my head as I reasoned it through. "No. First off, the only power I have access to right now is my hammer, and second, I didn't want anyone to be able to plug them back in and use them."

I looked toward Sarrlevi, worried about his reaction. He couldn't truly have wanted to turn into a dark elf—or be killed—but I had no doubt he had been willing to give up his life to save mine.

In that moment, it occurred to me how silly it had been for me to worry that he would leave me because I lost the ability to perform *bedroom* magic. As crazy as it sometimes seemed, he was into me. A lot.

Sarrlevi must have finished arguing with Zavryd because he stared stonily not at the dragon but at the now-dark hilltop, no hint of the orange glow remaining. Between my hammer work and the rockfall, I might have taken out everything magical in the laboratory.

"I do have a plan," I told him quietly, stepping over to stand at his side. I reached for him but paused, afraid he would push me away or reject the clasp.

Sarrlevi looked at my outstretched hand and at me, his face masked and hard to read, but he didn't step away. He wrapped his fingers around mine, his eyes growing bleak as he brushed his thumb over the dark-elven mark.

"I hope you're still willing to talk to me," I added, "because I need your help for it."

Sarrlevi cast a dark look toward Zavryd, who was waiting patiently for us. Because he resented the dragon pulling him out? Too bad.

Tell me what you need, Sarrlevi said.

For you to take me to a remote part of Veleshna Var. I assume when you visited the capital, you didn't find anything useful or a lead to a dark elf willing to lift my curse. I smiled without hope. He wouldn't have been here, trying to turn himself into one of their kind, if he had.

Unfortunately, I did not. My people believe the dark elves may be gone from the Cosmic Realms altogether since it's been so long since any have been seen anywhere but here on Earth, and if they are not even here anymore...

At least one *is.* I waved toward the rubble, though we didn't know the priest was around either. It might not have been that long since he'd propositioned Arwen, but, as I well knew, a lot could happen in a few months.

Sarrlevi shrugged, not appearing heartened, maybe because we hadn't seen proof that the priest had been here recently. For all we knew, the magic left behind in the laboratory, the pods and his recorded message, had been luring people in without his assistance for a long time.

While I was on Veleshna Var, Sarrlevi said, *I was permitted to attend an emergency meeting with King Eireth and his staff. It was called because a message arrived, the half-dragon Starblade delivering an ultimatum. It said that he and his colleagues wanted only to be left alone, but if Eireth didn't call off his searchers and convince the dragons and dwarves to likewise leave them be, there would be repercussions. Starblade said he knew all about the centuries-old magic of the elven capital and could destroy it if he wished.*

Hell, that's not going to make Eireth want to deal.

The king did not admit it, but I gathered from a few conversations with his advisors that previous messages had come in from Starblade, and that he had been more diplomatic in them, assuring the king that he didn't wish to harm the elven people. He'd been asking for asylum. However, because Eireth is being pressured by the dragons and King Ironhelm, he wasn't able to offer that asylum. Eireth also is doubtful about the sincerity of Starblade's claim that he and the other half-dragons only wish to be left in peace. He thinks Starblade wouldn't have freed more of his kind if he didn't intend to use them—and their power—to some end. Many believe the half-dragons wish to carve out a kingdom for themselves. Perhaps on a wild world but perhaps on a corner of Veleshna Var. It might not be a small *corner, and they might use it, the elves believe, to create more of their kind and become a threat to the order of the Cosmic Realms.*

I don't suppose they'd like to allow the dragons to mind-scour them to see if they're telling the truth about not wanting to do any of that stuff?

Even if the half-dragons volunteered for that, and they have not, they are powerful enough to affect a mind-scouring. Any information gathered would not be deemed reliable. Sarrlevi sighed into my mind. *I regret that I wasn't able to learn where on Veleshna Var they're staying or even with certainty that they are there. They can easily form portals to travel all over the Cosmic Realms.*

I have an idea about that. That's what prompted my plan. I shared what I'd learned from the dwarven librarian and my hypothesis about the location of the half-dragons.

Sarrlevi didn't reply, but a feeling of skepticism came through our link.

You don't think that preserve sounds like a likely spot? I asked.

It could be, but, even if they're there, if they don't wish us to find them, we will not.

I've been thinking about that, and I believe we need to take them a gift.

If you were able to enchant as usual, I would ask what gift you intend to make for them, but you cannot craft magical items right now, correct?

That's right. Even if I could, I doubt they would be that wowed by anything I could make.

Sarrlevi managed a smile. *Your soap dispenser was lovely.*

While I'm sure half-dragons have armpits as stinky as those of the next person, I assume they have the power to make whatever they need on their own.

I doubt any of them are enchanters. They were trained to be great warriors, to destroy, not build.

I waved away the argument. *Nonetheless, if they've been denied asylum, trinkets for the home aren't going to be on their wish lists.*

Sarrlevi frowned, as if he wanted to tell me not to dismiss what I could do—and I appreciated that—but I lifted a hand. *I have something else in mind. Maybe not as valuable as magical artifacts, but I would guess it'll be a suitable peace offering. Something they can't get on Veleshna Var probably, especially not out in the wilds, if that is where they are.*

What peace offering do you believe will appeal to beings greater than elves with many of the powers of dragons?

I pulled out my phone and waved to a restaurant I'd already pulled up. *I'm gambling on a hunch that their dragon blood gives them more than power.*

23

THE FROZEN TAIGA OF LOYLORA ON VELESHNA VAR WAS AS COLD AS
it had appeared in the photos, with an icy, insistent wind
sweeping across the snow. At least the sun was rising when
Sarrlevi, Dimitri, and I arrived, the rosy-pink sky reflecting off the
snow all around us as well as the stark mountains that jutted up
on the horizon. The surrounding flatlands were devoid of trees,
but some were visible on the distant slopes. A mile away, a herd of
animals browsed, pawing at whatever vegetation lay under the
snow.

"This isn't how I imagined the elven home world." Dimitri
hugged his arms to himself, shivering despite numerous sweat-
shirts and jackets he'd layered on over two pairs of sweatpants.
"Val always talks about forests with houses in the trees. She's never
mentioned *snow*."

"The capital city and most of the major population centers are
far to the north, across oceans and on more temperate continents."
Sarrlevi scanned the area intently, wrapping his camouflage
around all three of us, and I remembered that the cat-like predators here could also camouflage themselves. Or maybe it had been

that they shifted in and out of this dimension. Either way, they would be stealthy and dangerous.

"That's where Val and Zavryd went, right?" Dimitri sounded wistful. "Maybe I should have gone with them. You know, to help them with their diplomatic endeavors while you fight the bad guys."

Yes, not willing to remain on Earth while we undertook our journey, Val and Zavryd had taken a portal to the elven capital. What they hoped to accomplish there, I didn't know. I doubted they could talk Eireth into giving the half-dragons asylum, especially now that threats had been delivered.

"With luck, we won't be fighting anyone." I held up the pounds of foil-wrapped lamb and beef I'd ordered, a few pitas and toppings tucked in as well, since the restaurant owner had insisted that nobody would want *only* meat. He obviously hadn't been visited by many dragons.

"That may be more likely to lure the *daiyeesha* than the half-dragons," Sarrlevi said. "Remember that camouflaging magic hides people only from sight and magical senses. One can hear and *smell* those who've cloaked themselves."

"That's why I needed your help. To defend us against wild animals."

"Imagine my delight to have retired from my assassin career to become a game warden." Despite his snark, Sarrlevi wrapped an arm around my shoulders and nodded toward the mountains. "If you believe they are hiding in caves, we should walk in that direction. When we're closer, I'll sweep over the mountains with my senses and hope to detect something anomalous."

"Thank you." With the cold wind biting through my layers of clothing and scraping across my cheeks, I wanted to get moving. Hopefully, the mountains would provide shelter from the elements. "With luck, half-dragons have good noses and will naturally be drawn to us." I hefted the meat again.

Sarrlevi's skeptical look promised he believed the predators would more likely be drawn, but all he said was, "I hope your plan works. And that the half-dark elf has the knowledge and power to cure you."

"Yeah." I remembered Mom warning me that she had been raised by the same scientist-general who'd brought up the elven half-dragons. She might know more about *elven* magic than dark-elven, but I hoped she'd been curious and visited with and studied from her own kind at some point in her life. If not, there was always the priest, though I doubted *he* would be lured into doing a favor in exchange for gyro meat.

"How are we going to find anyone in all this wilderness?" Dimitri asked as we walked. "At least with a dragon, we could have flown around and looked for caves from the sky."

"The *dragons* are trying to obliterate the people we need," I said. "There's no way the half-dragons would come out of hiding if one was flying around."

"I'm still not sure why they would come out of hiding for us. I like gyro meat as much as the next guy, but do you really think it's going to draw magical super soldiers from hundreds of miles away?"

"We'll see. I *have* been wondering—" I considered Sarrlevi, "—do you think it would be better to walk without camouflage? So they see us wandering around out here?"

He looked at me, and I couldn't tell if that expression meant he believed it was a bad idea or if he was considering it.

"The predators could smell us anyway, right?" I added.

"Yes. Very well. I will drop it."

"Could you also call out telepathically to see if Starblade is in the area? As much as I'm sure we're a curiosity and they will, if they see us, wonder what we're doing, they may not immediately think greeting us is wise."

"What do you wish me to say?"

"That gyro meat is delicious, we have plenty for them, and I have a proposition."

Sarrlevi raised his eyebrows. "Do you?"

"I'm contemplating one."

"That means no, correct?"

"Not no. Just not *yet*." It had occurred to me that the half-dragons, if they wanted asylum, might consider Earth. Lots of magical beings took refuge there. Oh, nobody offered them asylum, but they found it a good place to hide out. And what if I offered to enchant a place for the half-dragons? To make it difficult to find, the same as the tiny homes I was going to make for the goblins?

Dimitri snorted. "Our fearless leader."

"Where's your faith?" I asked him. "My plan is going to work. You'll see. Also, after we're cured, I think you should agree to help me with the tiny homes for no pay. Or at least *reduced* pay."

"Hell, Matti. If this works, I'll build them *for* you." His eyes grew haunted as he looked at his palms, though gloves hid the glowing marks. "Zoltan says I'll die before the month is out if something isn't done."

I doubted we had a month, even with the dwarven blessing extending our lives, but I didn't want to make him feel worse. "I'll gladly accept as much assistance on the tiny homes as you're willing to provide after we survive this."

Sarrlevi held out a hand to stop us. "I've shouted telepathically as far as I can, letting Starblade know about your meal and proposition. We must hope that he's in the area and heard—and that no elven scientists or hunters are visiting the preserve and also heard. My noble status—*and* citizenship—could be revoked quickly if King Eireth finds out I am willing to deal with the half-dragons."

"You're not dealing with them; *I* am."

"Can you tell if anyone heard you?" Dimitri asked.

"*They* at least did." Sarrlevi pointed toward the shadow of the mountains where two great white cats were loping toward us. Off to their side, the herbivores we'd seen earlier scattered, fleeing fast and far across the taiga.

I winced, recognizing the *daiyeesha*. "Either that or they smelled the food."

"That is most likely."

"Do they consider the gyro meat to be the food?" Dimitri asked. "Or *us*?"

"Both, I suspect." Sarrlevi drew his swords and strode forward, putting some space between himself and Dimitri and me. To ensure they battled him and left us alone?

I handed the meat to Dimitri. Since he didn't have a weapon, he could stay back and hold stuff, but I wouldn't let Sarrlevi risk himself against two opponents when I was capable of helping.

Sarrlevi didn't appear surprised when I jogged up to crouch in a fighting stance beside him with my hammer in my hands.

"Side by side," he said, "instead of back to back. We don't want to let them past to your friend."

"Agreed."

"They're resistant to magical attacks, which is one of the reasons they're so formidable, but I'll employ some in an attempt to distract them."

"Okay." Already, the great cats had crossed more than half the distance to us, ignoring the herd of herbivores.

Even as we prepared to defend ourselves, the *daiyeesha* disappeared. Since I'd seen it in the recording, I wasn't surprised, but I promptly worried they would get past us and target Dimitri.

"*Hygorotho*," I said to Sorka, sensing Sarrlevi raising magical defenses of his own, then asked her, *Can you extend it to Dimitri?*

Only if he comes closer.

"Dimitri," I barked. "Come here. We need your moral support."

He'd fished out something that looked like a miniature crossbow and was juggling it with the meat I'd given him. He started to shake his head, as if I was nuts, but he must have sensed our barriers and gotten the gist.

"How close?" he asked as he hurried to stand behind me.

That is sufficient, Sorka said.

"You're in," I told him, not wanting him to get in the way of my hammer swings or Sarrlevi's swords. "But you won't be able to shoot through the barrier," I warned, doubting the little quarrel in his crossbow could do anything to thousand-pound cats anyway.

"If there's an opportunity, let me know. Zoltan gave me tranquilizer darts."

"To use against half-dragons?"

"To use against *anything*."

"Look out," Sarrlevi warned.

I whirled in time to see the first *daiyeesha* pop into view. The great spotted cat leaped for us, its saber-tooth fangs glinting in the morning light.

Sarrlevi sprang forward to meet it—and keep it from reaching Dimitri and me. He blasted it with power as he slashed with his blades. It roared, its innate magic deflecting his, and swiped toward his head with its long claws.

Movement to my side made me spin, losing track of Sarrlevi's fight as I jerked my hammer up to defend myself. Just in time. The second *daiyeesha* soared through the air toward me, paws the size of my head outstretched with claws like switchblades raking through my barrier and toward my face.

While dodging, I whipped Sorka up to protect myself. The *daiyeesha* twisted in the air and would have reached me if not for my hammer. Claws clinked off Sorka's haft, one sliding down toward my fingers. I let go with that hand, hooking the hammer toward the animal with the other, and managed to clip it in the flank as its momentum took it past me.

Not disturbed in the least, the great cat landed, snow flying as it spun without hesitation toward me. A tiny tranquilizer dart took it in the shoulder—Dimitri's contribution. The *daiyeesha* didn't so much as glance toward him as its powerful muscles bunched to spring at me again.

"*Hyrek!*" I cried and risked throwing my hammer at its face.

We were close enough that the cat didn't have time to dodge fully, but it *did* halfway evade my blow. Sorka struck its shoulder instead of its face.

Had I thrown a normal hammer, the cat would have shrugged off the blow, but lightning streaked from Sorka's dual heads. The air crackled as it branched around the creature. It screamed and jerked about, swatting at the lightning, as if it could knock the energy away.

The *daiyeesha* might have *some* resistance to magic, but it felt Sorka's attack.

With another command, I called the hammer back to my grip. When the lightning faded, the cat snarled and faced me again. But it didn't spring immediately. Instead, it crouched and considered me, its tail swishing.

A roar came from Sarrlevi's battle, followed by a squeal of pain, but I didn't dare take my eyes from the *daiyeesha* staring at me, poised to charge.

I raised Sorka again, tempted to throw her, but the cat appeared prepared this time. If the hammer missed, the animal would be on me, and I would be without a weapon.

Another roar sounded, this one in the distance and with such power that it made the hair on the back of my arms stand up. The cat looked in the direction of the noise, and I might have taken advantage and thrown the hammer, but another roar made me tighten my hands on the haft, not wanting to let go of my only means of defense.

That sounded like a dragon, one heading this way.

I risked glancing at Sarrlevi. The *daiyeesha* he'd been battling lay dead at his feet, its blood spattering the snow. My cat must have decided the threat of a dragon was too much to deal with. With a hiss of irritation, it whirled and streaked off across the taiga, as if a viper had bitten it in the ass.

Silence fell over the landscape.

"Do you sense anything coming?" I whispered to Sarrlevi.

Anything like a *dragon*?

"No," he replied softly, not taking his gaze from the direction of that roar.

He kept his weapons up. He might not sense anything, but he knew something was out there.

We heard the flap of wings, then snow crunching as whatever it was landed lightly.

With a whisper of power, Starblade appeared ten feet away from us, his aura abruptly noticeable as his camouflage dropped. His violet eyes flared as our gazes met.

He wasn't alone. A pointy-eared male with short silver hair, green eyes, and an equally powerful aura stood at his side. They both wore black clothing and magical armor and eyed us with similar cool stares.

I might have felt smug that I'd guessed right, that we'd found the half-dragons, but Starblade pointed a sword at us. The other half-dragon aimed a magical bow at Sarrlevi's chest.

Both weapons, I had little doubt, could pierce our barriers.

24

STARBLADE'S CLOTHING WAS TORN, HIS ARMOR DAMAGED, HIS HAIR mussed, and bags under his eyes suggested he'd been having a difficult time of late. His comrade looked equally rough.

"Hi." I lowered my hammer, activated my translation charm, and waved cheerfully with my free hand. "You may remember us. I'm Matti, and this is Sarrlevi and our friend Dimitri. We helped you escape from that stasis chamber on Dun Kroth." I knew Starblade hadn't forgotten, but his face was flinty and aloof, so a reminder might be wise.

I was about to repeat myself telepathically, not sure if they could understand, but Starblade said, "*Accidentally.*"

"Yeah, accidentally." I'd hoped he hadn't known that, but he'd read my mind before, so it wasn't surprising. "And you found a friend to also free. Isn't that nice?" I forced a smile, wishing the half-dark elf was the one with him. "I have a small but dire problem, and I'm hoping you—or specifically one of your buddies—can help. I brought an offering that might appeal to you, and I'm happy to pay or grant services in exchange for your assistance."

They gazed flatly at me, no sign of interest in their eyes.

"Dimitri," I whispered over my shoulder. "Show them the meat."

"Uh." He hefted the bundle without peeling back the aluminum foil.

I willed the scents to waft toward them, though it had to have cooled by now. After our walk across the taiga, it might be half frozen.

"We are not in a position to *assist* anyone." Bitterness twisted Starblade's mouth.

His silver-haired friend looked curiously at the meat.

"Nor do we want food that might be poisoned," Starblade added.

A wistful expression crossed the other half-dragon's face. Maybe he was willing to risk poison. He murmured something to Starblade that I barely caught. "*You've* had the opportunity to go out and enjoy the offerings of the various worlds. The rest of us have been dodging assassins and in hiding since we woke up."

"It's not poisoned," I said. "You can read my mind to check. I know you did that before, and my magical defenses are crap right now, so I'm sure you'll have even less trouble."

"I had no trouble before," Starblade said coolly. "Your human blood weakens your abilities."

"So I've been told."

Next to me, Sarrlevi's jaw tightened. He seemed willing to let me take charge of the negotiations—this was my plan, however lacking—but he tended to want to defend me. I appreciated it, as long as he didn't challenge Starblade to a duel.

"This *really* weakens my abilities." I pulled off my glove to show them my glowing palm.

Starblade regarded it without interest. The other guy was more intrigued by the gyro meat, but I'd wanted that, hadn't I? Maybe my guess that they shared a dragon's carnivorous tendencies had been right.

"You were cursed by a dark elf," Starblade stated.

"Yup. Any chance you can lift that curse? Or that your friend with dark-elven blood can?"

Starblade's eyes closed to slits. "Who told you about Gemlytha?"

"The dwarves and elves know about those you've released from prison."

"Not prison. From those torturous stasis chambers that keep you ensnared for all of eternity, plagued by never-ending nightmares."

I blinked. "You were aware in them? I thought they completely froze you and your bodies weren't active." Admittedly, I knew nothing about the science—the *magic*—that went into them, but Mom hadn't mentioned dreams.

They exchanged haunted expressions with each other.

"We are not assisting anyone at this time," Starblade said when he looked back to me. "My debt to you for accidentally freeing me has been repaid."

"That's true," I agreed. "That's why I'm willing to trade food, money, or service for further help. And it's your friend, Gemlytha, whose assistance I need. If you're not interested in what I can offer, maybe you could take me to see her."

"You have not listened to Mataalii's proposition," Sarrlevi told Starblade, speaking for the first time. "Is an interest in that not what prompted you to come out here?"

"We came out here to make sure you hadn't led dragons to us, dragons who would be a threat." Starblade eyed the sky. "You regularly spend time with one. You have his aura about you."

"Lord Zavryd'nokquetal is not looking for you," Sarrlevi said.

"If his queen wishes it, I'm sure he will be. He is here now, on this world." Starblade's eyes narrowed again. "Did you think I wouldn't know? You will tell him that you've located us, or he will see it in your minds, so we will have to leave this place."

"He will not see it in *my* mind," Sarrlevi said.

"Perhaps not, but those two will be easy for him to read." Starblade pointed at Dimitri and me.

The silver-haired elf knocked Starblade on the arm. "I'm hungry, and they brought something more appealing than roasted *hambda* meat. Let them speak with Gemlytha while we eat their food. She and Sleveryn will enjoy it too. We can relocate *afterward*."

Starblade squinted at him. "How is it that you once led troops in battle, Yendral? An enemy would have needed do no more than catapult a feast over your troops and into your maw to distract you during a crucial moment."

"Your wit has improved not at all during our centuries of imprisonment."

"It is my bitterness, not my wit, that marinated in those hellish chambers."

"Marinade." The half-dragon—Yendral—sighed wistfully.

I imagined I could hear his stomach rumbling.

Starblade looked over his shoulder. "Gemlytha comes. She can decide if she wishes to speak with that one."

I expected another elf to appear ten feet away as she dropped her camouflaging magic, but a dragon soared above the mountain peaks and flew toward us. A white dragon. I'd never seen one before and might have raised my hammer, but the half-dragons didn't react, merely nodding as if they expected it.

That's the half-dark elf. Sarrlevi stared, sounding awed as he whispered into my mind. *I hadn't realized they could shape-shift into dragons. I'd read that they were born as mammals, appearing fully elven, and there was some surprise from the scientists at the time. They believed the dragon blood would be dominant and the offspring would have many characteristics of their kind.*

Red eyes glowed from the dragon's albino head. That didn't make me feel hopeful about her assisting me. I'd seen enough movies and read enough books to know that helpful good guys *never* had red eyes. It was a rule.

The white dragon glided in to land behind Starblade and Yendral. Her talons sank lightly into the snow, and she gazed at us over their heads. She was about half the size of Zavryd, and when she shifted forms, she wasn't much taller than I, with skin as white as her dragon scales had been. Her elegant features included pointed elven ears.

I'd heard dark elves couldn't stand daylight, but Gemlytha didn't so much as squint at the morning sun glinting off the snow.

"You have visitors," Starblade said, glancing over his shoulder at her.

"Visitors? Or more spies?" Gemlytha didn't sneer, but she had a haughty tilt to her chin as she surveyed us, her gaze dismissive for Dimitri and me. It lingered longer on Sarrlevi. I couldn't tell if that was because she sensed he had more power and was the more dangerous of us or if she found him attractive, as so many women did.

It crossed my mind that Sarrlevi might be able to flirt with her, inasmuch as he did so, and, if she was interested, that might work better than bartering gyro meat. But after our recent encounter with Slehvyra, we'd agreed not to use his sex appeal as a bartering tactic with enemies. Or with anyone. I wouldn't suggest doing so now.

"The latter, likely," Starblade said.

"Uhm, no." I raised a finger. "We're not spies. We came to ask a favor, which is probably as annoying to you, I know, but as I said, I have a proposition that might interest you. And—" I took the meat from Dimitri, "—we've brought an offering. No strings attached." I walked it over to Yendral, since he'd been the most intrigued.

"Strings?" He accepted the foil-wrapped meat and rotated it as he studied it. Looking for strings?

"It's a saying. It means you can enjoy it and don't need to feel obligated to give us anything in return."

"Is it poisoned?" Gemlytha asked.

"Possibly," Starblade said, "though her thoughts don't suggest it. She intends it as a bribe, as if military commanders are moved to assist enemies by offerings of meals."

"We're not enemies," I said. "Or at least, I'd rather not be enemies. I have nothing against you guys."

"*You* are part dwarven." Gemlytha frowned at Dimitri and me, then gave no warmer an expression to Sarrlevi. "And the elves are proving that they will cast us to the *daiyeesha* rather than stand beside us these days. Once, they brought us into the Realms to assist them, but in this century, their relationship to us is no longer *convenient*." The way she said it made me believe she was quoting Eireth or some messenger he had sent. "Why have you come out here to speak with them, Starblade?"

Her voice was less dismissive and haughty with him, and I got the sense that he might have outranked her when they'd been soldiers. Maybe she still believed he did.

"Originally, to see if they represented a threat that needed to be dealt with." Starblade cocked his head as he regarded us. "They do not."

Sarrlevi lifted his chin, and I sensed that he wanted to object, but he kept his thoughts to himself.

"Now, I wonder if they can, like the others we caught, give us updated information on those who insist on declaring themselves our enemies." He sighed as he looked off toward the forests.

Was the elven capital in that direction? I didn't know.

"The elf will be more challenging to mind scour," Yendral said. "We should take them back to our base and eat first to improve our energy."

"*My* energy is sufficient for a mind scouring." Gemlytha turned her dismissive frown on him.

"Yendral seeks to test whether the food is poisoned for himself," Starblade said.

"I thought we might give a piece first to one of them. Just because *she* does not believe it's poisoned—" Yendral pointed at me, "—does not mean it isn't. I cannot read him easily." He nodded toward Sarrlevi.

"Poison isn't one of the extras on the takeout menu," I said. "It's pita bread, feta, tzatziki, and that's it. As to the mind scouring, you can." I winced at the thought of them forcibly reading Sarrlevi's mind, since I knew from experience that it was painful. "But we can also tell you what we know. As a gesture of good faith. The Assassins' Guild, pressured by the dragons, has named you all as their annual prestige hunt—as a former target, I *cannot* recommend that—so lots of random assassins are looking for you as we speak. And the dwarves may show up to help the elves hunt you. I think they just want you recaptured and put back into stasis."

All three of their faces twisted with such distaste—no, outright *rage*—that I wished I could retract that last sentence.

"The dragons, I'm told, want you killed," I said. "Because they consider you, uhm, an abomination."

Surprisingly, those two sentences didn't inspire a similarly visceral reaction.

"We know what they consider us," Starblade said softly, that same look in his eyes as he gazed off into the distance. Wistfulness? "We are aware of most of what you have shared," he said, bringing his attention back to me.

Most of? Did that mean I'd given them *some* new information? I hoped so. I wanted them to help me and also... I wasn't sure. Maybe Starblade had lied when he'd told King Eireth he and his colleagues wished only to be left alone and that they didn't plan to start a war, but maybe he meant it. My gut told me they weren't looking for trouble, but I didn't know how far to trust my instincts.

"They may know more," Gemlytha said. "We can't trust

anyone, certainly not any who are partially or all elven or dwarven."

"And who found us in our hideout," Yendral said.

"We told you why we had to look for you." I showed my palm to Gemlytha. "Can you lift a curse left by a dark-elven artifact? If not, we'll leave you alone."

"You will *not* leave," Yendral said. "Not until you've been mind-scoured and your motivations revealed to us."

He lifted a hand, fingers spread, then clenched them. A tremendous whoosh of power wrapped around all three of us, then snapped us together, my shoulders smashing against Dimitri and Sarrlevi. Once bundled, we were levitated into the air.

Again, tension tightened Sarrlevi's face, and I sensed him summoning his power to fight back.

We need their help, I reminded him, feeling we should go along with the half-dragons, at least for now.

Gemlytha didn't say whether she could lift the curse or not, Sarrlevi replied, but his shoulders slumped. *Their power is too much for me to break, regardless.*

Our three captors shifted forms, turning into dragons, each with scales similar in color to their hair. Their eyes remained the same, with only Gemlytha's red. From her dark-elven heritage, I supposed. Arwen was lucky she had her father's eyes.

"When you invited me along," Dimitri said, "I wasn't expecting to get this cozy with you two, though I'm more worried about the mind scouring. That hurts, doesn't it? A lot?"

"It hurts." I didn't point out that Sarrlevi was the one who the half-dragons would unleash their full mind-reading power on. I didn't want to remind him of that, not when he had only come along to help me. *Sarrlevi* didn't need anything from the half-dark elf—or any of them.

I need the same thing from them that you do, Sarrlevi spoke into my mind as a glowing golden rope of magic formed in the air, extending from Starblade's tail and lassoing around us. *For you to survive and the curse to be lifted.* He looked sadly at me. *I won't go so far as to say your pain is my pain, but when you hurt... I feel it.*

The downside of being fused, I suppose.

As the lasso wrapped tightly around us, Sarrlevi shifted so that he could grip my hand. *It is worth it.*

When the half-dragons sprang into the air, flying toward the mountains with us trailing behind by the magical rope, I squeezed his hand and closed my eyes, not sure whether this would lead to a solution to my problem or not. I'd told the half-dragons what I knew, but what if they found something in Sarrlevi's mind that made them mistrust us more? Or what if Gemlytha simply refused to help us?

That scathing look she'd given me when she'd pointed out my dwarven heritage promised these three hated my mother's people. After all the years—or decades?—they'd battled the dwarves, maybe that wasn't surprising, but it didn't bode well for her assisting me.

25

As the day grew brighter, the half-dragons flew us deep into the mountains, Starblade in the lead, Gemlytha a little behind and off to his left, and Yendral farther away and to the right. We floated after them, the ride smooth, but that didn't keep me from feeling queasy. Had I known we would end up flying, I would have brought medicine from Zavryd's anti-nausea collection.

After rounding a stark peak, the half-dragons flew straight toward a cliff, snow dusting ledges along the rock face. It looked like we would crash into it. There had to be an illusion over the entrance of a cave or something similar, but it was so realistic that I couldn't keep from tensing and squinting my eyes shut in anticipation of pain.

Dimitri swore and squirmed, jostling us. Bound by the glowing lasso, we were still packed like sardines.

"Be still," Sarrlevi said.

"You can detect an illusion?" I trusted nothing was dulling *his* senses.

"No, but it is there."

And it was. The half-dragons didn't slow down, simply soaring *through* the cliff, or so it appeared. We flew into a natural cavern, darkness replacing daylight. As we continued deeper, the walls narrowed so the dragons had to fly single-file. The darkness grew more absolute, and I soon couldn't see a thing.

"*Eravekt*," I whispered, though my arm was pinned at my side, Sorka flattened against my thigh.

Her silver-blue light flared, gleaming off rock walls, and more light appeared ahead. A level shelf thrust out of the back wall of the cavern, and a rounded man-made—or elf-made?—tunnel led deeper into the mountain.

The half-dragons alighted on the ledge, its size perfect for them, whereas it would have been a tight fit for larger full-blooded dragons. As Starblade's levitation magic brought us down on it, they shifted into their elven forms. Soft yellow light glowed from the tunnel walls, and a fourth half-dragon–half-elf waited for us.

"More spies?" he asked.

"We will see." Starblade nodded and with a flick of his finger continued to propel us along behind them.

The tunnel took us into a base with doorways leading to sleeping quarters, training halls, and storage rooms, a few with supplies inside, though they looked like shelf-stable items that had been there a long time rather than anything fresh. No wonder Yendral wanted some tasty gyro meat.

It had disappeared while he'd been flying, but he once again carried it, cradling it like a prize he didn't want to lose. Presumably, the half-dragons could create portals and travel to other worlds any time they wished, popping in to pick up exotic cheese like Sarrlevi did, but maybe they felt they had to keep a low profile. Mom had said something about there being a way to track these guys. I also remembered that Zondia, and presumably other dragons as well, could track people through portals if they'd been made recently enough.

The tunnel wound upward in circles, with a few other tunnels branching off, until we came to what I wanted to call a control center. Magical artifacts glowed from consoles and on walls, and a rectangular window looked out over the valley we'd flown through. There were a few tables and chairs, and someone moved beyond a gated doorway down a short hall.

My senses were so dull now that I couldn't tell who or what was back there, and my queasiness lingered, even though we weren't flying anymore.

An elf and a dwarf, Sarrlevi told me. *The captured spies they spoke of, I would guess.*

"I will have your thoughts," Starblade told Sarrlevi, his face and his tone detached and professional.

"I have little choice." Sarrlevi could barely shrug as long as we were pinned together.

Starblade flicked a finger, and his rope dissolved. The magic binding our arms to our sides and legs together loosened, but I still couldn't lift Sorka.

"I will have *your* thoughts," Gemlytha told me.

"Goodie," I said.

Dimitri looked warily at Yendral, but he ambled over to one of the tables, sat, plopped his boots on it, and started unwrapping the meat. The other half-dragon male joined him.

"Guess I'm okay with nobody wanting my thoughts," Dimitri muttered.

"Yours were simple to read," Gemlytha told him. "Humans have no power to resist mind magic, and your dwarven heritage is minuscule."

"Yup." Dimitri sounded more relieved than offended.

As Gemlytha approached me, fingers stretching toward my temple, I wished *my* heritage made her believe she'd already gotten everything. She probably already had. Thanks to the curse, I didn't have the mental strength to swat away a stray thought much less resist mind reading.

Next to me, Sarrlevi clenched his jaw as Starblade approached him, but he didn't summon his magic or try outwardly to resist.

"I only seek to learn if you endanger my people," Starblade said.

"I understand," Sarrlevi said, though he didn't look happy about the situation.

I'm sorry, I thought silently to him.

We remained close enough for him to squeeze my hand.

Do not be, Sarrlevi replied. *I would not be anywhere else except with you.*

You're being so supportive and romantic and not even teasing me. Is it because you're sure this won't work, and I'll die?

No.

Is it because I might die?

He hesitated.

I thought so.

Would you feel more optimistic if I did tease you?

Probably.

Then, if your proposition for these people is to plumb their base, I have not witnessed pipes that would suggest they need such a service.

I didn't bring my tools.

Short-sighted.

Most of them blew up when Xilneth blasted Hart's mansion into the lake. I haven't replaced all my wrenches yet.

Had I realized how dire your situation, I would have given you funds to purchase a new set.

It's hard to buy wrenches with gold on Earth.

It's such a benighted world.

I know.

Though she'd paused, as if to share an exchange with Starblade, I sensed Gemlytha's presence in my mind. I stopped thinking words to Sarrlevi, not wanting her to mock us for our banter or being close.

When she eyed our clasped hands, I braced myself for her to say something snarky, but she only looked at Starblade.

He, focused on Sarrlevi, didn't return her look. A hint of sadness crossed her face—even red eyes could convey that, I found—before it disappeared and she turned resolutely toward me.

Did she have feelings for him? More than the feelings of a subordinate toward a commander? If so, I didn't get the feeling that he returned them.

Her elegant white eyebrows drew together as she focused on my face, and I suspected she was tracking my thoughts. And didn't appreciate my insight.

She didn't address it, however, instead asking, *How did you find this place?*

Before I could form words to answer, she raked through my mind, stirring pain as she dug for the truth. I thought of the dark-elven artifact and how I'd been marked—*cursed*—and hoped she would see that it had led me down this road, that I wouldn't have bothered them if I hadn't so badly needed a cure. I also thought of the dark-elf priest, wondering if he'd been here, if she'd seen him.

Gemlytha sneered into my mind, though I thought the feeling was directed toward the priest rather than me. *He came here looking for me, yes. Wanting to* breed *with me, or at least take my blood so that he could use it to magically and scientifically create mostly dark-elven offspring. Apparently, he didn't mind that any of my children would have some dragon blood. He liked that. It would make any dark elves that were born more powerful than usual.*

I wondered how the priest had thought he would birth and raise babies without the help of a mother. Kidnapping human women and inserting fertilized eggs into their wombs to carry to birth? Was that possible? I shuddered at the thought and wished we'd been able to get rid of him, not only his base.

I was not impressed by his offer, Gemlytha said, then scraped through my mind again.

Though I knew by now that this was part of the process of a mind-scouring and she didn't necessarily want to hurt me, I couldn't help but gasp in pain. Whether intended by the perpetrator or not, this shit always hurt.

I am even less impressed now that I see he first propositioned a mongrel human, Gemlytha said, *but that is not important.*

What's important to me—

Yes, I know. You wish your curse lifted. I do have the power to do that—though he who created us was elven, he ensured that dark-elf tutors came to teach me how to use the magic of my heritage—but why should I help a half-dwarf? The dwarves are the reason we were imprisoned for centuries and why so many of our kind were put to death.

I had nothing to do with that. That was a long time ago.

Not to me. You will tell me how you found us and who else knows you're here.

Alarm surged through me. It hadn't occurred to me that they would try to figure that out.

Zavryd and Val knew. Zoltan. And of course—

A scythe of pain carved through my mind, and I couldn't keep from gasping and remembering being in the library on Dun Kroth. My mom's face floated through my mind.

Gemlytha jerked her fingers back from my temple and hissed.

Starblade also stepped back from Sarrlevi, letting his hand drop. He appeared less concerned about what he'd seen, but he frowned at Gemlytha. "What is it?"

"Her mother is the dwarven princess, Rodarska," Gemlytha said. "They were together when she decided she would search for us in this place."

"So Ironhelm and the dwarves know where we are," Starblade said.

"I'm sure they told the elves too. And the *dragons*." Gemlytha gave me a scathing look.

Sarrlevi stepped closer to me, though their magic hadn't fully released us. I still couldn't lift my arm—my hammer.

"She might not have told the dwarven king." I wished I could have said that with more conviction.

"Your *grandfather*," Gemlytha said.

"Yes, but that's not my fault. Did you see my proposition?" I smiled hopefully. "Are you interested?"

Sarrlevi arched his eyebrows. I hadn't explained my idea to him, in part because I'd so recently thought of it, and in part because it might be dumb and of little interest to them.

"We do not need a *mongrel* to assist us with hiding," Gemlytha said. "A mongrel who would tell the dwarven princess everything she knows."

That was possibly true, especially since I would need Mom's help for the enchanting... But would Mom object if the half-dragons were hidden away and not killed or captured? They had battled the dwarves before her time. How much of a grudge could she hold? Mom wasn't even a grudge-holding kind of person.

"Hiding?" Starblade asked.

Before Gemlytha could explain, Yendral and the other half-dragon rose to their feet.

"Dragons are coming," Yendral said. "Dragons and more."

He and the other half-dragon had been at the table, sampling the food—I had no idea if they'd given it to one of the spies to test before tasting it—but, now, they charged to the window. Or what I'd thought was a window. When Yendral touched it, it shimmered, something like a TV display replacing the valley view.

It showed six dragons soaring high over an ocean, trailed by two dwarven dirigibles like I'd flown in before. Numerous elven warriors on *evinya* flanked the dirigibles. It was a large combined fleet, and I had little doubt it was heading this way.

"She led them to us." Gemlytha scowled at me once more.

Starblade's face, so often more wistful than warlike, grew

masked and determined now. He looked every bit the veteran military commander when he addressed his people. "Gemlytha, Sleveryn, man the defensive stations. Yendral, lock our visitors up with the others."

Power tightened around Sarrlevi, Dimitri, and me again, lifting us into the air. Yendral strode ahead, using his magic to open the gate down the short hallway—a cell door. If that fleet was about to attack this base and we were locked inside, we might be destroyed right along with the mountain. It wasn't as if dragon magic was *subtle*.

I looked in anguish at Dimitri and Sarrlevi, realizing I might have doomed us all.

26

"CAN'T YOU GUYS PORTAL YOURSELVES OUT OF HERE?" I ASKED AS Yendral opened the cell door and used his magic to nudge Sarrlevi, Dimitri, and me inside.

"Not without leaving a trail," he said with distaste, then pushed open his shirt, revealing a dragon tattoo on his left pectoral. It glowed a faint silver.

"Is that... an enchantment?" I asked.

"The elven council of our era ensured we wouldn't disappear on them. They created us and trained us, but they trusted us only so far. None have *ever* trusted us fully."

With a wrenching of power, Yendral tore Sorka from my grip and one of Sarrlevi's swords from his. After thrusting us inside, he clanged the door shut. Another surge of power activated the lock and made the bars sizzle with energy. With our weapons in his hand, he stalked back into the command room to join Starblade. The other two half-dragons had already taken off to man the defenses. Wherever they were.

"Why'd he leave you one of yours?" I waved at Sarrlevi's remaining sword—he had a number of daggers as well—before realizing the answer to my own question. Yendral had taken the sentient one, the more powerful of the two. Maybe he'd believed Sorka and Sarrlevi's sword would be capable of breaking the magical bars that restrained us.

Sarrlevi nodded, no doubt following my thoughts.

Dimitri bent and gripped his knees. "Next time you want to help me by taking me on a quest, I'd just as soon wait to join you until after you've defeated all the bad guys and have the solution."

"I'll keep that in mind." I turned around to survey our prison.

A dwarf and an elf looked curiously at us from opposite corners of the cell. With wild hair and bloodshot eyes, they looked tired and frazzled but not injured.

Other than the two cell occupants, a trough with water flowing through it was the only thing in the square prison. It was probably for drinking and waste. I almost joked to Sarrlevi that there *was* plumbing in this place, but I had no tools and no magic. There was nothing I could do.

The prisoners weren't armed and had unremarkable faces and clothing. Maybe they were spies, but I doubted either of them could help us escape, not unless they were so valuable to their people that the fleet commanders would call off the attack so their lives wouldn't be risked. That might work with the elves and dwarves, but I doubted the dragons cared if a couple of *lesser species*, as they so often called us, were killed in their quest to destroy the half-dragons.

It is your *presence that is more likely to sway the dwarves.* Sarrlevi gripped the bars to test them, but they buzzed against his skin. It must have been painful because he let go quickly and stepped back.

Probably only if Mom is with them. Maybe my grandfather. I thought about General Grantik, a more likely person to be commanding a dwarven contingent, but I doubted he would halt an attack for my sake. *Let me know if you sense either of them when they get close, please.*

By the time they are close enough for me to sense, the attack will be underway.

Comforting. Any chance you can make a portal to get us out of here? I suspected he would have already offered if he could. Lately, we'd been wandering into a lot of underground bases with insulating magic or barriers that prevented the formation of portals.

Not since we flew into the cave.

I was afraid of that.

If this base is destroyed sufficiently, its defensive magic may falter enough to allow me to create a portal.

Would that be before or after the entire mountain has caved in on us?

Ideally before.

What's that tattoo of his—of all of theirs?—do exactly? I asked. *Do you know?*

Not for certain, but it appears to be a permanent elven enchantment. I've seen such magical tattoos before. On prisoners to keep them from escaping.

They can make portals though. We've seen Starblade do it.

Yes. It's likely they weren't ever treated as prisoners, not by the elves, at least not until the end, but if it's as that one said, any portals they make might be trackable. Or they specifically might be trackable. The enchantments might act as tags that can lead those familiar with their magic to them. I am certain there is a range, or they would have been found earlier.

They look kind of rough. Like they have *been found a few times, and had to fight their way out.*

Perhaps. Many seek them. That must be why they chose this distant continent as their hiding place. Sarrlevi looked upward, though the stone ceiling was unremarkable. *I can sense the dragons now. They'll be here soon.*

"It's not too late," Yendral's voice floated to us from the command room. "We can get out before they reach us, portal to another world and make a few hops to lose them. Didn't you say some of those wild worlds you visited have such weak magic that it would make it harder for the trackers to find us?"

"Harder but not impossible. They would have a range of perhaps fifty miles instead of one hundred." Starblade paused, then continued so softly it was hard to catch. "You all told me you didn't want to spend the rest of your lives running, that you'd rather make a stand and die fighting than live like that. Is that not why we worked on rebuilding the defenses of this place? This place that has been abandoned for centuries and is little like what we remember from our youth."

"I just know I don't want to go back into those stasis chambers. I'd rather die than spend another eight centuries having nightmares in that perpetual limbo from which there is no escape."

"I know," Starblade said. "We will stay and hope we are enough to defend this place, to turn them away. The dragons will be difficult to kill unless they change forms to come into our tunnels. If they do so, we will confront them. But if not, we will focus on the elves."

"On our own people?"

"If we battle them ferociously enough, perhaps they will decide it is better to cede this place to us and leave us be. No elves live or train in the area now. It is a preserve for them."

"I do not think that *killing* elves will make Eireth more likely to give in to our demands."

"Then what do you suggest?" Starblade asked, short for the first time.

"Attack the dwarves, drive them and the dragons out, and then negotiate with the elves. I do not believe they want us dead. Perhaps they would even like knowing we are here and that we would come to their aid if their alliances faltered in the future."

"Would we?" Starblade asked softly. "After they abandoned us, allowing us to be locked up as if we were *criminals* and not the model soldiers they'd made us? No elves were locked up in the stasis chambers with us. Did you see?"

"I know. I saw."

"What does Gemlytha think?" Starblade asked.

"She'll do whatever you wish."

"Because I'm her commander, and that is what soldiers are *supposed* to do, Yendral of the many questions."

"Because she'd rather be on a private beach with you, fondling your ears. Since I have no similar inclinations toward your ears, I speak my mind."

"*Your* inclinations are toward food."

Yendral laughed shortly. "That's not untrue."

They moved farther from our prison, their words growing too soft to understand.

A wave of weariness swept over me, that nausea never far away now, and I flopped down on my back on the floor. My palm itched madly, a reminder that even if we got out of this, I hadn't found anyone to lift the curse. Gemlytha had gone to another part of the base, and I didn't know where. Even if we could escape, she wouldn't cure me. She *could*, but she wouldn't. Because I was half-dwarf. Or just because she didn't give a shit.

I rubbed my gritty eyes. Logically, I knew there was no reason for her to care and couldn't be surprised; still, it was hard not to feel bitter and frustrated.

Water gurgled behind me as it flowed through the trough, but I couldn't sense the pipes or do anything that could free us. Sarrlevi poked at the gate with his other sword, applying magic to try to break the bars, but even if he found a way out, two of the four half-dragons remained twenty feet away. They would halt our escape before it began.

A distant *thwump* sounded, reverberating through the stone

floor. The first attack? Or a weapon firing from within the mountain?

Sarrlevi left the gate and knelt beside me. *You are ill?*

I've been better. I clasped his hand, wishing I hadn't brought him or Dimitri with me.

He smiled sadly. *Who would have carried the meat for you?*

The elf prisoner made a disgusted noise, and muttered, "They know I am here, yet will press the attack instead of sending in a rescue party. Never should I have volunteered for this mission."

The dwarf grunted in agreement. Maybe they were both in telepathic contact with their people.

I do not sense Princess Rodarska or King Ironhelm on either of the dirigibles, Sarrlevi told me.

So neither of the people who might have hit pause until I could be retrieved were here.

I believe I sense General Grantik. Do you wish me to reach out to him?

I sighed. Did I?

As I'd been thinking earlier, I doubted he would stop the attack to save me. He wouldn't go out of his way to kill me, but I couldn't imagine him sending in a party of warriors to rescue me before they unleashed everything they had on the half-dragons.

Sarrlevi rested his hand on the cold floor beside me. *You cannot sense the pipes under the ground? Or the stone itself? I sense magic in the walls, ceiling, and gate, and also the floor, but there is, I believe a gap, perhaps where the pipes are. The water must flow in here from somewhere, so maybe that spot isn't as reinforced.*

I'm sorry, Varlesh. I can barely sense you holding my hand right now. I've lost my power, my hammer, everything.

Not your knowledge.

If my knowledge is what has to save us, we're in trouble. More trouble.

You know a great deal—about plumbing. Sarrlevi shifted my grip so that my hand rested atop his, the one he had flattened to the ground. *Maybe we can use my power and senses, and your dwarven affinity for the earth and stones and pipes.*

I snorted softly. *Can that work?*

Let us see. I am lowering my mental defenses. Step into my mind as you did the other night.

I had less power now than I'd had the other night.

I will assist you. He nodded encouragement.

Three great *thwumps* reverberated through the rock. Then an explosion sounded, muffled and distant but ominous. Were the dirigibles bombing the mountain?

The attack has begun. Sarrlevi showed me not the fleet that had to be flying above our mountain but a sensation of metal embedded in the floor.

With my meager remaining power, I willed my mind and magic to join with his—to *fuse* with his—and tried to surf on his power to the source of the water for the trough. An underground well? A hot spring that didn't freeze like the taiga outside?

It wouldn't, I supposed, since underground temperatures remained relatively stable and well above freezing.

But what could I do even if we found the source? Create a great surge of water that would come up, burst the pipes, and flood this whole level? How would *that* help?

A distraction? Sarrlevi suggested. *Our weapons are in the control room with those two. If they ran off and left them, I could levitate my sword, and Sorka would come to your call.*

Through the gate? Of course, if I ordered Sorka to bash herself against the bars, she would. But would that be enough magic to break through without me also swinging her with all my might?

"The defenses are holding," Yendral said, their voices audible again.

"For now," Starblade said. "Their defenses are holding as well. The dragons are protecting the elves and dwarves."

"I know."

"I'm goading the dragons," Starblade said.

"Something that's *always* wise."

"We want them to shift into a lesser form and come into the tunnels so we can face them that way. Our power will be closer to equal."

"They still outnumber us."

"That's why I said *closer*."

More explosions sounded, creating tremors we could feel through the floor. This reminded me of the organization's underground lair on the Olympic Peninsula. It had been reinforced to hold up against attacks too—against a war, if necessary.

Mataalii? Sarrlevi prompted.

Sorry, I'm thinking. I'm not sure what to do. Stopping up the toilet is only going to get us wet, not bother them.

As Sarrlevi lent me his magic and his senses, I delved deeper into the mountain, below us, to the sides, and above. With his help, I detected liquid in pores in the rock, something more viscous than water. The mountain all around us was like that, and it took me a long minute to puzzle out what we were sensing.

"Hell," I muttered, wincing when another muffled explosion sounded.

Mataalii? Sarrlevi asked again.

Even though we sensed the same thing, an elf wouldn't have much experience with oil. We'd seen electricity in the dwarven capital, so they probably burned oil or coal or some other natural resource, but every modern amenity that I'd seen on Veleshna Var was powered by magic.

We could be screwed if one of those explosions gets through, I told him. *For more reasons than the roof caving in on us. I think this base is built into a mountain with deposits of crude oil. Probably natural gas too. That stuff is all flammable. Be ready to put a barrier around us, please.*

Would a barrier be enough if the whole mountain blew? Was that possible? I didn't know. I shared a memory with him of a news report I'd once seen on a crater in Turkmenistan where natural gas had been burning out of control for decades.

I see, Sarrlevi said. *I am prepared.*

"The dragons are coming in," came Yendral's excited voice.

"I am aware." Starblade sounded distracted.

Though it had seemed like they were only hanging out and chatting in the other room, they were probably using their magic to defend against attacks while their colleagues sent attacks of their own into the skies.

Yes, Sarrlevi agreed with my thoughts. *A great battle is going on above the mountain. I can sense it all. Between the power of the dragons and that of the half-dragons, it is quite alarming. The elves and dwarves are trying not to be caught in the crossfire more than they are assisting.*

It... occurs to me that I could ask you to contact General Grantik and have him direct the dwarves to try to intentionally ignite the oil and gas. I didn't *know* there was gas, since we hadn't sensed it, not the way we could the oil, but I was fairly certain the two were often found together. Didn't drillers often have to flare natural gas away so they could extract the oil? *A big enough chain reaction might take out the half-dragons. And the entire mountain.*

Given our current location inside the mountain, that plan seems flawed.

Yeah.

If I grasp correctly the explosive potential, my barrier may not be enough to protect us.

I know.

The barriers of the half-dragons wouldn't be enough to save them *either,* Sarrlevi mused, though he didn't sound enthralled by my idea.

Maybe not, but I'm not that sure I want to see the half-dragons destroyed.

Certainly not before the female lifts your curse.

I snorted. I doubted that would happen. The best we could hope for was to escape and return home. If we were free, maybe there would still be a chance to locate the dark-elf priest and convince him to fix me.

Maybe not at all, I added. *They don't seem that bad, honestly.*

They would seem better *if the female cured you.*

Gemlytha. We ought to use the names of people we want help from.

Gemlytha, Sarrlevi agreed.

"Four of the dragons are veering for our tunnels," Yendral said.

"I sense them," Starblade said.

"They'll have to change forms to fit inside. This is our chance."

"Yes. I'm going to face them."

"*We* will face them. You won't have a chance four-on-one."

"Four-on-two against dragons isn't much of a chance either."

"Yes, but better to die fighting. As we decided."

"Agreed," Starblade said. "Tell Sleveryn to join us. Gemlytha can handle the defenses by herself."

They're leaving, Sarrlevi said. *Both of them. The command room is empty.*

Any chance they didn't *take our weapons with them?*

Sarrlevi rose to his feet. *They did not.*

"*Vishgronik,*" I called to Sorka, pushing myself up as well.

Dizziness swept over me, and heat flared in my palm. Sarrlevi caught and steadied me.

"Thanks," I whispered as Sorka came into view, floating in the air along with Sarrlevi's sword. They stopped, hovering on the other side of the gate.

I bit my lip. We still had a problem.

When more explosives blew in the distance, the ground shuddering, I couldn't help but wince in fear. Now that I had a better idea of the extent of our *problem,* I *really* wanted to get out of here.

Any chance you can bust through that gate on your own, Sorka?

There is a limit to what I can do without my wielder, she admitted.

You smashed your way into Hart's library and lightning-struck the crap out of his ceiling fixtures nicely.

I did, yes, but these bars are more of an impediment than the simple device that was designed only to alert when magical weapons went through it.

Try anyway, please. We may not have much time.

I glanced at Sarrlevi, who could sense the true extent of the battle. He kept eyeing the ceiling warily. The elf and dwarf, their senses no doubt in working order, also paced and eyed it.

"Are your hammer and sword going to break us out?" Dimitri asked hopefully. Like me, he was more focused on the gate and the possibility of escape.

"*Yes,*" I said firmly.

Sarrlevi's eyebrow twitched—I wondered if he'd had a similar conversation with his sword—but he didn't object. Outside the gate, his sword rotated until its tip pointed at the bars. At the bars and *us*.

"Stand to the side." He waved for everyone to get out of the line of fire.

Remembering how his sword could blast an orange beam of energy from its tip, I hurried to flatten my back to the wall.

The others did the same, and the beam burst forth, striking one of the bars. Some of the power slipped through, splitting around the bar, and streaming into our cell. It pounded into the back wall and blew out chunks.

Sorka reared back, as if she were in an invisible person's hands, and hammered against the same bar the sword was assailing. I wondered if they'd had a conversation with each other about their plan of attack.

The bar is weakening, Sarrlevi said, though his gaze remained upward, his senses toward the battle.

Booms came from the tunnels below the command room, then

distant clangs accompanied by what sounded like gunfire. But neither dwarves nor elves used firearms, did they?

The great crash of something that might have been a tunnel collapsing followed. The tunnel we'd come in through? I hoped not.

As the weapons continued working on our jailbreak, a presence entered my mind, and a cold chill went through me.

Starblade.

Damn it, wasn't he busy fighting dragons?

I looked away from sword and hammer, as if that would keep Starblade from seeing through my eyes and realizing we were escaping. But as the cool fingers of his mind scour swept through my brain, I knew it wouldn't.

27

You did not share your proposition with me, was not what I expected Starblade to say into my mind.

Uh. Again, I avoided looking at Sorka banging at the bars while Sarrlevi's sword cut into them. Between the noise and sparks of magical energy flying in all directions, that was difficult. The sentient weapons had gotten through one bar and were working on a second. *I think your friend plucked it out of my mind. Gemlytha.*

She said you believed we could hide on Earth. A long pause followed, more clangs and gunfire coming from the tunnel below. Was Starblade in the middle of a *battle* as he chatted me up? A battle with a *dragon? I've been to your world, and the lack of substantial magic in the earth would not be sufficient to keep dragons from tracking us.*

I'm enchanting a tiny home village for some goblins in a forest more than fifty miles from Seattle—where the dragon Zavryd lives. My mom is going to help. It'll be a great enchantment. I'm sure you could also hide there.

With goblins. How someone in the middle of a battle could

manage to make those two words so dry and dismissive, I didn't know, but Starblade did.

It'll be perfect, I assured him as Sorka busted through the second bar, beating Sarrlevi's sword into the cell. *We enchanters are great at hiding people.*

Okay, I hadn't practiced that yet, but Mom had made it sound easy.

Sorka floated into my grip, emanating smugness that I felt even with my diminished senses. The sword followed, levitating into Sarrlevi's hand.

The elf and dwarf charged out of the cell and didn't look back.

Nobody will think to look for powerful half-dragons among goblins, right? I kept talking to Starblade, hoping the conversation would keep him from noticing we were escaping. Maybe he would even be interested and want to take me up on the offer. *And there's plenty of room in that forest. It's not like you'd have to shack up with the goblins. But I do need to survive to build the sanctuary and enchant the village. Any chance you can lift this curse? Or direct me to a dark elf who can?*

"We're busting out of here, right?" Dimitri took a step toward the gate but frowned at me.

I hadn't moved yet. Sarrlevi also frowned at me, but he must have figured out what was going on. He wrapped his mental defenses around me, trying to push Starblade from my mind.

For a moment, it worked, his presence fading. Again, I had the sense that Starblade was in the middle of a battle—the clangs and gunfire-like sounds that kept sounding below helped convey that.

But, again, he brought his attention back to me. With a magical shove, he knocked aside Sarrlevi's protection. This time, suspicion laced Starblade's mental touch. Maybe Sarrlevi pushing him out of my mind hadn't been a good idea because Starblade raked through my thoughts, as if certain I was hiding something.

It wasn't as painful as Gemlytha's touch had been, but I bent forward and leaned my elbows on my thighs for support. I sensed him getting everything about my surroundings, including the now-open gate and Sorka back in my hands. He also scraped through my earlier thoughts, catching information about the oil and gas reservoir I believed existed all around his base.

Interesting.

More like *concerning.*

You did not tell the dwarves, Starblade said.

I didn't want them to get the bright idea to blow up the mountain with us in it.

No, he thought softly. *But you could have used that knowledge to help them destroy us.*

That's not my goal here.

I see that now. Perhaps we should have listened with more consideration to your words, but we have learned to mistrust all but our own kind. The few that there are left.

You don't know us well. It's understandable. Come to Earth, and we'll do coffee. I know this great place that serves an extremely *caffeinated blend.*

More explosions boomed. If Starblade said anything else, I didn't catch it. Maybe I should have tried to tempt him with something more valuable than the Goblin Fuel blend from the Coffee Dragon.

"Mataalii." Sarrlevi reached for me, as if he might sling me over his shoulder.

"He's gone. I'm coming." I hurried out of the cell after Sarrlevi and Dimitri, and we ran into the control room.

Four smaller displays now filled the window-like screen, as if we were seeing the feeds from security cameras. One continued to show the fleet in the air, dirigibles, elves riding birds, and two dragons soaring around the peak and lobbing magical explosives.

One screen showed the mouth of the cave where we'd flown in. Two others focused on tunnels, but one was filled with rubble and nothing appeared to be moving inside, though I glimpsed the legs of a body sticking out from under a rock pile. A half-dragon? A shape-shifted dragon? I couldn't tell, but it was hard to believe a rockfall could have taken out a full-blooded dragon. Unless he or she had already been badly injured when it came down.

In the fourth display, Starblade and Yendral battled two elves in the tunnel that we'd passed through before. No, the eyes glowed on those *elves*; they were shape-shifted dragons.

The two pairs of fighters not only engaged with swords but also used magic, hurling everything from wind to fire to vines that grew into writhing snakes as they flew through the air. Magic *and* blades moved with awe-inspiring speed, the half-dragons standing toe-to-toe against their more powerful cousins. The ground and walls shook around the combatants, but their defenses were strong enough to protect them from falling rocks as well as each other's attacks.

Mostly. Another body lay off to the side, crumpled and unmoving. Again, I couldn't tell if it was one of the half-dragons or a dragon that had fallen while shape-shifted.

"Unless there is another way out, we will have to run past them to escape." Sarrlevi pointed toward the tunnel we'd come through, the clamor of battle echoing from it. Whatever was firing gunshots, we couldn't see it on any of the displays, but the noise continued.

"Our camouflage magic will work in here, right?" I touched my pocket—the half-dragons hadn't taken anything but our weapons, so I had my charms. "And we just have to get out of the mountain before you can form a portal?"

"I believe so. We will have to be careful going past them. With the power they are employing, their magic could kill us by accident."

"Like a fly hitting a windshield?"

He looked at me.

"Never mind."

"This adventure gets better and better," Dimitri said.

A series of *thwumps* coursed through the floor. Not far away, another rockfall started, bangs and thuds thundering through the tunnel leading out. A cloud of dust wafted into the control room.

"That wasn't the sound of us being trapped in here, was it?" Dimitri asked.

"I can move rocks aside if necessary." Sarrlevi jogged toward the exit. "Come."

With the mountain shaking under the assault from above, we ran into the tunnel, the floor sloping downward. We didn't make it far before running into an obstacle. The rockfall we'd heard half-filled the passageway.

Sarrlevi kept running, clearly planning to climb or levitate over, but he paused when a clanking rumble came from beyond the rubble. The gunfire we'd been hearing rang out, louder now, accompanied by white flashes that threw stark shadows against the walls.

Sorka wrapped her barrier around me, and I grabbed Dimitri to extend its protection to him. Sarrlevi also raised a barrier around himself. Just in time. Projectiles struck our defenses with little flashes, then pinged off, hitting the walls.

One clipped off a boulder in the rockfall, struck the ceiling in front of me, and bounced downward, gouging into the floor. It was similar to a bullet but longer, a five-inch stake of metal that could have killed any of us if we hadn't been protected.

"Someone's coming ahead of the dwarven construct." Sarrlevi placed himself in front of Dimitri and me.

Dwarven construct? Was that what was firing those projectiles? I hated not being able to sense magic anymore.

"The half-dark elf," Sarrlevi added. "I believe she's injured." His voice turned grim when he added, "There's also a dragon traveling with the construct."

If the dragons realized Sarrlevi and I were here and believed we'd been helping Starblade and his allies—those they considered abominations—would we end up back in the valley of their council? Being questioned and mind-scoured? Being threatened with punishment and rehabilitation? Or worse?

More gunfire rang out amid the sounds of machinery rumbling closer.

I was about to activate my camouflage charm, hoping we could somehow squeeze past the construct and the dragon without being noticed, when Gemlytha ran up the rubble pile and into view. Blood streaked down her pale face and matted her hair, and she leaned on the sword she carried as if it were a cane.

She spotted us, then spun and threw something—a magical grenade—over the top of the rubble pile. As she hurried toward us, it blew.

White light burned my eyes, and a tremendous blast of power erupted. It threw Gemlytha toward us even as it knocked us flying.

Our barriers kept us from crashing into the walls but couldn't keep us from rolling all the way back to the control room. Clatters and clanks sounded as pieces of the dwarven construct hit the walls, some flying over the rubble pile—what remained of it—and skidding after us.

An angry roar erupted beyond the rockfall, and more boulders tumbled down into the tunnel. They landed atop the debris from the previous rockfall and blocked the tunnel completely, another cloud of dust flooding the air.

Dimitri groaned. Sarrlevi had somehow kept his feet and landed in a crouch, his swords in hand. Gemlytha had avoided the rockfall, but she was sprawled on her stomach in the tunnel, blood saturating her white hair.

She'd blocked the passage behind her—at least until the dragon could move aside those rocks—but why? That was the only way out, wasn't it?

Her head lifted, and she looked blearily at us—no, at me—with blood dripping from her chin.

I squeezed past Sarrlevi, though he might have grabbed me to stop me if he'd had a free hand, and knelt beside her. "Can I help you?" With all the blood, I feared she'd taken a mortal wound—a number of them—but I added, "Sarrlevi isn't a bad healer."

"Just tell him." She wheezed, then coughed, blood dribbling from her lips. "Tell him... I did... as he wished."

Before I could ask what or who, Gemlytha gripped my wrist. A tremendous rush of alien power coursed into me, centering on my palm.

Behind me, Dimitri gasped and dropped to his knees.

As her power scoured the mark, removing it from my flesh, Gemlytha thrust an image into my mind. A trapdoor accessible from the control room and a secret tunnel that would lead out of the mountain—if it hadn't collapsed.

Why? I asked, startled that she'd given her life to come back to lift my curse and show us a way out.

Because you gave us—him—a way out. Gemlytha shared another image, Starblade's face, and I caught the gist of her feelings, the same I-would-do-anything-for-him feelings that I had for Sarrlevi.

A final rush of power ran into my hand before her grip loosened, and she slumped back to the ground. Muffled gunfire sounded, and something rammed against the rock pile. Another dwarven construct trying to clear the way and get to us? To Gemlytha?

"Varlesh," I rasped, looking at my palm—my skin now free of the mark. Tremendous weakness overtook me, as if it had taken my body's own energy to lift the curse, but as long as it was gone, I didn't care. Assuming we could survive the next twenty minutes and escape. "There's another way out. But can you heal Gemlytha? And carry her?"

We couldn't let her die after she'd rushed back to give her life to help us.

"It's too late." Sarrlevi picked me up instead of Gemlytha. "She's dead."

I slumped.

"She was mortally wounded before she reached us," he added.

I wanted to protest being carried, but my legs felt rubbery. My whole body did, and tremors coursed through me.

Sarrlevi had to help Dimitri to his feet, and fresh fear washed over me. She hadn't touched him. What if she hadn't healed him?

But as he staggered upright, he blinked, removed his gloves, and looked at his palms. His marks were also gone.

More distant explosions sounded outside the mountain, and the ground shook harder than before. The base was losing more and more of its integrity under the onslaught.

"You said there's another way out?" Sarrlevi asked.

"Yeah." I brought up the image of the trapdoor Gemlytha had shared with me, hoping he could read it in my mind.

He nodded and, with one arm securing me over his shoulder and the other gripping Dimitri, he hurried back into the control room. The trapdoor wasn't obvious, but, with the directions, Sarrlevi found it and used his magic to pry it open.

Dust clogged the tunnel below, and it was pitch-black. Trusting Sarrlevi to lead us out, I hung limply, letting myself dangle in his grip, my cheek to his back. Tears trickled from my eyes as I couldn't help but feel regret and loss for the half-dragons. Would any of them survive this? Had staying here and fighting to the death truly been better than being recaptured and returned to the stasis chambers? I couldn't imagine it, but I hadn't experienced what they had.

Several times in the tight tunnel, Sarrlevi and Dimitri had to climb over rockfalls, but eventually cold, fresh air reached us.

"There are still dragons out there," Sarrlevi said. "I'm camouflaging us."

"If you want to move your hand from my butt to my pocket," I said, "you could rub my charm for added magic."

"I like my hand where it is," Sarrlevi said, humor in his tone for the first time in hours—or maybe days. "You do too."

"It's all right." I'd barely noticed it since his hard shoulder was jammed into my stomach and we were running for our lives.

"All *right*." He sniffed.

I kissed him.

Soon, a hint of daylight reached us, and he slowed down. Panting, Dimitri leaned a hand against the wall for support. He'd had nobody to carry him. Feeling guilty, I squirmed off Sarrlevi's shoulder. We'd stopped at the mouth of the tunnel, the snowy valley and surrounding mountains visible outside.

Though I trusted Sarrlevi could extend his magic around us, I rubbed my charm and gripped Dimitri's hand, willing it to wrap around him as well. To my surprise, I could sense him and Sarrlevi again. Not only that, but I could detect the dragons, dwarves, and elves above. They continued to drop explosives, one missing the mountain and going off when it landed in the valley below. Snow and rock flew hundreds of feet, and the ground quaked.

"Brace yourselves." Sarrlevi wrapped his levitation magic around us and lifted us from the tunnel. "We'll have to go slowly so we don't risk breaking the camouflage and being seen."

"There's no hurry now," I murmured, eyeing my palm but also looking back at the mountain. I tried to tell if the dragons and other half-dragons were alive in there, but, with all the magic in that base, that was a lot to ask of my slowly reemerging senses. "Not for us, anyway," I added softly.

"Maybe," Sarrlevi said neutrally. Not believing we were out of danger?

He probably wanted to get away from the battle and all the witnesses before activating a portal.

It is possible, he told me telepathically as we floated across the valley, *that the dragons never realized you—we—were here. I would like to keep it that way.*

Since I hadn't recognized any of the dragons, I hoped that was true, that if they'd been aware of anyone inside besides the half-dragons, it hadn't registered as significant to them.

Then we glimpsed movement in the valley below, two figures crouching behind snow-covered rocks as they watched the battle. The elf and dwarf had made it out. A part of me was glad they'd escaped, but they were also witnesses, witnesses who might tell their people that they'd seen us. From there, someone might tell the dragons.

I shook my head bleakly. We could worry about that later.

Sarrlevi took us out of the valley and started to round another peak. I happened to be glancing back when an explosion far greater than any that had gone before blasted from the base. The top of the mountain blew off, as if it were a volcano, and smoke poured into the air. Rubble struck the dragons, dirigibles, and elven birds.

Their defenses kept them from being knocked out of the sky, but they flew away from the mountain, their attack halting. When the smoke cleared, a crater existed where the peak had been, and fire roared upward from it, burning the flammable resources within.

The attacking fleet dispersed, avoiding the smoke roiling from the remains of the mountain.

Sarrlevi paused, the three of us levitating in place, to stare at it. What an ugly scar that would leave on the beautiful elven world, especially if the fuels kept burning indefinitely, as I'd been thinking about earlier. Maybe with magic, the elves would find a way to put out the fires.

"I do not know if that was accidental or intentional," Sarrlevi said, "but I do not sense anyone left alive in the mountain."

"Who would do that *intentionally*?" Dimitri asked.

I thought of Gemlytha's words, *You gave him a way out,* and wondered.

Though I wasn't an expert on the flammability of fossil fuels, that had been more of an explosion than I thought nature alone could have provided. Had Starblade and whichever of his people survived staged their own deaths? Maybe, even with those tattoos, they believed they could finally find a suitable hiding place—if everyone believed they were dead.

"Come," Sarrlevi murmured, levitating us farther from the burning mountain. "Once we're out of range of the fleet and their senses, I'll take us home."

"I look forward to it." I eyed my palm again, hardly able to believe Gemlytha had given her last breath to lift my curse. "I have a forest sanctuary to build and enchant."

28

Almost a month had passed since the death of Gemlytha and the lifting of my curse, but I still felt pleasure as magic trickled out of me, flowing into the boards I was using to frame the last of five tiny homes lined up on wheeled trailers in the warehouse in Ballard. A part of me had wanted to say *no way* to leasing it, since all my troubles had started here, but the owner had lowered the rent even further. So, here I was, working hard and hoping to finish The Wrench's project before Christmas. Given how short the days were this time of year, it was nice to have an indoor workspace.

Rain fell outside, and we'd had to fix a few leaks in the roof, but the electricity was on and I'd moved a lot of my tools over. It had turned out to be a decent place. Abbas and Dimitri were helping with the framing, so the pounding of hammers rang from the walls.

Tinja was here today too, though her assistance largely translated to her wandering around with her blueprints and pointing and tut-tutting if we strayed from her design. With the paint arriving next week, she could shift to decorating, which was one of her fortes. She'd already selected curtains, linens, vases, and throw pillows, saying that *of course* rural goblins who currently lived in lean-tos would appreciate matching accessories.

Sarrlevi came and went, occasionally using his magic to help, though now that the threat to my life was past, he seemed restless. If I'd had an assignment from Willard, I would have invited him along to assist with the fighting. More than once, he'd asked if I'd heard about any more yetis that needed to be dealt with. Never had someone looked so hopeful when inquiring if mountain creatures were beheading pigs and other livestock.

At lunchtime, Val arrived with meals from Nin's food truck for everyone and dropped off tools that Dimitri had asked her to bring. Amber was with her and walked around, openly jangling the keys to her mom's Jeep, letting everyone know that *she'd* been the one at the wheel. Her driver's education was apparently going well, and she hadn't yet careened off a cliff or into a lake.

"Five down, and fifteen to go?" Val smirked as she offered me a paper-wrapped meal and a carbonated water.

"We haven't finished these five yet, but we've got a system, so it won't take too long."

"I saw the curtains and assumed that was a finishing touch." Her smirk widened. "Along with the decorative vines growing around the door and windows of that one."

"Those are, yes."

"Willard wants to know how your health is doing and if you'll be game to take on new assignments soon. I think she's going to call you later."

"Yeah, I can thump bad guys in between hammering nails."

Val opened her mouth but paused. "I was about to say you're a woman of many talents, but I think those are the same talents."

"It's true. As for my health..." I looked down at my palm, the mark long gone. "It's been fine, and my magic has returned fully, though I haven't... Well, there's something I've been wondering about."

"Something bad? Anything I can help you with?"

"Probably not." I lowered my voice. "Unless you know a doctor who specializes in magical beings and knows how dark-elven curses affect the human, er, *mongrel* body."

"Dr. Walker does reconstructive plastic surgery and was in the military, so he has experience with wounds and burns and such." Val looked me up and down. "What happened? You look okay."

"It's not a wound." My voice dropped even lower. "It's more of a lady problem." I rolled my eyes at the silly term, but with guys working all around us in the warehouse, I didn't want to go into great detail about female ailments.

As if he was drawn by my discomfort and wanted to be supportive, Sarrlevi headed over.

"Like an infection or something?" Val asked.

"No. I haven't had my period since the curse. I'm wondering if it, you know, affected things." I waved vaguely at my abdomen, then closed my mouth.

I hadn't voiced my concerns to Sarrlevi. It wasn't that he wouldn't be supportive and help me with any problem, but I didn't want him to worry or contemplate that I might have lingering health issues that could make it difficult going forward if we wanted to have kids. He'd warmed to the idea, and I had too, damn it. As soon as life settled down and we finished the tiny homes, I'd thought we might start trying.

"Uh." Val looked at Sarrlevi, though he'd stopped a few feet away, clasped his hands behind his back, and wasn't saying anything. "Are you sure the *curse* is the reason for that absence?"

"I don't know what else it would be. It *did* almost kill me and messed with my aura and all that for a while. It seems logical that it might have interrupted my cycle. That happens when people are stressed, right?"

"Well, yeah, but—" Val looked at Sarrlevi again then whispered, as if his sharp ears wouldn't pick it up, "—have you taken a pregnancy test?"

"I... no. I'm on birth control."

"You know that's not one hundred percent though, right?"

"Of course I know that, but it's always worked fine before. I don't think half-dwarves are that fertile." Admittedly, before I'd hooked up with Sarrlevi, I hadn't been having sex every day, often *multiple* times a day. My previous boyfriends hadn't inspired me to pounce on them quite as often, and there had been long gaps without male company. Hell, was it possible...?

"Your fit and virile *elf* may be fertile," Val said.

Sarrlevi lifted his chin, as if to say, *Of course, isn't that obvious?* All he vocalized was, "Yes."

He managed to look contemplative as he glanced toward my midsection and smug and full of himself at the same time. Elves were so haughty.

"I'm not— We weren't— I haven't had morning sickness," I finally settled on. My sister had complained about that. A *lot*. "Getting airsick on a dragon while cursed doesn't count." At least, I didn't *think* it counted.

"Maybe dwarves don't get morning sickness. You're from a stock of hardy people, after all."

"I'm sure I wouldn't be that lucky."

"Better take a test." Val winked at me. "Then you can decide if you need to see Dr. Walker."

"Willard's lion-shifter boyfriend is not who I would go to about pregnancy. Or anything else going on in my lower regions."

"Probably a good idea. He's a *marsupial* lion shifter, after all. He might be confused by your lack of a pouch."

"You're terrible, Val."

"Yup. Enjoy your lunch." She waved at me, gave Sarrlevi an

ironic salute, then rounded up her daughter and headed for the door.

Amber sprinted ahead, jangling the keys.

"It is a possibility that you carry offspring?" Sarrlevi asked quietly, joining me and wrapping an arm around my waist.

"I guess it is."

"You are pleased?" He regarded me. "Or not?"

"Just surprised. We *were* talking about this, so I think if that *is* what's going on, I would be... happy." I tamped down the mixture of feelings threatening to burble up, telling myself to wait until I did a pregnancy test. "Maybe daunted though."

Sarrlevi nodded. "Raising an elven child, even a half-elven child—one that will likely possess great physical, magical, and mental ability—could be taxing."

"I meant daunted because I have so much work to finish first." I waved at the tiny homes, thinking of the fifteen that hadn't yet been started. "Though I'm sure your offspring *would* be a pain in the ass and challenging to raise."

His eyelids drooped, but he didn't appear offended in the least. "*Your* offspring will have frequent temper tantrums."

"Meaning a kid of mine would be a pain in the ass too?"

"A *challenge.*"

"Good thing you like challenges."

"I do." He kissed me gently.

If Dimitri and Abbas hadn't been hammering nearby, I might have let him take me off to a private nook where we could explore his *fertility* more thoroughly.

After a moment, Sarrlevi broke the kiss. "You will wish to wed now? Before the child is born? Is there a stigma among humans for having children outside of an official mating?"

"Maybe for some people, like my sister—" I wrinkled my nose, "—but she's not the one who matters most." I rested a hand on his chest. "I want to marry you because I love you. It can be now or next year or whenever."

"If we accepted your roommate's proposition to wed us, it could be soon." His eyelids drooped. "And then we could celebrate our future together with elven mating sex."

"Elven *mating* sex? Is that different from all the other sex we've had?"

The corners of his eyes crinkled.

"Hell, it doesn't involve trees, does it? *Multiple* trees?" After all, we'd already had sex hanging from a branch.

"Vines of Binding," he said.

"Uh." I envisioned some BDSM scene with vines chaining me to a bed like shackles.

"Nothing like that." He smirked. "They bind us to each other and are erotic."

"Erotic vines. It's amazing how much Tolkien left out of the elf lore."

"Some rituals are not shared with outsiders," Sarrlevi said, though I doubted he had any idea who Tolkien was. "Tonight, I will give you more details so you know what to expect. And after we are mated..." He smiled suggestively.

"I'll talk to Tinja and see if she's still willing, though we could visit the justice of the peace anytime." That would make it official. I suspected Tinja's *goblin* wedding vows would only make our mating official among her own people. "After all, what girl would want to put off experiencing erotic vines?"

"None." Sarrlevi kissed me again before wandering off, his lips and magic teasing me, making me think that I wanted to go home with him instead of staying to work. But if there was a chance I might be pregnant, I had a lot to get done in the upcoming months. And I needed to find out how far into a pregnancy it was safe to swing hammers.

My phone rang, Willard's name popping up.

Trying to adopt a professional tone and put my meandering thoughts aside, I answered, "Hello, ma'am."

"You'll be pleased to know, Puletasi, that the remaining yetis have moved back into the high-mountain wilds and shouldn't threaten any more farmers."

"That is what I've been most concerned about lately."

Willard snorted. "I assumed. With my blessing, your former roommate has put the wayward scheming goblins who were responsible to work. I understand they'll be living on your street. How's your home security?"

"Good."

"You might want to add some Dobermans and pit bulls to the property to further deter trespassers."

Just the kinds of animals an expecting mom wanted roaming the premises. I kept the thought to myself. Until I took a pregnancy test, there wasn't any point in bringing up motherhood.

"You might be more curious about the latest development on the dark-elven artifacts," Willard continued.

"I hope the latest development is that they've been incinerated with the ashes dumped in an active volcano."

"It pertains to the specific artifact that resulted in your curse. Well, the *pair* of them that we now have locked up in the basement."

"A volcano would be a better place for them."

I thought of the mountain on Veleshna Var we'd last seen in flames and wondered if the elves had been able to put the fire out. I also wondered how many bodies they'd found—and if Starblade had gotten away. Did the fleet that had attacked the half-dragons believe them all dead now? I didn't know. Mom hadn't visited me on Earth, and she'd been on the elven world when I'd gone to Dun Kroth to let her know that my curse had been lifted and I was okay. I'd left a vague note, sparse on details, and trusted the dwarves had gotten it to her.

Since then, I'd been hesitant to use her portal generator to visit again, instead waiting for her to come here. If the word had gotten out that Sarrlevi and I had been a part of the half-dragon battle, however inadvertently, the dwarves might not be happy about it. The dwarves, the dragons, the elves... For both of our sakes, it had seemed a good idea to stay on Earth and lie low until things blew over.

"I don't have a *volcano* in my basement," Willard said.

"The Army overlooks a lot when they design their buildings."

"No doubt."

Sarrlevi, who might have heard the word *yetis*, reappeared, fresh from adding more decorative vines to one of the tiny homes. As he'd informed me earlier, he assumed goblins would appreciate a touch of elven magic. I was less sure about that but planned to tell them, if they objected, that the vines were part of the enchantment that would make the homes blend into the forest.

"Anyway, the artifacts are safely locked up down there," Willard said. "What I thought you might be curious about is that the first one you found wasn't originally put in that Ballard basement decades ago by the dark elves, like we thought."

I remembered that skeleton and the LED lantern—and how that death had seemed more recent. "Oh?"

"According to a half-orc informant who got back to me late after I put out a call requesting information on the artifacts, it was put there by a pack of scavenging orcs who found it and a few other dark-elven items in the Seattle underground in the aftermath of Val's battle. They learned that the curse would eventually kill those who touched it, which made them believe they had found a good way to eliminate someone slowly and over time. Someone they hated and whose death might result in retribution. They believed that by using the artifact they could kill this person without being caught for the murder they planned."

"Whose murder did they plan? Who that might have accidentally stumbled across an artifact magically hidden in a sealed basement that hardly anyone could have known existed?"

"Val's," Willard said.

"As far as I know, Val doesn't have a lot of hobbies that require she rent a giant warehouse. Or did they think she would need it to hold all the commercial kitchen equipment she's had to buy for her mate?"

"She used to live in an apartment in Ballard a few blocks from there. They assumed she would one day be walking around, sense the artifact, and be drawn to it. If that didn't happen, I gather one planned to send a note to her with clues in it. A couple of things happened to throw a wrench in their plan. First, Val's landlord got tired of all the violence she drew to her apartment building—not to mention the dragon that kept smashing the patio chairs when he landed on the rooftop deck—and raised her rent, which inspired her to move. Second, the orc scavengers succumbed to the curse themselves and died. My informant wouldn't have heard of this plan at all if it hadn't taken a number of days for them to die. Lesson being: don't play with fire, or you'll get burned. Dark-elf fire, in particular."

Yeah. I rubbed my palm at the memory.

"The skeleton we found belonged to a half-orc, not a full-blooded human," Willard continued. "We're not sure how exactly he was involved, and we may never know."

"I'm not real broken up over the loss of the orcs."

"I assumed not. Val won't be either, I'm certain."

"I'm glad we succeeded in keeping her from touching the artifacts," I said. "It was hard enough to convince Gemlytha to cure *me*." Thinking of her made me regret, not for the first time, that I hadn't thanked her before she died. Since Willard didn't know the details, I forced lightness into my tone and added, "And we know how charming and delightful *I* am."

"Uh huh. You hit anyone with your big hammer yet today?"

"Just some nails, and I don't use Sorka for that. She objects."

Yes, I do, she agreed from where she leaned against one of the trailer tires.

Even though the last few weeks had been quiet, I never left her too far from where I was working.

"I'll bet," Willard said. "Is Sarrlevi with you?"

"Yes, he enjoys assisting me and holding my tools." I arched my eyebrows at him, certain his keen ears could pick up both sides of the conversation.

"I enjoy holding certain of your assets; that is correct." He wasn't so overt as to ogle my chest, but I knew what he meant and smirked at him, giving my *assets* a wiggle.

"What did he say?" Willard, not having keen elven hearing, might not have heard that. Good.

"He agreed that holding things for me is an honor."

Sarrlevi snorted but didn't disagree.

"Tell him the goblin surveillance network reported a mysterious cloaked magical being with two swords leaping to the defense of two women jogging around Green Lake a couple of days ago. A lion shifter who got kicked out of a home he'd made in the zoo was living in the park and assaulting women. I was about to send you or Val to hunt him down. Then his body was found floating in the lake, his head lopped off."

I looked at Sarrlevi, but he didn't give any acknowledgment that he'd been responsible. I also couldn't tell from Willard's tone if she approved or she was exasperated. She almost always sounded a little peeved, and she hadn't liked my *vigilante* crime fighting, as she'd once called it.

"If the shifter was mauling women," I said carefully, "is there anything to object to?"

"My *objection* is primarily about leaving a headless body floating in the water by the park trail for every jogger and dog walker in the area to stumble across."

"Well, I don't think Sarrlevi has your number or knows about the corpse mobile." I didn't want to confess on his behalf, but I trusted he would have objected by now if he hadn't been the person responsible.

"Give it to him, and ask him if he wants a job."

I blinked. "A job? Working for you?"

"As Val has pointed out, he knows more about the Cosmic Realms than all my agents combined, most of whom are from Earth or have lived here a long time. And he's a capable fighter and mage. If he's willing to take orders and follow directions, I could find a use for him."

"Work for the human military leader?" Sarrlevi curled a lip.

"She would send you to hunt yetis regularly." I smiled, loving the idea of my restless former assassin doing work for the good of humanity, work that ought to keep him suitably stimulated, more so than magically growing decorative vines around windows. "Maybe even more exciting enemies than yetis."

"Hydras have shown up in Deception Pass again," Willard said. "Someone who can levitate and doesn't have to steer a boat out to reach them could be the ideal agent for the job."

"Yetis *and* hydras," I said. "What do you say, Varlesh?"

"What rate of payment is the human military leader offering in exchange for the heads of enemies being delivered to her office?" Sarrlevi asked.

"You're independently wealthy," I said. "Why do you need to be paid?"

"Since I spend more time on this wild world now that we are fused, it would behoove me to acquire Earth coinage. Even though humans reputedly find gold desirable, I have rarely been able to purchase goods and services using my coins. The clerks either do not know how to value gold, or they are incapable of... *making change* is, I believe, your term."

"Yeah, it's hard to pay for a latte with a gold bar worth two thousand dollars."

Sarrlevi nodded.

I thought about mentioning that we could find a pawn shop and get some of his gold converted to dollars, but I was fairly certain those guys had to report the exchange of large sums to the IRS. What form would an elf from another world fill out to stay on the up-and-up with tax collectors?

I repeated his question to Willard, including the bit about the delivery of heads.

"The heads don't need to come to my *office*," Willard said, lowering her voice to a mutter to add, "It's bad enough that goblin ten-pound cakes show up here regularly. As for payment, the same as you and Thorvald get plus combat bonuses."

"That is a sufficient amount for a mate wishing to contribute to his family's welfare?" Sarrlevi asked me.

"Assuming there is a steady supply of yetis and hydras and such terrorizing the greater Seattle area, yes. It might even buy fertilizer for your vines."

"Excellent."

"I won't ask," Willard said, apparently catching that last.

"Good idea, ma'am."

EPILOGUE

THE PREGNANCY TEST WAS POSITIVE, AND A CHECKUP WITH MY human doctor—not the marsupial shifter, thank you very much—confirmed its accuracy. If everything went well, next summer, I would have not one but *two* half-elven-quarter-human-quarter-dwarven babies.

"Talk about mongrels," I muttered, though I never intended to use that word with my children. I *did* wonder if the human attributes would come out on top in all that or if I would have to explain oddly pointed ears to my doctor. "Here's hoping the kids at least won't have to visit a wax salon as often as I do."

"Is speaking to yourself a part of the enchanting process?" Sarrlevi asked, joining me at the edge of the goblin encampment.

With my portion of the work largely done, I was watching with contentment as goblins jumped up and down, directing the placement of the last of the tiny homes in the forest northeast of Arlington. We'd lucked upon a sunny day in January for the delivery. The two batches of ten tiny homes trundling up I-5 in the slow lane, pulled by a combination of steam-powered lorries the goblins had dug up—or made—and shiny new Ford trucks

The Wrench had provided, had offered quite the show for commuters.

"It is. I like to talk my magic into existence."

"And this is effective?"

"Yup. It's a dwarf thing."

"Interesting. I wonder if our offspring will possess this ability." Sarrlevi brushed his arm against my shoulder and eyed my abdomen, having informed me a few times that he could *sense* the twins forming and that they were healthy. Though I'd recovered from the curse, my ability to detect such things wasn't as strong as his, and I mostly sensed a couple of blobs. But it pleased me to know they were *healthy* blobs.

Tinja wandered past with Work Leader Yurka, highlighting all the features of the tiny homes and asking about recording videos for her social-media channels. Feast preparations were underway, with numerous goblins tending fires while others brought whatever roadkill they'd managed to find to stick on spits. The smell of baking ten-pound cakes wafted through the air. I couldn't say the aroma was tantalizing, but it smelled better than one might expect, given the ingredient base.

"Our children will probably have a unique blend of abilities," I told Sarrlevi, "framed by the dwarven tendency toward temper tantrums and the elven tendency toward haughtiness. All I know for sure is that they'll like cheese since we both do."

"Oh?" Sarrlevi asked. "You believe that is conveyed through the blood?"

"It must be. I've seen Mom and King Ironhelm hoover down cheese and charcuterie trays like nobody's business."

After all the months he'd spent on Earth and around me, Sarrlevi had heard most of my American vernacular and didn't cock his head in puzzlement as often, but that statement did earn me a such-strange-things-come-out-of-your-mouth look.

Several goblin children ran by, ostensibly foraging for food for the feast but mostly goofing around. The boy with glasses was among them, and he waved heartily at Sarrlevi as he passed. Sarrlevi inclined his head, still stiff and aloof, but, earlier, he'd deigned to toss the ball with the kid. By the time our children were old enough to play with, he might relax enough to enjoy such endeavors.

"When your mother arrives, she will assist with further enchanting?" Sarrlevi extended a hand toward the forest.

"I think so."

The homes were already emanating magic that included enhanced durability, self-cleaning, and an illusion that would ensure mundane humans passing through the area wouldn't notice the cedar-shingled structures among the trees. But The Wrench wanted the sanctuary hidden from magical beings as well, something I also desired, and that was beyond my knowledge and ability. Enchanting things I was building wasn't hard, but enchanting a miles-wide swath of the forest? I wouldn't know where to begin. By wandering around and willing my power into each tree? There were a *lot* of trees.

"I'm summoning my resolve to go get her," I added, waving toward a backpack I'd brought, the portal generator inside. "She did say she would help."

"You have not visited her since we returned from Veleshna Var." *He* had been the one to deliver a message to her about Enchanting Day, though I didn't know if he'd gone in person or used the equivalent of the goblin post.

"No, and you know why." I slanted him a sidelong look. "You haven't visited the elven capital either. Nor the dragon home world."

Sarrlevi snorted. "I would *never* voluntarily visit there."

According to Zavryd, his fellow dragons weren't looking for Sarrlevi or me, and the queen hadn't mentioned us at all. I had my fingers crossed that our presence at the battlefield—the battle *mountain*—had gone undetected by the dragons, but I'd been worried that the escaped spies might have said something about us. I'd been reluctant to ask around to find out. If people started thinking things through, they might realize it was strange that, after my wide-ranging quest to lift the dark-elven curse, the problem had abruptly resolved itself.

I hadn't known what to say when Gondo, the biggest blab in Seattle if not on Earth, had asked how I'd gotten rid of it. Thankfully, the fast-thinking Val had explained a magical loofah we'd found that could excoriate flesh-based curses. I didn't know if Gondo had believed that, but he hadn't pried further. It helped that Tinja had chosen that moment to flirt with him to distract him. Since I didn't think she sought a mate, I appreciated her sacrifice.

"It looks like they've picked their neighbors," I said as goblins detached the last tiny home from a truck. "I guess I'll go get Mom."

"Can dwarven enchanting repair smashed foliage and tire marks?" Sarrlevi pointed to the torn-up ground, an unfortunate byproduct of the trucks driving the tiny homes into the forest to drop them off.

"I think it could *hide* the damage. An elf would be better at repairing it." I patted him on the arm. "Maybe with vines."

"Vines? In a place where vines do not naturally grow?"

"Oh, like that's stopped you before. I've seen you sprout them out of siding and carpets."

He started to answer, but magic swelled nearby, and he paused. It wasn't goblin magic.

I started to reach for Sorka but recognized a dwarven signature. I hesitated, not certain if we were safe or not. Why would dwarves show up out here?

Surprisingly, the ever-vigilant Sarrlevi didn't reach for his swords or blink in surprise at the formation of the portal. Ten familiar dwarves hopped out of it, armor clanking. My mother's bodyguards. They were the ones to blink in surprise, peering at their forest surroundings. Had they expected to arrive at my house? Whoever had made the portal had known where it would come out.

After the dwarves fanned out, eyeing the goblin village uncertainly as they fingered their weapons, my parents arrived. They didn't look peeved, not in the least. Mom's expression was delighted as her gaze locked onto me.

I looked at Sarrlevi—he must have told her where to find me —and he gave me a knowing smile. *Your roommate has offered to wed us in the goblin way today, so I invited your parents to witness the event.*

Oh, thank you. We were already officially married, thanks to a visit to the justice of the peace, but it would be nice to have Mom and Dad here for the goblin version of our wedding. I clasped his hand, still bemused that Mikki the Wrench, of all people, had come up with a complete packet of identification papers for Sarrlevi, claiming he was a Swedish citizen legally living in the United States. His new name was Sven Larsson, and the documents were so convincing that I was afraid the government knew all about Sven and would expect him to start paying taxes.

You are welcome, but Work Leader Tinja insisted, Sarrlevi said as Mom and Dad headed toward us, *that your parents be here for you.*

Mom must not know we were at the mountain? I guessed, doubting he would have risked inviting them if he'd been worried there would be repercussions.

As soon as they reached us, Mom and Dad engulfed me in hugs.

I did not bring it up when I went to Dun Kroth to request that they visit today, Sarrlevi continued. *I did mention that you had news you wished to share with them.*

When Mom and Dad released me, Mom keeping a handclasp

as she looked down at my abdomen, I realized they already knew we were expecting.

You told them I'm pregnant? I asked Sarrlevi, not annoyed, but I might have liked to tell my mom myself.

I did not. But when I said you had news, I apparently appeared... full of myself—I believe that is how your mother put it. She said it was an Earth saying and that you would know what it meant.

Yeah. And she was right, I'm sure.

"Twins?" Mom asked. "Oh, yes. I sense them. No wonder your elf was smug. Oh, they already have strong auras. That's fantastic. They'll be powerful enchanters—or whatever they wish. And they appear very healthy."

"Mom," I said, realizing she would have immediately sensed that I was pregnant even if Sarrlevi hadn't inadvertently warned her, "they're embryos."

Was that right? They might qualify as fetuses now. I couldn't remember the exact development calendar. Either way, it was early to start thinking they'd be the next Gandalf the Greys.

"They're wonderful," Mom said, smiling into my eyes.

"Congratulations, Matti." Dad patted me on the shoulder. "I have to confess, when you were a little girl and I wondered what your future would be like, I didn't envision..." He looked at Sarrlevi.

"Grandchildren with pointed ears?" I didn't think Dad objected to Sarrlevi—*Mom* had a lot more reasons to dislike him, and she seemed to have forgiven him for the past. Even so, it might take some time for him to get used to the idea of half-elven grand-children.

"Yeah." Dad shrugged sheepishly. "But it's all good. I under-stand there's to be a small ceremony today too? After the enchant-ing? Not that we would require that, just so you know. After all, *we* never married, and we're happy." He smiled at Mom.

"We never married," she said, "because you were wanted by

your military, and I was wanted by... everyone who desired the powers of an enchanter."

"Also because you're not an Earth citizen," Dad said.

"We have an acquaintance that could hook you up with citizenship if you want to get married here." I smirked and gripped Sarrlevi's arm.

"Would she also receive the name *Sven*?" he murmured, not sounding delighted by it.

"Nah. Mom looks more Russian or maybe German. She could be an Olga."

Dad's expression was dubious. Considering the name Rodarska didn't roll off the tongue, *Olga* might not be a downgrade, but I didn't say so.

"*Nika*, may I have a word?" Mom waved a hand toward a private spot between the trees.

"Are you still willing to enchant the area to hide it?" I followed her, worried Sarrlevi had been wrong and that she would bring up the half-dragons and say King Ironhelm and everyone else planned to ostracize me.

"Yes, of course. I'm relieved not to have to do it in the aftermath of your death." Mom nodded gravely toward me and glanced at my hand.

"Me too." I showed her my unmarked palm before realizing she would ask how I'd resolved the problem. Or did she already know? The message I'd left had been vague, but Sarrlevi might have given her a few details.

"You haven't been by these past few weeks," she said quietly.

"I've been busy building." I waved toward the tiny homes. "And, uhm, you haven't come to visit me here either."

"I know. I've been busy too, working with my father and his advisors to iron out the elves." Mom tilted her head. "Is that the right saying?"

"Uh, iron out the kinks with the elves, or smooth things over with them. I believe elves object to having hot irons applied to them."

"Yes. They're a sensitive people." Mom rested a hand on my shoulder. "I'm not sure how you were involved with the battle in their preserve, but I believe you were there long enough to find a dark elf?"

"Yeah. It was Gemlytha, the half-dragon female, who healed me. I never did run into the priest." Which was good since he might know by now that I'd destroyed his laboratory.

"Ah. She did it before her death?" Mom raised her eyebrows. "The elves found the charred remains of her body in the aftermath of that battle. A quite explosive battle, I'm given to understand. General Grantik shared the story."

"Yeah." I tried not to squirm and feel guilty even though I hadn't had anything to do with the outcome. Sarrlevi and I had never raised a hand against anyone in that fleet. It wasn't my fault that Starblade had learned a crucial detail from my thoughts...

"I do not blame you for anything, *Nika*," Mom assured me, "and I have not told anyone, even your father, that you were there. I did some historical research into the half-dragons, and while there were many that were horrendous and used their power to be cruel during the war, Starblade and the three he freed were not among those with such reputations. Perhaps, if he and the other two have survived, they will not make trouble. No one is certain if they *did* survive or not. No other remains were found, but the great explosion and collapse made it difficult to search. The dragons who hunted the area said they believe that the escapees all died there."

"It's possible they did," I said.

Mom nodded. "Yes. Regardless, I have told nobody that you visited that area, nor will I."

"Thank you, Mom." I hugged her again.

"I have something for you." She released me and reached for a belt pouch.

"Oh?" My senses picked up magical items in it.

"You did not exchange rings with Sarrlevi?" She waved at my bare fingers.

"Not yet. I've been super busy, and I actually didn't know we were going to do this today."

"Your own wedding is a surprise to you?" Her eyebrows rose.

"Not *entirely*. I guess that's weird, huh?" I thought about explaining that we'd already formalized things with the justice of the peace, but my eye caught on two small wooden boxes that she drew out.

"Unusual perhaps. It is good that I came prepared." Mom opened the lids, revealing two handsome silver rings, one embellished with hammers—was that *Sorka*?—and one with trees and swords. Even though they featured different decorations, there was no doubt that they matched. "As soon as Sarrlevi told me, I visited the smithy to make these for you two."

"Thank you, Mom," I whispered around emotion that welled up in my throat.

"Elves do not exchange rings, but it is very common for dwarves, and I assume he will not protest."

"I'm sure he won't. Especially when they're enchanted." I touched the hammer ring—*my* ring—with reverence. Numerous subtle enchantments laced the silver, expertly intertwined. "What do they do?"

"As long as you wear them, you will heal more quickly from illness and injury in battle, and—" Mom's eyes crinkled with amusement, "—I've added an enchantment to increase your mental defenses to make you better able to resist compulsions."

"So I'll be less likely to touch malevolent artifacts?"

"Precisely."

"This may become the most valuable item I own."

"Yes." After handing the rings to me, Mom pulled out a red velvet bag held shut by a gold drawstring at the top, more small magical items inside. "This is a gift that you should wait until tonight to open." The humor in her eyes turned a touch wicked. "In the bedroom."

I accepted it gingerly between thumb and forefinger. "More elven sexy toys?"

By now, I was familiar with my mother's ribald streak.

"*Dwarven* pleasure devices. You can educate your elf in the ways of our culture."

Well, it couldn't be any worse than the mating vines.

"Thanks, Mom. We'll, uh, treasure everything."

"I believe you will." She winked and waved toward the forest. "Shall we begin the enchanting? We can make a lesson of it."

"I look forward to it."

"I will attempt to finish quickly, so as not to interfere with the goblin feast."

"We're all invited to that, actually, though you might want to go home before then. Or maybe not. If dwarves like my grandma's peanut brittle, they might eagerly chomp down ten-pound cakes."

"Our people are known to enjoy hearty desserts."

"What about *heavy* desserts?"

"Sometimes, yes."

As we walked back to join the others, I sensed Zavryd approaching with Val on his back. Maybe Tinja had invited them to come for our little ceremony. Surprisingly, I picked up another elf aura on Zavryd's back.

Tinja ran over, waving cheerfully. "The mother of Sarrlevi and the grandparents of Matti have arrived. Now we can start the ceremony."

"You invited my mother?" Sarrlevi asked Tinja in bemusement.

"You invited my grandparents?" I wasn't surprised she had and that they'd agreed to come; I was shocked, however, that my eighty-five-year-old grandparents were riding on a dragon's back.

"You don't think they will enjoy seeing you married?" Tinja asked.

"My mother will enjoy *knowing* we are officially mated," Sarrlevi said. "I am less certain she desires to attend a goblin wedding."

"Oh, she does." Tinja clapped. "They all do."

Zavryd came into view, flapping his wings sedately as he flew low over the trees, four people riding on his back—two hanging on for their lives. I winced in silent apology to my grandparents. I was fairly certain *ride a dragon* wasn't on either of their bucket lists.

"You arranged for everyone to come?" I asked Tinja.

My grandparents wouldn't have been that difficult, but how had she reached Meyleera on Veleshna Var?

"Of course, of course. A work leader must think of her clan and what's best for them. A wedding should be attended by one's close family. I sent offerings of meat to the dragon to convince him to travel to Veleshna Var and the town of Marysville to collect your kin. I also attempted to invite your sister, Matti, but she huffed at the idea of you getting married in the woods and said she would arrange something more *appropriate* later."

"Hell, we may end up at the country club yet," I muttered to Sarrlevi. Maybe I could talk Penina into just doing a reception there. As much as I loved Sarrlevi, I didn't want to get married a *third* time. Oh, well. My grandparents were more easygoing, and it would be nice to have them here.

After landing, Zavryd levitated them gently down to the ground, though Grandma's eyes were wide with concern as she looked around at the woods, the goblins, and all the bonfires cooking mystery meat. She clutched a large cooler to her chest, and Sarrlevi stepped forward to take it from her. She clasped him for support, saying how alarming being carried off by a dragon had been.

"Dragons can be *quite* alarming," he agreed, enduring her embrace. "Especially if you attempt to do a favor for them by cleaning their scales."

You cannot tell that story, Zavryd spoke telepathically to us, *without informing them that you used a* sword *to engage in your brutish cleaning.*

"A sword?" Grandma asked. "Goodness, that would be like using a scouring pad on fine china."

Yes. Zavryd sounded pleased that someone agreed.

Sarrlevi sighed, though it might have been because Grandma was still smothering him with her hug. That was what he got for once carrying her luggage and cleaning her car for her. And being so handsome that even octogenarian women couldn't resist his allure.

Less unsettled, Grandpa walked up to one of the homes—Zavryd had landed close enough to it that he could see it through the camouflaging enchantment—and patted it. Admiring the craftsmanship? He nodded to me.

I lifted my chin, delighted that he'd been able to tell it was my work, even without the ability to sense magic.

"We brought food for the wedding feast," Grandma told me, peering toward the goblin cook fires.

"Oh." I brightened, glancing at the cooler. Grandma's American desserts might be appealing only to strong-jawed dwarves, but her Samoan food was delicious, and I would love having something to eat that didn't come from the roadkill family.

"Roast pork, corned beef, and boiled taro," she said.

Pork? Zavryd, still in his dragon form, lowered his snout toward the cooler. *Beef?*

"We may only get some of the taro," I murmured to Sarrlevi.

"I will prong that dragon in the nostrils with my sword if he attempts to eat your wedding food," Sarrlevi said.

Zavryd turned baleful eyes on him.

Val patted Zavryd on the flank. "I believe that female goblin who keeps winking at you has dragon fare prepared."

Hm. Zavryd sniffed the cooler once more before turning his gaze toward the cook fires. *Numerous* female goblins waved tongs and spatulas at him, and his nostrils twitched with interest.

I am pleased that you are well again, Matti, Meyleera spoke into my mind, *and that you are marrying my son.*

He's a good elf. I'm glad he's willing to marry me.

As am I. I never would have thought he would turn out to be... respectable. She beamed pride at Sarrlevi.

I didn't know if she'd said anything to him yet, but he lifted his chin, as if to say *of course* he was respectable. He always had been, even as an assassin.

I am also pleased that there will be offspring, she added, smiling at me. *I hope you will consider bringing them to visit so that I may teach them of elven culture and show them how to paint.*

I will, and I'm sure they'll love that.

With only one-quarter dwarven blood, the kids would probably be a lot more into swinging from trees and running across rope bridges two hundred feet in the air than me.

"It is wonderful that you are all here." Tinja waved toward Sarrlevi's mother and my parents and grandparents. "Now we may begin the ceremony."

"Here?" I pointed at the pine needles underfoot, though it wasn't as if there were chairs set up anywhere. Goblins tended to squat or perch on logs rather than build seating areas.

"Here." Tinja nodded firmly. "The feast is nearly ready, so we must hurry."

"You did promise us brief," I said.

"Yes. Goblins prefer their joinings to be done quickly so there is more time for eating."

"I believe that."

Sarrlevi extracted himself from Grandma's grip, pausing to give his own mother a hug on his way to join me. Once we stood side by side facing Tinja, the rest of the goblins came over, forming a circle around us to observe the ceremony. For some reason, the children had been shooed away.

Tinja lifted her arms. "I am here today to link two foraging partners in a chain of great durability."

Similar to being fused like trees, Sarrlevi told me silently, *but less romantic.*

To goblins, chains are romantic, I replied.

Such a strange people.

Unaware of our commentary, Tinja continued. "Do you, Varlesh Sarrlevi, promise to forage for and care for Matti Puletasi and all offspring you might have together?"

Sarrlevi clasped my hand. "I do."

"Do you, Matti Puletasi, promise to forage for and care for Varlesh Sarrlevi, especially in the event that he is maimed or dismembered in a crafting or engineering accident?"

I blinked. Did that happen to goblins often enough that they needed to incorporate it into their wedding vows?

Tinja nodded to answer my unspoken question.

"I do," I said formally, and then added, "There's no telling when his vines will go awry and maim him."

"It is more likely that your hammer," Sarrlevi murmured, "flying during an outburst of your temper, would club me in the head."

As much as I wanted to object, that was probably true.

"Excellent. You have jewelry of binding to exchange?" Tinja looked toward the ring boxes in my hand—I'd tucked the drawstring bag and *its* contents into my backpack.

"We do." I showed the rings to Sarrlevi.

"Ah, gifts from your mother." He nodded in approval, smiling as he brushed a finger over the swords on his. "This is perfect." He lifted the hammer ring from its box to look at the outside and also the inside of the band, and his eyes twinkled. "And I see yours is perfect too."

"I think that's Sorka."

"Sorka and cheese." He smirked as he showed me the inside.

I almost laughed. I hadn't noticed the wheels and pieces of cheese engraved along the inside of the ring.

When I consulted Sorka on the matter, Mom spoke into my mind, *a couple of months ago when I realized you two would eventually become mates, she insisted the cheese go on the inside. If you can imagine it, she said pieces of cheese weren't elegant or stately enough to be pictured next to her fine likeness.*

I can imagine it. Varlesh is right. It's perfect, Mom. Thank you.

Sarrlevi slipped the ring on my finger, and I did the same for him.

"Excellent." Tinja nodded. "As soon as you kiss the bride, you will be formally joined."

"Kiss the bride?" Work Leader Yurka scratched her head. "The goblin vows call for vigorous mating. Optionally but *ideally* in front of witnesses."

Our goblin onlookers giggled and nudged each other with their elbows. No wonder they'd shooed their kids away. They'd expected a show.

"As I have learned," Tinja said, "humans and elves prefer to do such things in private, so I have amended the vows. Also, they have already mated vigorously. Many, *many* times. As a roommate with ears, I can attest to this."

I leaned against Sarrlevi but refused to blush. It was true.

Not getting the show they'd expected, most of the goblins slumped in disappointment. Then someone announced that the ten-pound cakes were ready, and their cheer returned. Excited by the promise of food, half the goblins ran away before Sarrlevi and I even kissed.

We will mate vigorously later, he assured me as our lips touched.

Not with the erotic plants again, right?

You did not enjoy the elven mating vines? Many enthusiastic cries came from your lips.

Yes, but they were mixed in with alarmed cries whenever a vine slithered over my leg.

You did not find that stimulating? Half-dwarves are almost as odd as goblins.

Elves are odder than either.

Perhaps this is so. Sarrlevi broke the kiss but clasped my hands and gazed contentedly into my eyes.

I gazed back, looking forward to having his children and spending the rest of my life with him.

After Mom and I enchanted the village and a great swath of land around it, and after dark came and we all finished picking the edible items out of the feast, I grabbed Sorka and headed into the woods. To make use of the all-natural goblin facilities, I told my family, but there was something I wanted to check on before we headed back to Seattle.

Mom's enchantment had covered enough square miles to include the laboratory in the hill, or what remained of it. I wanted to make sure the dark-elf priest hadn't returned to cause trouble. Even though I'd never met him in person, he was the *last* person I wanted to have a protective sanctuary here. I also wanted to make sure those pods hadn't been repaired in my absence.

But when I came to the top of the ridge, pausing where the goblin shaman had stopped all those weeks ago, the gully and hill looked nothing like I remembered. Enough of a moon lit the land-scape for me to make out the changes.

Not only had the orange lightning stopped, but I didn't sense any dark-elven magic coming from within that hilltop. The boul-ders had been covered in dense vegetation that sprouted large leaves. The sides of the hill, where only stumps and bones had existed before, were covered in ferns, salal, and salmonberry shrubs. Pine, fir, and cedar saplings, similar to the trees growing in the surrounding forest, had also erupted from the gully. It looked like years had passed, nature returning to take over what the dark-elf priest had denuded, and a hint of magic clung to it all. A hint of *elven* magic.

A shadow stirred on the hilltop, someone looking across the gully toward me. I didn't *sense* anyone, but two violet eyes flared briefly in the darkness. Starblade?

Before I could say anything, he disappeared from my sight as well as my senses. If not for the foliage, I might have doubted that I'd actually seen him.

But he was there. I didn't know if the other male half-dragons had made it, but Starblade had taken me up on my offer of sanctuary.

THE END